TROLLING PRISONS

TROLLING PRISONS

MANTLE AND KEY PARANORMAL AGENCY™ BOOK EIGHT

RAMY VANCE

MICHAEL ANDERLE

DISRUPTIVE IMAGINATION®

Copyright © 2022 by LMBPN Publishing
Cover Art by Jake @ J Caleb Design
http://jcalebdesign.com / jcalebdesign@gmail.com
Cover copyright © LMBPN Publishing
A Michael Anderle Production

LMBPN Publishing
PMB 196, 2540 South Maryland Pkwy
Las Vegas, NV 89109

Version 1.00, October 2022
ISBN (ebook) 979-8-88541-388-6
ISBN (paperback) 979-8-88541-946-8

THE TROLLING PRISONS TEAM

Thanks to the JIT Readers

Dorothy Lloyd
Veronica Stephan-Miller
Dave Hicks
Jan Hunnicutt
Deb Mader
Diane L. Smith
Jackey Hankard-Brodie

If we've missed anyone, please let us know!

Editor
The SkyFyre Editing Team

CHAPTER ONE

The prison's walls seemed to close in on her like a trap as Maine hobbled forward. Behind her, the sounds of inmates fighting renewed as guards started intervening.

"Look out, yo!" Noff squeaked in a high-pitched Mickey Mouse voice from the pants pocket of her prison uniform. Considering he was the size of a mouse, it was a wonder she could hear him over the sounds of the riot behind her.

Maine evaded to the side of the corridor as a tattooed prisoner lunged at her from one of the doorways. She elbowed him in the face as he fell past her and kept moving forward. The corridor was long, and when she reached the end of it, she groaned.

"I've got to go up there now?" Maine muttered when she came to the stairwell leading up to the exit.

"There she is!" a voice called from behind her.

She barely had time to turn as three inmates entered the corridor and rushed her, a vampire, a goblin, and a rhino shifter. As they fell upon her position, mouse-sized Noff blasted out of Maine's pocket and sunburst in front of the first prisoner's face. The vampire went cross-eyed, and the rhino shifter trampled him. Noff blasted to the side and sunburst a second time, blinding the other two with a miniature dazzling fireworks display. While they threw up their hands to guard their eyes, Maine dispatched them with quick jabs to the chin and solar plexus. Maine had already turned before their groaning bodies slumped to the floor.

Maine muttered, "Mantle, can you give me a little more energy?"

The invisible demonic cloak hissed in her mind. *I am nearly depleted. You need healing.*

Maine grunted and placed her foot on the first step. Safety lay at the top beyond that door. She had to make it there.

Hurry! the Mantle hissed.

Exhausted, Maine inhaled and started up the steps.

Before she could get far, two ogre prison guards stepped into the corridor behind her, eyeing her warily and hungrily. Behind them, three mythical gang members with their arms and necks sleeved in arcane tattoos cracked their knuckles.

So close and yet so far, the Mantle hissed. *You're outnumbered and spent. You'll never make it up the rest of these steps.*

Maine turned and descended the few steps she had climbed. "You don't scare me," Maine shouted in challenge to the five newly arrived opponents. She tried not to wobble, but her body ached all over. She was so tired.

The first guard threw himself forward, leading with his fist. Maine blocked his uppercut and shoved him to the side. Then the second ogre guard grabbed her by the arm and shoulder, holding her in place like a bully.

"Shiv!" Noff squeaked, but it was too late.

While Maine focused on dealing with the second ogre

guard, one of the gang members had shot forward, plunging a thin, sharpened piece of metal into her side.

She grunted, slipped out of the guard's hold, and swiveled away from her attackers, heaving in a breath and pausing long enough to clutch her side. Warm red liquid oozed through her fingers.

As she backstepped and lost her footing, the Mantle hissed disappointedly.

Congratulations. That is a fatal wound. I always knew your blood would stain my cloth.

Maine reached out for the wall for support, but her hand slipped off it, and she collapsed backward. She blinked and realized she was seated against the wall with her five attackers looming. As her eyes fluttered shut, she heard Noff's frantic Micky Mouse squeaks in her ear, telling her not to go to sleep.

Sleep. Ah, yes, that seemed like such a good idea.

Her eyelids fluttered closed.

CHAPTER TWO

Seven Days Earlier

"Mantle, seriously, what am I looking at?" Maine asked. She was standing in the mansion's study, holding the framed painting of the quaint countryside in her hands. The countryside was alive. Grass swayed and the pond's surface rippled in the breeze. Two suns shone in the sky, and a troll hunkered beside the pond, fishing. A troll who was the spitting image of her father.

Her dead father.

I've already told you, I do not know, the Mantle hissed.

Her cyclops ghost butler Al looked equally unsure in his ghostly formal attire.

Footsteps sounded in the study's doorway, and she turned to see Sage enter. He looked concerned.

"Maine, what's going on?"

She looked uncertain. "This painting. It's... Well, take a look." She handed him the painting.

"It's a painting of a hillside..." Then Sage blurted, "It's got two suns! And it's—"

"Moving," Maine finished. "Yes, I know. I don't think this is a painting. You have any idea what it really is?"

"Not a clue. But I can look into some identification spells we can try casting on it. How about you call Maki-Mae over? She'll be able to help us."

Maine was about to do so when Noff padded into the study. "What's up with all the racket in here?"

"Ever see a moving painting before?" Maine asked.

The miniature dire wolf yawned and glanced up at her. "Uh, yeah."

Maine's heartbeat quickened. "Where?"

"Harry Potter movie marathon last night. Where else?"

Maine groaned. As she stepped out of the study to call her stepmom, Noff blasted into the air and gawked at the painting.

"Wow, ya ain't kiddin'. It really is alive. And it's got two suns..."

An hour later, Maki-Mae and the rest huddled around the painting, now propped up on a sofa in the study. "We need to take a closer look at it," Maki-Mae prompted. "Is that a fishing troll?"

Maine nodded earnestly. It felt good to have her here. Between Maki-Mae and Sage, they had a lot of magical knowledge. Maki-Mae also had a lot of magical contacts she could probably use to help unravel this mystery.

Sage set a spell tome on a coffee table. "This magnification spell should help us to look for any distinguishing details." He uttered an incantation, and a transparent magical viewing pane appeared in the air before them in front of the painting.

"How does this help us?" Maine asked.

Sage only grinned at her, then pressed his thumb and forefinger together. He touched them to the magical viewing pane and pulled his fingers apart. In response, the viewing pane zoomed in on the painting.

"Nice," Noff barked. "Kinda like an iPad screen. Too bad I ain't got no opposable thumbs."

Sage was zooming in on a tuft of grass. He zoomed in so close that they could see the veins in the grass.

Then Maine reached toward the magic screen and made a reverse-pinch gesture over the troll fishing in the pond.

"Dad?" Maine muttered when the magnification enhanced the troll's face. He wore a placid smile as he sat on the embankment, waiting for a fish to bite. He looked so at peace.

Maine waved at him. Through the enhanced view, it looked like she was standing right across from him. He didn't see her, though. He sat there bobbing his head good-naturedly. His lips pursed as he whistled a tune she couldn't hear.

"Seriously? What's going on?" Maine asked. "Who is that guy? Where is he?"

"It's so damn lifelike," Noff barked. "Like we're watchin' a movie."

Maki-Mae placed a hand over her mouth to suppress a gasp. "That *is* Valkious. I know it is."

Maine shook her head slowly. "But he's dead. Is this a recording?" That was a weird idea, but it seemed plausible. Maybe her dad had recorded this sometime in his life. "Wait, if this is Dad, when was this recorded? I don't remember him ever expressing an interest in fishing when I was younger. He was always too busy with work to relax. I don't recognize that hillside from anywhere."

"Me neither, and I've been around the block," Noff barked.

Sage and Maki-Mae admitted the countryside wasn't familiar to them either.

Maki-Mae straightened her kimono as she stared at the troll in the painting. "I don't think this is a recording. I'm not sure how it's possible, but I think it is happening in real-time."

"That's impossible," Maine said. "What makes you think that?"

Maki-Mae gently met her eyes. "Because in this painting, Valkious is doing something he never did before you were born."

"What?" Maine asked.

"Smile."

"You're joking, right?"

"No." Maki-Mae brushed some of her barbed hair to the side. "It may sound cliché, but you were the light of his world."

Maine frowned. "You're right, that is cliché. I thought detective work and solving cases was my father's passion."

"It was. You were an altogether new and brighter passion."

"If I was so important to him, how come he never made an effort to get to know me?"

"He did. He took you on rides in his muscle car along the coast to see the ocean and lighthouses. Also, he liked taking you to watch baseball games. And he liked playing soldier with you when you were little."

Maine recalled instances of all three of Maki-Mae's situations. The car rides were fun. Baseball games were interesting. She had almost forgotten about the two of them playing soldier when she was little. She hadn't thought about that in a long time, but it all made sense now, knowing that Valkious had been a badass leader in Troll War II. The memory of her father giving her a grinning salute made her blink back the formation of tears.

Sage's hand fell on her shoulder. "You okay?"

"Yeah. Just remembering something silly my father used to do when I was little." She gave Sage a mock salute, and he laughed good-naturedly.

"Hey, I don't get no salute?" Noff barked.

Maine tilted her head down at him and saluted again.

"Much better, partner." Noff raised a paw to his furry head and saluted back.

Maine turned back to Maki-Mae. "Look, I'm not trying to be selfish, but if I was so important to his happiness, then why didn't he make more time to spend with me?"

Maki-Mae paused. "He worked his cases to always know what was going on in Rainwater. He worked so hard and so tirelessly to protect this town and everyone in it, you most especially."

"Yeah, but how do you know that?" Maine asked.

Maki-Mae's eyes glazed over as she recalled something. "He never said the words," she said at last. "He didn't have to. I could see it in his eyes."

Silence fell over the tender moment until Noff barked, "Yeah, yeah, but what does that got to do with this paintin'?"

Sage rubbed his chin, then turned his attention back to the enlarged troll in the painting still sitting by the pond waiting for a bite. "Assuming this isn't a magical recording, it means that this is somehow Valkious, or at least Valkious sometime after Maine was born."

"I attended my dad's funeral," Maine said. "I know the Veil and magic in general are wonky, but how is this possible?"

Noff scratched behind his ear with his hind leg. "I'm stumped."

"Me too," Sage said. "I've never seen or heard of anything like this."

"Perhaps the answer lies in the frame and not the painting itself?" Maki-Mae suggested.

Maine moved the magic viewing screen to the side for a closer look at the frame. It appeared to be an old, plain picture frame. When she picked at it with her fingernail, nothing came off like the painting. She flipped the image over and inspected the backing. It was solid and scratching revealed nothing there either. Sage cast an identification spell on the back with the same result—nothing out of the ordinary.

Maine flipped the painting back and concentrated, trying to unravel the mystery. In her hands was a magical painting-thing that had been painted over in another painting set in an ordinary frame. Why?

Camouflage was the only reason she could think of. It was made to look like a painting to conceal it from all but the one who knew what it truly was.

Her eyes narrowed as her mind spun faster now. The person who knew what it truly was. Who would that be?

She had only one answer: the mansion's previous owner. The person who had murdered her father.

Maine glanced up at her friends gathered around her. "I think we need to talk to Noolie."

At first, they looked confused. Then Sage smacked his forehead. "It's his painting. Why didn't I think of that before?"

"Uh, 'cause he's in a magic supermax prison," Noff barked.

Maki-Mae's head bobbed as she considered. "We can't be certain that he knows what this painting truly is. Maybe he inherited the painting. Or maybe he bought it on the black market in the Beneath without knowing its true value."

Maine shook her head. "There's no way it's a coincidence

that Noolie doesn't know what this is, not with his, uh… connection with my dad." She pointed at the troll sitting by the pond.

Maki-Mae's face tightened at the mention of this. Likewise, Sage's and Noff's features tensed as well.

"I'm going to have to talk to Noolie," Maine said.

"He's in prison," Sage said. "Say you go to visit him. You think Noolie is even going to see you? You put him in jail. You un-Mythed him, took away his magic. He was a supernatural criminal underworld boss. That was the worst punishment you could have dealt him."

"Yeah, you're right." Maine thumbed her knee as she thought. "He probably won't agree to talk to me."

Noff's tail began to wag vigorously. "I got it! We try the ol' inmate approach."

"The what?" Maine asked.

"You know, go undercover as an inmate. I saw it on a cop show. And in a prison movie. And on Brooklyn Nine-Nine. It's a common prison trope—it'll work."

"Get myself thrown in prison so Noolie will trust me?" Maine considered that. "I like your thinking, but…" Maine gestured at herself. "There's just one problem. I don't exactly look like prison material. Besides, the last I heard, Noolie was in an all-male magical prison."

"Details, shmee-tails," Noff barked. "We got magic on our side. We can brew a potion or cast a glamor to make you look like some big male brute."

Maine bit her lip. "If you really think it's possible, I'm in."

Sage threw up his hands. "Whoa, hold on, you can't be serious about going undercover in a supermax prison, are you?"

Maine smirked at him. "Are you volunteering instead? You're the only other male here."

"Hey now," Noff warned.

"Dire wolves don't go to jail," Maine pointed out. "Do they?"

Sage nervously tugged at his shirt collar. "What? Me in prison? I wouldn't last a day."

Maine laid a hand on her fiancé's shoulder. "I know, dear. That's why it has to be me." She spun toward Maki-Mae. "You're the magic attorney and master negater of chaos. Do you have any ideas for how to get me looking like male convict material?"

Noff barked in protest. "Ya ain't havin' all the fun. I love prison shows—I'm comin' too!"

Maine added, "We also need a way to smuggle Noff inside. I could use the backup."

As Maki-Mae considered this, Maine watched the painting. In it, the troll's fishing line quivered. The troll gave his rod a single jerk, and a large orangish fish promptly leapt out of the pond and into the troll's burly arms. The troll's face was awash in joy.

"We've got this, team," Maine said. "I'm going to prison. What can possibly go wrong?"

The Mantle hissed. *I am not going to answer that.*

CHAPTER THREE

"Your plan is to get thrown into prison *tomorrow?*" Sage all but shouted a few hours later after they had discussed the plan at length, including how she would get arrested and thrown in jail.

"Look, it will be fine," Maine said as she pushed past Sage into the bedroom.

Sage followed her. "Can't we at least talk about it?"

Before she reached the adjoining bathroom, she turned back to face him. "What's there to talk about? We've got to figure out what's up with that painting. To do that, I've got to chat with Noolie."

Sage sighed. "Why do we have to get to the bottom of the painting in the first place? Why can't we let this mystery go?"

Maine's fists quivered. "I never really got to know my dad. My mom died when I was young and my dad… Look, I've got to do this. It's my dad."

Sage backed off. "I know. I owe your dad a lot for what he did for this town and how he helped me in my life when I was at a crossroads. He was the best. But this isn't him—it can't be.

If anything, I say it's a trap. What if Noolie planted it for you to find one day in case you beat him?"

Maine scoffed. "That doesn't even make sense. Noolie never expected me to 'beat' him. He tried to have me assassinated or have you forgotten?"

"No. I just—"

"Besides, that magic painting was hidden in plain sight behind a coat of paint. I don't think Noolie intended anyone to find it, let alone recognize it for what it is."

Sage massaged his temple. "We still don't know what it is. Maybe it's not a trap, but that doesn't mean it's not going to be dangerous if we continue to pursue this thing."

"What's *not* dangerous behind the Veil?" Maine asked. "There are giant clam-shaped dumpsters that will eat you if you fall in. Magic card games where opponents summon monsters to fight each other to see who's stronger. Chicken huts that mutate into T-Rex brick houses. What's one more dangerous and unknown situation to navigate?"

"It's a supermax prison for the worst magical creatures."

"So? I've defeated a rogue Fate. I've beaten the Corruptor, the world's most dangerous demon. Hell, I stopped Chaos from breaking reality. I think I can handle a prison full of sweaty prison hunks."

Sage shook his head forlornly. "Maine, I don't want to argue."

"Too late. We are. You think I can't handle myself?"

"It's not that."

"Then what is it? Maki-Mae said that a supercharged guise spell will keep me completely unrecognizable to all the other inmates. For all intents and purposes, I will *be* one of the guys."

"Yes, this 'guise' spell. What if it wears out sooner than

intended? What if one of the other inmates can see through it and blows your cover?"

"Maki-Mae said it won't wear out before its duration. Also, she said it will fool any mythical creature. Period. Even Death won't know it's me under the guise spell."

"Why are you so for this idea?" Sage asked.

"Why are you so against it?"

"Isn't it obvious? Because we've gotten involved with plenty of dangerous situations over the last year. Is it too much to stop seeking out trouble for once and to play it safe, enjoy life?"

"This is something I have to do. You can't change my mind."

Sage stepped forward and clasped her hand between his. He locked eyes with her like a long-lost lover. "When are you going to be done with these crazy crusades? I want to marry the love of my life—not worry that she'll get shivved in a prison shower."

Maine was about to fire back when she recognized the distraught look on Sage's face. "I'm sorry. I guess I am letting my emotions get the better of me. I didn't mean to yell at you." Her voice softened. "You know that I have to do this, right?"

After a long moment, Sage nodded. "I know. Once you set your mind to something…"

"And I have the supercharged guise spell. I'll even be able to wear the Mantle while I'm in prison. I'll see any shivs coming from a mile away."

Sage sighed. "I know."

"Don't forget, Noff will be inside with me the whole time. An extra-concentrated shrink potion will make him the size of a mouse and Maki-Mae said she'll cast a guise spell on him to make him look like a mouse." She giggled, and Sage joined in, the tension between them beginning to ease.

"That will be hilarious," Sage said softly, pulling her close to him.

She let herself be pulled in and embraced him back. "It will be like a mini vacation—prison edition. Like we discussed, Blue Dots will smuggle a magic earmic into the prison, and I'll be able to talk to you guys the whole time."

"It is a good plan," Sage relented finally. "That doesn't mean I like it."

Maine brushed the back of her fingers against his cheek. "I wish it could be another way, but this is our best option on such short notice."

"You sure it's the best option? What if we appealed to the prison warden and asked to interrogate Noolie? You defeated the Corruptor. The warden would probably do anything you asked."

Maine made a clucking sound with her tongue. "Nope. We don't know who we can trust in there. What if the warden is on some bad guy's payroll? There could also be corrupt guards in the prison. Maki-Mae is researching the current inmates and staff, but in the meantime, we're going in blind. Do you really think Noolie would talk to us? After what I did to him?"

"You're right."

"Part of me is excited to go undercover. It reminds me of one of my dad's old cases when he went undercover in an aswang counterfeiting operation."

"There will be no shortage of excitement and nerves," Sage admitted.

"All that is left is to pick out what my guise will be. I'm thinking wendigo, but Noff thinks I should be an ogre…"

Taking her lightly by the shoulders, Sage tipped her backward, guiding her onto the bed. "Babe, I don't care what monster you look like. You'll always be my troll."

Maine slapped his hand playfully away from her. "Aw, that's the sweetest thing you've ever said to me." Then they were together again, kissing as they rolled over on the bed.

When Sage was on top of her, he puffed some hair out of his eyes. "Let me give you a suggestion. If you want immediate street cred when you get to the prison, you'll want to go with an Oni demon guise."

She batted her eyes at him. "Oh?"

"Yeah," Sage said. "Besides, female Oni demons are kinda hot."

"The guise spell will make me look like a male Oni demon, though."

Sage winced. Then he chuckled. "Trust me. Oni demon is a sure bet for prison material."

"I'll consider it." Maine twined her arms around his neck and pulled him down to her. "Now that we're on good terms again, how about I act out your biggest Oni demon fantasies?"

"Or we could just cuddle," Sage said innocently.

Maine tapped him playfully on the cheek.

CHAPTER FOUR

The next day, the road hummed under them as the tech van sped down the highway. When they hit a pothole, Maine, who was pacing in the back, bumped her head on the ceiling.

"Maybe slow down a bit?" Maine called toward the van's front.

Blue Dots the dragonfly fairy cocked her sexy head back at the tech van's rear. "I know how to drive."

"Then can you please face the road?" Sage blurted.

The dragonfly fairy turned just in time to correct the van's trajectory before running into an oncoming truck. "Ha ha, right. Um, so you guys ready back there? The destination will be here before we know it."

"Almost." Maine rubbed her head and turned to Maki-Mae, Sage, and Noff, who occupied the back of the tech van with her. One interior wall contained sleek monitors and computer equipment. Her friends would be able to monitor Maine's and Noff's situation inside the supermax prison. Blue Dots also had a computer set up in the mansion's study.

Sage cradled Noff's shrink potion in his lap, waiting to

administer it to Noff when they got closer to their destination. Sitting on Maki-Mae's lap was a spell tome containing the potent guise spell she would cast on Maine and Noff. Maki-Mae had already "supercharged" her magic through a night-long ritual she had undertaken at the mansion.

As Maki-Mae flipped through the book, she said, "Where was I now?"

This was it. Time for final preparations. Time to get thrown into prison.

They had calculated the how and were now nearing that objective. Before Maine got herself incarcerated, it was time to learn more about the supermax prison and her target.

Maine spoke up. "You were about to tell us about Noolie."

"Of course." Maki-Mae stopped flipping pages and glanced across the van at her. "Have you ever heard of the Five Gangs of the Veil?"

"No?" Maine sounded uncertain. Her stepmom's uneasy tone indicated that Maine probably should have known already.

"C'mon, partner. Ya serious?"

Maine nudged Noff lightly with her foot. "I'm guessing these Five Gangs are bad news?"

"Bad news?" Noff barked with delight. "They're the baddest motherf—"

"Hence my concern." Sage nudged Noff as well. "Hearing that the prison has some Five Gangs members in it, I think maybe we should rethink our plan."

Maine shook her head. "No, it'll be fine. So what if a few members of the Five Gangs of the Veil are in there?"

Maki-Mae corrected, "it's not only *some* gang members. It's a lot of them. Also, I'm not sure how it happened, but all five gang leaders are there. It's the first time I'm aware of that they have all been in one spot together, which is odd..."

"Woohoo!" Noff barked. "I always wanted to meet a real shot-caller."

"Oh." Maine tried to understand the gravity of this development. "Why would that change anything?"

"You're right," Maki-Mae agreed. "It shouldn't change anything, assuming you stay out of their way."

Sage folded his arms and looked surly. "The Five Gangs of the Veil hate each other's guts. Luckily there's an unofficial standing truce between them all for the moment, but the situation is still like a loaded power keg. Stay clear of them, Maine. Don't want you to spark a gang war or a riot while you're inside the prison."

Noff barked, "That would be awesome."

"I'll lay low," Maine said. "Promise. I don't need to talk to any big bad gang leaders. I only need to talk to Noolie. Is he in one of the gangs?"

Her stepmom nodded grimly. "Yes. He's a high-ranking member of the Seeing Eye gang."

"Ooh, sounds spooky," Maine said.

Sage blinked at her as if he couldn't believe her.

Noff cleared his throat with a bark. "Partner, the Seeing Eye gang ain't to be messed with. Well, none of them are. But them in particular. Ya don't wanna see what they do to traitors. And with their special abilities, they can 'see' through deceptions and shit like that."

"Will they be able to see through Noff's and my guise spells?" Maine asked Maki-Mae.

"No. As far as I know, the guise spells I will be casting on you two will fool any person or creature. Even if someone suspected you were utilizing a guise spell, they wouldn't be able to see through it unless they determined the exact guise spell I cast and performed an equally exhaustive ritual as I did."

"Okay, that's good," Maine said. "And we have five days until the guise spells wear off?"

"Five more minutes 'til we're there!" Blue Dots called from behind the van's steering wheel. The van swerved sharply, then corrected. "Sorry!"

Noff wagged his head. "If that chick don't kill us on the road, I think we'll be all right."

"So Noolie," Maine said. "He's like some big shot-caller?"

Maki-Mae frowned. "Not exactly. He's the gang's tattoo artist."

"That's ominous."

Her stepmom added, "He is a rather high-ranking member, considering he has only been in prison for a year."

Noff barked excitedly. "So either he's the best inker in the joint, or he's servin' in some other kind of nefarious role for his gang."

"So he likes tattoos," Maine said. Noolie didn't have his magic anymore so he probably wouldn't be that big of a threat to anyone. "I hope my guise has plenty of tats."

"Mine too!" Noff barked.

While Maine gave Noff a blank look, Sage cautioned, "There's still time to back out. But if we are to go through with this, it's time to cast the guise spells."

"Oh, we're goin' through with this, ain't we, partner?"

Maine nodded.

Noff wagged his tail excitedly. "Hey, Maki-Mae, got any info on the prison's warden? They say the best thing an inmate can do is make friends with the warden."

Maki-Mae frowned. "I could not find that information.

Which is highly strange. I'm not sure why that information would be blocked to the public."

That was interesting, Maine thought. But they weren't going to be in prison long enough to need to get to know the warden.

Maki-Mae found the correct page in the tome. "I guess it's time then. Are you ready?"

Maine and Noff both assented.

"Remember," Maki-Mae continued. "No matter how realistic these guise spells will look, they are not real. If someone physically interacts with you, they will feel the guise's appearance—not yours. But if you maintain physical touch with them for too long, the guise will temporarily fade, and they will begin to see through it."

"Sure, okay." Maine wondered how real her disguise was going to look. Maki-Mae had said this was a supercharged spell. Maine hoped her stepmom's night-long, intense ritual paid off.

Sage squeezed Maine's hand, then sat back in his seat. After clearing her throat, Maki-Mae read off two quick incantations, one directed at Maine, the other at Noff.

A few moments passed.

"I don't feel any different," Maine noted. When Sage's eyes suddenly bulged, she glanced down at her arms. They were bulging and tanned like the hide of a demon.

"Whoa," she blurted, flexing her intimidating Oni demon claws. She flexed her biceps. They looked like they belonged on an Olympic weightlifter's arms. Intricate tattoos and inked script flowed up both her arms. "This is awesome!" Her legs had equally enlarged beneath her jeans. It was curious to note that while her body looked enlarged, her smaller clothing conformed to the guise spell's specifications. "Anyone have a mirror?"

Maki-Mae drew a compact from her purse with professional grace and handed it to Maine.

Maine flicked it open and raised it to face height. "Now this is what I'm talking about…"

Her head no longer resembled her own. Instead, it had the dark bat ears of an Oni demon complete with upturned tusks on her lower jaw, a smashed-up snout, and glaring eyes. Her thick neck contained the same kind of demonic-looking tattoos as her arms.

Such a lovely guise, the Mantle hissed. *I am impressed. It really matches your true inner self.*

Maine ignored the Mantle. She wondered what a human would see if they looked at her so she quickly lifted the Veil and peered once more into the compact mirror. Instead of a jacked-up Oni demon, she now resembled an evil Vin Diesel.

She lowered the Veil again and turned her attention to the awed gazes of Sage and Maki-Mae. "Hey, wanna kiss me?" she asked Sage with a demonic smirk.

Sage swallowed. "It's just a guise. It's just a guise…" He leaned forward and kissed her on her upturned lips. "Wow, your fangs feel so real." He pulled slowly back.

Maki-Mae spoke up. "Remember, anyone will be able to start to see through your guise with prolonged physical contact. Be cautious when you must interact with others inside the prison."

Maine nodded. She had no intention of blowing her cover before she got the lowdown from Noolie about the painting and why her father was in it. She lifted both of her massive arms in front of her. "I know what all these tattoos are for."

Sage grinned. "Noolie should be impressed. I studied some

of his artwork that Maki-Mae sent me in preparation for the guise spell. He'll notice your tats."

"But not your tits," Noff squeaked, prompting everyone to adjust their gazes to Maine's chiseled, very male-looking chest.

"That was rude…" Maine began. Then she noticed how Noff's guise spell had changed his appearance. He looked like a tomcat-sized hairy mouse with oversized buck teeth and a long pink tail. She laughed.

"Hey, what's so funny?" Noff squeaked.

Maine turned the compact around and flashed it his way. Instead of recoiling away from his appearance, he bobbed his head like a cool kid at school. "Lookin' sexy," he squeaked.

The Mantle hissed. *Make fun of his buckteeth. Then, while he cries, punch him in the big fat mouse nose.*

Blue Dots twisted around from the front of the van and shouted, "Nearly there!" She paused to take in Maine's and Noff's new guises. "Wow, those are really good—"

"Road!" everyone shouted and the dragonfly fairy turned in time to avoid running off the side of the road.

When it was clear they weren't going to die in a horrible road accident, Maki-Mae caught Maine's and Noff's attention. "The guise spell I cast has a unique effect when the two of you are close. Essentially, Noff will become invisible when he is next to you. If he squeaks, those around you may or may not be able to hear him so be careful."

Maine and Noff both nodded that they understood. Then Sage lifted the shrink potion off the seat next to him. "Noff, you ready to become the size of a mouse?"

Noff rolled his mousey shoulders. "Ain't my first shrink potion. Lemme have it." He tipped his head back, and Sage poured the potion down his throat.

A few seconds passed, then Noff shrank to the size of a mouse.

"All right, partner!" he squealed in a comically high-pitched voice. "Let's go get ourselves thrown in prison!"

"Here's our stop," Blue Dots announced half a minute later as the van stopped outside a juice bar with a giant bamboo umbrella on the roof. Several police cars sat in the parking lot. "If you're going to get arrested, this is the place in Rainwater."

Maine squinted at the giant umbrella atop the roof through the front window. "A juice bar? I thought cops were into donuts."

"What a racist!" Noff squeaked.

"That wasn't racist," Maine said.

"He means you're stereotyping," Maki-Mae offered politely. "Yes, it probably is strange for you to see, coming from the human world."

Sage grinned. "In Rainwater, having to deal with mythical baddies that go bump in the night, the cops take care of themselves. You do not want to disrespect them."

Maine shook her arms and legs and prepared to climb out of the back of the van. "You're sure the cops will take me straight to prison and not to some county lockup jail cell?"

"Of course," Sage confirmed. "Magical law doesn't mess around. If you do the crime, you do the time. Assaulting an officer is a very serious crime."

"Ain't no such thing as due process beyond the Veil," Noff squeaked as he sat up on his hind legs on the seat.

"I'm always learning something new about magic or the Veil." Maine cracked her imposing knuckles against her palms. "Okay, I'll see if what you guys say is true."

"You've got this, girl," Blue Dots slid out from behind the steering wheel and maneuvered back to the wall of electronics

in the van's rear. "Oh, I almost forgot, I had to create a ficti-
tious new identity for you. Here you go." She handed Maine a
driver's license with a rough-looking photo of her guise on it.

Maine read the name on the ID card. "My name is Johnny
Mantle? What kind of name is that?"

A very good name, the Mantle hissed.

Blue Dots made a cheesy face. "I figured it would be easy
to remember. You know, since you wear the Mantle. I fudged
a minor criminal record for you as well."

I like this new identity of yours.

"Thanks," Maine offered. "It's perfect."

"Good luck." Sage leaned in and kissed her again.

Maine savored it, knowing Sage had to feel awkward
kissing a massive male Oni demon. Then she opened the van's
back door and hopped to the ground. Her Oni demon body
carried the weight of the guise with it, and she nearly tumbled
to the asphalt. She caught herself on her callused palm and
picked herself up. She felt powerful. She felt in charge.

"Wait for me," Noff squeaked. He blasted out of the van
and landed on her shoulder. Under all her new muscle, she
didn't even feel him land.

"Good luck, dear," Maki-Mae called from behind Maine.

There was no one outside the juice bar watching her so
she turned and nodded silently. Then she spun and faced the
juice bar.

It was time to get arrested.

CHAPTER FIVE

As Maine stepped inside the juice bar, she took in her new surroundings. The juice bar was small but orderly. There was a high-topped counter next to the cashier and several tables and booths. A couple of millennials sat at some tables glued to their laptops and smartphones while five police officers perched upon stools at the counter.

She wondered how she would "assault" one of the magical police officers without hurting anyone. Would insulting an officer be enough to warrant an arrest? That sounded pretty lame, but she wasn't a criminal.

I've got some ideas to get the juices flowing... the Mantle hissed. *Flip a table. Smash a laptop over a millennial's head. Shove a smartphone down someone's throat—*

"Hi, can I help you?" a middle-aged woman asked from behind the counter as she saw the rough-looking Oni demon that was Maine.

Maine didn't know what to say. Should she order something, then get thrown in prison? How did one go about these things?

"Say something!" Noff squeaked in her ear, perched on her shoulder. As Maki-Mae had said, Noff's guise spell made him invisible to everyone around them whenever he was close to Maine.

"I'll have what they're having," Maine said as gruffly as she could, nodding at the officers on the stools.

The officers eyed her closely for a few tense moments, then turned their attention back to the green drinks in front of them. Apparently, they didn't perceive her as a threat.

She sidled up to the bar, overemphasizing each motion of her gait to maximize the Oni demon-ness of her guise.

She nodded at the cops and raised her eyebrows. "Yo."

One of the officers nodded at her. They seemed to be in the middle of a low conversation.

She cleared her throat. "Nice day today, isn't it?"

"What are ya tryna do?" Noff squeaked. "Win good citizen of the year award? Ya gotta piss 'em off!"

The waitress behind the bar started making Maine's drink.

Maine stepped up to one of the officers' stools. She gave it a soft kick, holding back her full strength. She didn't want to hurt anyone.

The officer whose stool she had kicked faced her. "Excuse me?"

"Oh, sorry," Maine said unconsciously.

"What are ya doin'?" Noff squeaked.

You really are the worst at this, the Mantle added.

Maine gruffly cleared her throat and popped her knuckles. "I mean, hey, officer, I'm looking for a fight. Know where I can find one?" She puffed out her chest and eyed the officer warily like she wanted a confrontation.

Behind the bar, the waitress turned on the juicer, which

began to shake and make an incredibly loud noise as green juice sluiced down into a glass.

The officer appraised Maine for a time, then rubbed his jaw.

The juicing machine quieted, and the officer gestured at the front door. "There's a gym a few blocks away. It's got a sparring ring. That's what you mean, right?"

Maine nodded unconsciously.

"You're such a bad criminal," Noff squeaked.

You must do something bold, the Mantle hissed.

This all felt so weird to Maine. She didn't hurt good people. Her bottom lip quivered as she pondered her next words and actions.

Then it came to her when the waitress set a glass of green juice in front of her. It was frothy and smelled like celery.

She picked up the glass and in one quick motion, upended it onto the nearest magic police officer. As it soaked his uniform and dripped to the floor, she was already apologizing, saying it was an accident. She had such clumsy hands.

The officer wiped green juice out of his eyes with his palm and gave her an easy smile of understanding.

Dammit! She'd done it again. It was hard being bad.

Maine's mind was frantically trying to figure out the next thing she could try when the officer stepped forward and gripped her shoulder with quick precision. In the next instant, he spun her around and slapped handcuffs on her wrists. She tried to break free, but even her strength was no match for the magic binding her wrists together.

"You're under arrest for assaulting an officer," the lawman said. He turned to the other officers still on their stools. "Someone want to run this punk out to the bus stop? I need to get cleaned up."

"Bus stop?" Maine grunted.

"To take you to prison," one of the officers clarified. "You know the rules."

"She really doesn't," Noff squeaked hilariously.

A clumsy ploy, but it worked, the Mantle hissed. *Congratulations, you're going to prison.*

Half an hour later, she was driven out to an empty parking lot. The mythical police officer let her out and ushered her toward a prison transport bus. Maine lifted the Veil for a moment and saw that it looked like a normal school bus. But with the Veil down, it was a dull rust color. As she stepped closer to it with her cuffed wrists *clinking* together in front of her, rough-looking faces leered at her from behind the bus' windows.

"Up you go now, bye-bye," the officer directed, and the bus door opened with a *whoosh* of accordion pneumatics.

Maine's gaze traveled up the flight of steps to the driver, a bigfoot with scraggly gray hair and spectacles perched on his nose sitting behind the wheel. The driver thumbed backward down the bus aisle as he started the engine. The bus rumbled to life, and Maine slowly boarded and walked down the center aisle. One or two mythical creatures already occupied most of the seats. There seemed to be two general types of inmates on this bus. Big muscled brutes and scrawny wild-eyed ne'er-do-wells.

Maine didn't feel like she belonged here. A glance down at her tatted-up Oni demon arms reminded her that she looked like she should be right at home here.

Fake it to make it, the Mantle hissed.

With that thought in mind, she moved with confident indifference. Now that she was falling into her planned role, she had to act the part.

A couple of the handcuffed prisoners in the seats gave her amused looks. Others didn't even look her way, their gazes unfocused or pointed out the smudged bus windows.

She saw orcs and minotaurs and even a gnome. When Maine spotted a troll sitting upright like a statue with slumped shoulders, she did a double-take.

Not because he was a troll but because she recognized him.

Sort of.

He had a scruffy beard now and less hair, but he reminded her of one of the trolls who had fought with her father in a grimoire vision she'd had of Troll War II.

Yes, it is one of the trolls under your father's command, the Mantle hissed. *I remember that day well.*

Interesting. There was an open seat behind him, and she took it. Air deflated out of the seat cushion as she sat.

The bus took off with a jolt, and she vaguely wondered if maybe Sage was right and she had bitten off more than she could chew.

CHAPTER SIX

Maine took in the prison bus' sights, sounds, and smells. This was a rough crowd, and she guessed maybe half of them hadn't taken a shower in days.

Noff did the same, peeking over the bus seats from his spot atop Maine's shoulder, twitching his whiskers and pawing at his nose due to the smell.

Maine realized she didn't have access to her magic. The Mantle informed her that the prisoners' cuffs and the bus were suppressing all their magic. She was far from helpless, though. She still had her innate strength and agility, and the Mantle could enhance her abilities and read weaknesses.

She sat in silence for a few minutes, watching the other prisoners as the scenery passed outside the bus window.

The troll sitting in front of her intrigued Maine. She was about to tap him on the shoulder and ask his name when a prisoner a few seats ahead of them, a satyr, turned and asked, "So what are you guys in for?"

An ogre smacked a palm against his chest, causing his

handcuff chains to rattle back and forth. "They accused me of robbing a bank and having a shootout with the human police."

Maine nearly gasped. She had heard about that incident on the news but hadn't looked at the suspect's photo. Now, on the bus, she lifted the Veil to see what humans would see when they saw the ogre. He looked like a roided-up WWE wannabe. Maine lowered the Veil again.

A minotaur sitting across the aisle from the ogre shook his head and chuckled. "Oh yeah? Well, I was falsely accused of breaking and entering some rich guy's house and setting it on fire."

The satyr nodded understandingly and mockingly passed his goatish gaze over some of the other prisoners in the seats behind him. "Magic law is such a travesty. Is there anyone among us who is guilty?"

This elicited a couple of laughs from some of the prisoners.

Then a third prisoner, a green-skinned leshy, the Mantle informed her, raised both palms peaceably. "I was busted at an underground Corrupter rally. I am NOT innocent."

To this, it seemed that all the prisoners cheered with wild grins. Well, not everyone. The troll seated in front of Maine like a lifeless statue remained quiet.

Maine turned her attention back to the leshy and the other inmates on the bus. One thing was certain. Among this crowd fighting for the Corrupter was street cred. She would need to be careful. She would probably have to pretend to support the Corrupter too, or she could blow her cover.

Suddenly, the troll seated in front of her grumbled, "The Corrupter is an ass."

Handcuff chains slithered over laps as everyone turned to look at the troll. He went quiet, bearing the inmates' glares with utter stonelike indifference. Eventually, they disregarded him but not until after the leshy made a throat-cutting gesture in his direction. Soon, multiple conversations broke out among the prisoners until the bus driver shouted for silence, or else they'd all be thrown in the "hole" when they got to the prison.

Maine didn't know what that might entail, but with magic involved, one could only imagine.

The rest of the bus ride continued in silence accompanied by sparse hurtful jeers and chuckles. Maine kept wanting to talk to the troll in front of her, whisper in his ear to learn if he had fought in Troll War II, but this wasn't the right time. They were in hostile territory.

At last, the bus pulled into the prison.

It looked about how Maine expected. Giant barbed wire fences surrounded a series of interconnected ugly concrete buildings.

The bus passed a gate that closed behind them, and Maine saw the electricity coursing through the outer chain-link fencing.

"Oh, electric fencing," Maine commented, wondering how much voltage it was. Then she saw the signs posted at regular intervals along the fencing. *Warning: 1,000,000 volts.*

Noff squeaked with energy. "Day-um. This is more excitin' than watchin' a prison show on Netflix."

"Your new home." The bigfoot bus driver chuckled as he worked the door lever. The doors accordioned open with a pneumatic *hiss.* "Welcome to hell."

The prisoners filed off the bus in a more or less orderly fashion starting with the front. When it got near Maine's time to leave, she nudged the troll in front of her on the shoulder and said, "Hey, did you fight in Troll War II?"

The troll gave her an impassive look, then stood and took his place in line to get off the bus.

Maine was perturbed. Didn't the troll want to talk to another troll? Then she remembered that oh yeah, she looked and sounded like an Oni demon, not a troll.

Once they all climbed out of the bus, they had to step through a magic metal detector and receive a pat down. Then the guards took their handcuffs off.

After that, they lined up on the asphalt and listened to a harsh speech by one of the head prison guards regarding how they were expected to behave while in prison. Also announced were the times for meals and lights out. There was a brief talk about opportunities to work in the prison's kitchen or laundry room for good behavior and the privilege to access weightlifting equipment and some basketball courts in the rec area once a day after lunch, behavior permitting.

"Does he ever shut up?" an inmate said.

The guard heard him and called him out. "No privileges for you!"

After the introduction to prison life speech, they got in another line and received an orange prison jumpsuit one by one. Slowly, the line progressed, and Maine received her jumpsuit. The bright orange contrasted sharply with her demon skin.

She had lost sight of the troll and was trying to find him again when Noff squeaked, "Wow, we're really here. It feels so real."

"That's because it is real," Maine muttered, trying not to be overheard by anyone.

An ogre pointed at her. "Hey, an Oni demon that talks to himself."

Maine snarled, jabbing her lower tusks into the air. "What of it?"

The ogre straightened, intimidated by her presence. "I didn't mean nothing by it." He turned away.

Wow. Sage had picked a good guise for her. It seemed that Oni demons ruled the block here.

She saw the troll then. He was a few yards ahead of her.

She also saw the leshy stalking toward him. Before she could call out, the leshy cocked his fist back and slammed it into the troll's side.

The troll staggered and caught his balance. He spat some blood on the asphalt, having bit his tongue during the hit, Maine guessed.

Maine wasn't the only one to see the leshy strike the troll. It seemed like all of the bus prisoners had seen it while all the prison guards had not.

The prisoners flashed each other greedy looks, then fell onto the troll in a wave.

"So much for your troll friend," Noff squeaked. "He's 'bout to be jelly."

CHAPTER SEVEN

Raising her palms, Maine attempted to conjure twin fireballs, but she couldn't even conjure a flicker of a flame. The same as on the bus, the prison's warding prevented her from accessing her magic.

You're in prison now, the Mantle hissed. *New rules, same old tactics. Use your fists!*

Maine threw herself toward the troll getting attacked. Before she reached him, the troll threw off his attackers and staggered to his feet. The leshy drew back to punch him again, but the troll punched him first, squarely across the jaw.

The leshy wiped blood from his lip. "You shall pay for disrespecting the Corruptor!"

Meanwhile, two ogres rushed the troll. Maine grabbed one of the ogre inmates and slung him backward. The troll knocked the second ogre off him and kicked him in the gut.

Then the troll narrowed his eyes at the leshy. "Like I said, the Corruptor is an ass. A failure. Couldn't even start the apocalypse with the help of his demonic weapons."

"Shut up!" the leshy roared. He charged, but the troll was

much quicker. He stepped aside and tripped the leshy who went sprawling. When one of the ogres ran at the troll, the troll tripped him too, and shoved him sideways.

The other ogre tried to pummel Maine's face, but she backstepped, then kicked him in the crotch. When the leshy got back up, Maine focused on him.

Leshy, the Mantle hissed. *Greatest strength: super-endurance. Resistant to physical attacks. Weakness: fire.*

The leshy charged the troll again, and this time he managed to get in a few jabs to the troll's chest. When the troll staggered forward, the leshy body-slammed the troll to the ground.

"Leshies are no joke to fight," Noff squeaked. "They can take a beatin'."

She couldn't conjure fireballs. But there was another weakness she could manipulate.

She cupped her hands over her mouth. "Yeah, the Corruptor's a real weakling. Resorting to special weapons instead of using his fists."

The leshy was trying to put the troll in a headlock on the ground. Upon hearing Maine's insult, he looked up at her, giving the troll the opportunity to break free.

The troll elbowed the leshy in the cheek and rose to his feet, assuming a fighting stance. "Hell, I heard the Corruptor got beat by a girl. A troll girl. Hah!"

The leshy threw a drunken punch that the troll knocked aside while the two ogres got up and rushed Maine. She caught one by the elbow and swung him to the ground, then exchanged blows with the other ogre. Soon Maine was back-to-back with the troll. Where the hell were the guards?

"Hey, Oni demon," the troll said. "You fight pretty good. Got a name?"

Maine deflected a punch with her forearm. "You can call me Mantle."

The troll ducked under the leshy's next attack and chopped the leshy in the neck. The leshy staggered to the side but got up. "I think I'll call you Oni. My name's Hank."

"Nice to meet you," Maine said. Then one of the ogre inmates tackled her to the ground, taking the wind from her lungs. As Maine struggled with the ogre, she recalled the warning about her guise spell only lasting so long before physical contact would cause it to fade.

She promptly kneed the ogre in the groin and rolled him off her.

A fish-like creature was smacking the troll over the head with his fins when a group of guards ran over with telescoping batons in their hands.

"Everyone, down on the ground, now!"

Maine dropped flat to the ground with most of the other inmates. A couple of the inmates didn't comprehend in time and were still standing when the guards reached them.

The guards flicked their wrists and electricity from the tips of their batons blasted into the inmates. They weren't standing for long.

They crumpled to the asphalt with the smell of scorched clothing and jaws spasmed shut, preventing them from screaming.

As Maine lay on her chest with her cheek to the asphalt, she caught the troll's eyes. He gave her an almost imperceptible nod but didn't say anything. Noff stood on his hind legs a few feet away from her.

"Did you see that?" he squeaked in amazement. "That dude's shirt caught fire!"

The nearest guard whipped his head from side to side, listening. "What's that high-pitched squeaking sound?"

Noff darted up to Maine so he would stay invisible to everyone else.

A few moments later, the guard continued. "You're all getting on my nerves already. Wait until the warden finds out about this flagrant disrespect of the rules. He won't be pleased."

Some of the prisoners cursed. Maine wondered who the warden was.

Next came the reckoning to see who had started the fight in the first place. It wasn't hard to see that it had been everyone against Maine and the troll so even when an ogre tried to say that the troll had started it, the guard shook his head in disdain.

There were more threats that the warden was going to come and deal with this batch of "lowlifes" himself, but since the only ones involved were the new prisoners, and it was their first day, they ended up getting off "easy." The prisoners were all rounded up and ushered to their cells without punishment.

"Woohoo!" Noff squeaked as a guard led Maine into the prison. "Ya dodged a bullet there, partner. Now, I can't wait to see who they room you with!"

CHAPTER EIGHT

Her cell wasn't as bad as she thought it might be. It was composed of three solid walls and a vertical barred wall out front where the door was. It had a sink, a toilet, two bunk beds...and a roommate.

Fortunately, that roommate was Hank. The guards must have roomed them together since the two of them had been on their own fending off the rest of the inmates. That was more than fine by Maine.

Unfortunately, the troll was in no mood to talk to her.

She asked him twice if he had fought in Troll War II. His only response was an impassive stare at the cell's opposite wall.

"Can you at least nod or blink your answer to me?" Maine flexed her sore muscles. Luckily, neither she nor Hank had been injured during the fight, but they'd gotten scuffed up pretty good.

Hank resembled a depressed statue as he sat on the edge of the bottom bunk bed. What was it going to take to get him to talk to her?

"Is it because I'm an Oni demon?" Maine asked.

Finally, Hank turned to her. "I don't care what kind of creature you are. Look, I appreciate what you did out there, having my back, but I don't owe you any answers. I keep to myself, and that's how I prefer it."

"But you and I are the same."

"Huh?"

"We're on the same side. You know, Team Anti-Corruptor."

"Oh. That."

"I probably dislike him more than you do."

The troll looked at her. "An Oni demon?" He scratched behind one of his ears. "Something tells me there's something different about you. Maybe you're telling the truth."

"Fine, we don't have to talk about the war. Can you at least tell me a little about yourself? How someone who stands up against the Corruptor ended up in prison?"

"How did you get here?" he asked in turn.

Maine couldn't tell him the truth. She was wearing a guise. That was no way to build up trust. "It's complicated. I threw a green smoothie on a police officer."

"That's not complicated."

Maine chuckled. "I guess maybe not. Except my reason for throwing it was."

Hank looked at her for a few moments, then dropped his head low to match his slumped shoulders. "You seem new to prison life so let me give you some advice. Join a tribe."

"A tribe?" Maine asked.

"A gang."

"Oh. What gang are you in?"

The troll gritted his teeth. "None. I have no tribe."

"Then why are you telling me to join one?"

"It would be easier for you. People would have your back. Me? I've never lived what you would call an easy life."

Maine leaned against the cell's wall and crossed her arms as she regarded him. "What do you mean?"

"For a while now, I've been in and out of the system. You know how it is…" He gave her a knowing look as if to confirm that she knew what he meant.

She didn't.

He's a drifter, the Mantle hissed into her ear.

Hank was starting to frown at her when Maine said, "You were a drifter."

At that, the troll gave the hint of a smirk with the corner of his mouth. "Exactly. I've been all over, never staying in one place for too long. Not setting down roots, just always…you know, moving on."

"Must be a hard life," Maine said conversationally.

"Eh, you get used to it. Like I said, I don't have any friends."

Maine focused on the troll, trying to read him.

He's lying, the Mantle hissed. *He had plenty of friends during the war, after the war too.*

Maine was going to try to press him. "What about the war? Didn't you have friends then?"

For the second time in their conversation, the corner of Hank's mouth twitched into a sort of half-smirk. Then his face matched his slumped shoulders again. "That was a long time ago. I don't want to talk about it." He rubbed his face with his palm, then met her gaze seriously. "Why's an Oni demon want to know my life story anyway? You a spy?"

"What? No."

"You're saying you wouldn't lie to me?" Hank asked suspiciously.

Be careful, the Mantle warned. *Don't get caught in a lie.*

"I'm just curious is all. And I really don't like the Corruptor. You seem like good people."

"Hah. Well, you'd be the first to say that about me since Val —" He shut his mouth when he realized what he had been about to say. "Look."

His eyes took on a grim, determined glint. "Maybe you're an all-right guy. How am I to know? I just met you. But let's get one thing straight. If I find out you're playing a game with me…"

He breathed in a tight breath between his clenched teeth. "But, if you're on the up and up, I think we can get along, demon or not."

He extended his hand and Maine accepted it. She was about to withdraw her hand, recalling the warning about prolonged physical contact, but Hank pulled her in and clapped a hand on her back and shoulder.

What are you doing? the Mantle hissed. *Social distance!*

Maine tried to pull away, but the troll held her tightly to him in a brotherly embrace.

"Want me to bite him?" Noff squeaked.

When she was sure her guise spell would fade, Hank eased up his grip on her, and she slipped out of his grip. When Hank gave her a suspicious look, Maine coughed. "I uh, well…"

Lie!

"I'm not a handsy guy," Maine finished. "Psychiatrist says it's from a traumatic childhood."

Hank nodded seriously. "You know how many people have tried to get me to see a psychiatrist? Hell, I almost did once. But they can't help me. No one can."

Maine didn't know what to say to that. Luckily, Hank changed the subject.

"So you said your name was Mantle?"

"Yeah, it's my last name," Maine said.

Hank tasted the name on his tongue. "It's a strong name. You know that one of the Corruptor's weapons is a Mantle?"

"What? Uh, yeah, I do. Funny coincidence, huh?"

Kill him. He's seen through your guise and is about to blow your cover.

"That is my favorite demonic weapon," Hank said. "The Mantle is the one I would want if I had to choose one of them."

Never mind, I like this guy.

"Why the Mantle?" Maine asked.

Hank's words were slow, sad, and honest. "Isn't it obvious? Because then I would get to see others' weaknesses. Is there anything that beats that?"

"I don't know. The Clawhammer is pretty damn formidable. And the demonic Timepiece is nearly impossible to defeat with its time-altering powers."

"True," Hank said.

"Then there's the Needle. It can reshape the fabric of creation."

"Yeah, but I would rather be able to see others' weaknesses."

I really, really like this guy. He truly understands me.

"Why?" Maine asked.

Because he feels a great weakness inside, the Mantle hissed. *He wants to see that he's not alone, that deep inside, everyone's as messed up as he is.*

Hank didn't admit to any of this. He was about to say something when the dinner bell sounded. "Have fun at meal-time," he said.

It was clear he was done talking about himself. In their

short time speaking she had learned a lot about him. She moved toward the cell door, but the troll didn't budge. "You coming?" she asked.

"Nah. Not hungry."

He's lying, the Mantle hissed.

"Okay," Maine said, not wanting to press him. He was probably sore from the fighting and didn't want to interact with the other inmates. "I'll see about bringing some food back if I can. In case you get hungry later."

Hank looked at her for a few moments, then he lifted a hand to his forehead and saluted her.

Except, it wasn't an ordinary salute. It was the exact same salute her father would give her as a child when they were playing soldier.

"That's an interesting salute." Maine lingered in the cell's doorway.

The troll's sigh was heavy. "It was my special regiment salute in Troll War II. It's a troll thing."

At that moment, Maine's heart pattered hard for a second. She had always thought her dad was being silly when he saluted her when she was little. Now she could confirm it was from his days in Troll War II. It also reminded her of her mission—why she was in prison in the first place.

She nodded at the troll and saluted him. She could almost hear her father addressing his troops. "Carry on, soldiers!"

She turned and ducked out of the cell, heading for the cafeteria.

CHAPTER NINE

It was a long walk to the cafeteria, not so much in distance but in taking in the sensations around her as she did so.

For one, the prison stank. What it smelled like, exactly, she couldn't quite place. It was a combination of BO, farts, and lunch.

The whole was worse than the sum of its parts. She couldn't imagine spending more than a few days in here. How all the guards standing around could bear the smell was beyond her. Didn't inmates get to take showers?

As she continued toward the awful smell of lunch coming from the cafeteria, she thought maybe she should have watched some of those cop shows with Noff before coming here.

As she took a turn, she saw an open doorway leading to the showers. A muscled minotaur inmate stood inside the doorway with a wrapped-up towel in his hand. Whenever someone new would come in or out, he would lash out at their rear with the towel. A guard stood outside the showers, alert but slowly shaking his head, not taking any action.

From inside the showers came the echoing shouts, cries, curses, grunts, and growls of inmates taking showers or whatever inmates did in public showers.

The thought of going in there with all those naked, smelly mythical beasts made her stomach turn. The smell of the cafeteria food wafting down the aisle didn't help.

Her stomach made a hungry warbling sound, though. She kept walking past the showers.

If the smells didn't drive her nuts, the Mantle was going to. Every time an inmate passed her or even looked at her funny, it would hiss a weakness and suggestion of how to manipulate it.

For a bald gnome: *self-conscious about not being able to grow a head of hair. Tell him it's all downhill now, and he looks like a dick.*

For a cross-eyed kobold: *he can't see straight five feet ahead of him. Poke him in both eyes and tell him he can't see* anything *now...*

For a stout ogre: *depressed. Tell him his mother never loved him and while he's contemplating his love-less life, punch him hard in the babymaker.*

In short, the Mantle was in heaven. It belonged in a prison.

Maine didn't.

The guys all around her were animals, some literally. She resolved then and there not to shower or do anything she didn't have to do. She was only doing this for her father—to find out what he was doing in that living painting.

Her stomach grumbled again as she reached the expansive cafeteria filled with rectangular tables and a serving line. The stench of hopefully not rotting food filled her nostrils, and she wanted to turn and run.

A guard shoved her forward into the cafeteria. "Watch it. Keep moving."

Maine swallowed the gross feeling and surveyed the prisoners inside the cafeteria before heading toward the food line. To the untrained eye, it might have looked like a hodgepodge of convicts. To her eyes, and with the Mantle's help, she saw that the prisoners gathered in the lunchroom belonged to five main sects. Six if you counted the oddballs and misfits sitting off to the side. Their shoulders were tight and their glances furtive as they kept a constant lookout for danger despite all the guards posted throughout the cafeteria.

Were these the Five Gangs of the Veil? She didn't know for sure, but she could tell them distinctly apart from the others. It was in the way they held themselves. The magic-dampening devices were placed throughout the prison, out of sight behind walls and ceilings like wireless routers. Instead of projecting free Wi-Fi, they instead suppressed your magic. It suppressed even the guards' magic, or else they would have used magic instead of those electrified batons when the inmates had ganged up on Hank and her.

She wanted to know more about these five factions. She would have to ask Hank later.

A guard shoved her lightly in the back, and she started forward toward the food line. As she walked, she searched for Noolie but didn't see him anywhere. He must not have shown up yet. Maybe he was taking a shower, she thought in disgust at the idea of her target baring it all in the public shower room.

Finally, she reached the food line. Some of the cooks behind the food tables looked like semi-respectable cafeteria cooks. The rest were inmates wearing hairnets. They looked at Maine like she was fresh meat, something to be fed upon later.

At the Mantle's urging, Maine bared her fangs and growled. The inmates took a step back from the food table, and a guard stepped in and warned Maine to behave.

Yes, yes, the Mantle hissed. *Keep up the tough guy façade. Shiv a few punks in the showers, and you'll be a prison shot-caller in no time.*

Maine inwardly grimaced at the Mantle's suggestion. She outwardly grimaced when the first big scoop of prison food slop landed on her plate.

Her stomach churned.

Right now she missed the food at the Sacred Sourdough and her friends back in Rainwater. When her tray was loaded, she searched for a place to sit. Since Hank wasn't here to sit with, she decided to sit at one of the tables of oddball inmates who weren't in any of the Five Gangs.

She glanced up at a surveillance camera as she passed it, wondering if her friends were watching her.

CHAPTER TEN

Sage leaned over Blue Dots' shoulder, staring at the huge computer monitor on the desk in the mansion's study. The monitor was split into numerous security camera views of the supermax prison Maine was currently in.

Gods, he hoped she was doing okay. He was against this idea from the beginning and still was, but they'd all agreed to it. Now he and the rest had to provide Maine with all the support and backup they could. The quicker Maine could fit in, get the info she needed and get out, the better.

Blue Dots had a pretty nice setup here. Zombie Icarus had helped carry everything in from the tech van. He kept groaning that they had better not make a mess of things.

"Where's Maine?" Sage asked as one of the prison cameras showed the entrance to the public showers. He grimaced. Surely she knew better than to take a prison shower, no matter how sweaty or dirty she was. Not that she should be sweaty or dirty—she was supposed to lay low, not get into fights or make enemies.

The tech fairy's fingers flitted over the keyboard. "I'm still searching. There aren't cameras everywhere, and she's probably in a blind spot right now."

The camera views switched to an empty outdoor recreational area complete with a couple of weightlifting benches and a basketball court.

"What if she already got shanked?" he blurted in horror. He leaned in closer, and Blue Dots waved him out of her space. "Check the infirmary," he said.

"I'll find her, okay? Your fiancée is as tough as they come. And she's half-troll." Blue Dots twisted her dainty head around at Sage. "She can handle herself."

Sage stood tall and ran his hands through his hair. "I know, but she's never been up against anything like this. Gods, I hope she doesn't get thrown in the 'hole.'"

The door to the study opened, and Maki-Mae stepped inside. "Don't worry. She's wearing the guise of an Oni demon. I agree with Blue Dots. Maine can take care of herself. Although I wish she would have chosen a different method to gain her information, I have every confidence Maine will be fine."

"That's what I keep telling him," Blue Dots said. "Now can you please distract him long enough for me to find—oh, got her!"

Sage leaned over the desk, his face inches away from the monitor. After giving him a sharp look and reprimanding him not to touch the screen, Blue Dots highlighted a live video feed of the cafeteria. It was lunchtime and all the inmates seated there seemed to be grouped into six main groups. Five of the groups looked like hardened criminals, each of their members possessing a similar body language and stance. The sixth group, whom Maine was sitting with, looked like a hodgepodge of inmates who didn't belong in the prison system.

Sage groaned. "Oh no, are those the Five Gangs of the Veil?"

"Yes," Maki-Mae said.

"Crap!" Sage's hands were in his hair again, tugging until he flinched. "There's so many of them. If she gets on one of their bad sides..."

"She won't," Blue Dots said in an exasperated voice.

"She *will*," Sage said. "I know her better than anyone, and she is going to piss off some bad guys. I didn't think there'd be that many." His eyes widened as another thought hit him. "All of the Five Gangs rep the Corruptor. If Maine's guise fails—"

"It won't," Blue Dots said.

"—she won't last half a day. They will tear her apart if they learn she's the one who defeated the Corruptor and prevented the apocalypse. I knew this was a bad plan..."

As he started to hyperventilate, Maki-Mae placed a hand on his shoulder to calm him. "Maine still has Noff and the Mantle to watch her back. The magic dampeners inside shouldn't affect the Mantle much, and the Mantle will be able to spot threats and identify weaknesses."

"How long do you think Maine could realistically hold out if the entire prison was after her? And we haven't vetted all the prison staff to look for threats there."

Maki-Mae gave him a look that said, we'll get through this and so will she.

Sage glanced back at the video feed of the cafeteria. It looked like Maine was trying to talk to some of the other oddball inmates, but they weren't responding to her. As Maine ate, she kept a watchful eye on the room around her.

Sage sighed in relief, and Maki-Mae smiled. "I'm so glad she's all right," Sage said. "But what is she eating?"

Maki-Mae fanned her face with her hand. "Oh, dear."

"That looks disgusting," Sage said. "They call that food?"

Blue Dots zoomed in on Maine's plate. "What is that? Cooked spinach and oatmeal?"

"Zoom out, zoom out!" Sage gasped, pulling his shirt collar over his mouth. He felt like he was about to vomit. "Wait, do you see Noolie anywhere in the cafeteria?"

"I don't see him," Blue Dots said calmly. "I'll start checking the rest of the cameras. Maybe he's in his cell or somewhere."

As she worked the keyboard, Sage turned back to Maki-Mae. "Oh, I forgot. What did you find out from your legal contacts?"

Maki-Mae smiled grimly. "About that, I have good news and bad news."

"Worse than Maine being stuck in prison with the Five Gangs of the Veil?" Sage asked. "Good news first, unless it's really, *really* bad news, then I want to hear that first."

Maki-Mae bowed professionally, then straightened her kimono. "The good news is that I pulled some strings and got you a conjugal visit in a few days."

Sage's eyes nearly exploded. "What? A conjugal visit?" His face wrapped itself up in a crazy grin. "That's excellent! Thank you, you're the best future stepmother-in-law ever!"

He rushed forward, nearly tripping over his feet, and embraced her. "I can't wait to see and touch her again…" He pulled back from the harionago, eyeing her suddenly tense barbed hair standing all around Maki-Mae's head. "Wait, what's the bad news?"

"Remember that Veil judge who owes me a favor, who said

he could get Maine out of prison if we could prove extreme circumstances for her arrest?"

"Yes…" Sage squeezed his eyelids almost shut as he waited.

"He turned down my special request to extract Maine under Magic Rule 143A, Clause IV, Part 2C—"

"Shit," Sage said. "What does that mean?"

Maki-Mae shifted uncomfortably, then put on her best "I'm afraid you have cancer" doctor face. "It means we won't be able to get Maine out of prison after she connects with Noolie."

"What? But her guise spell only works for five days…" Sage felt like he was going to puke for real now.

As he swallowed bile, there was a knock on the study's door, and Al peeked hesitantly inside.

"Master Maine, I know you said not to disturb you, but there's a, uh, visitor to see you."

"A visitor?" Sage said.

Maki-Mae stepped over to the study's door and pulled it wide open.

She cleared her throat and blinked at the new arrival in the doorway. "Oh gods, not you."

CHAPTER ELEVEN

Lunch passed without Maine getting shivved, and she managed to take a tray of cold unappetizing slop back to Hank who thanked her with a silent nod and ate it gratefully. Then it was time for rec hour. Maine was a bit surprised when the troll got up to go with her to the rec yard, which was right outside the cafeteria.

"You won't go to the cafeteria, but you'll go outside?" she asked.

The troll shrugged. "Vitamin D is good for you."

Maine chuckled. "That was funny."

"I didn't mean it to be."

Tell him his face is funny, the Mantle hissed. *Then smash it in with your fist!*

"Come on." Maine waved him after her. "Let's go."

The recreation area was hot. The sun was beating down, and there was no airflow anywhere. Prisoners stood around on the even hotter asphalt, many with crossed arms and scowls as they joked with each other under the watchful eyes of the guards. Tall chain-link fences surrounded the rec yard, topped with barbed wire.

As Maine searched for Noolie, she asked Hank, "So what do we do?"

Hank grunted, then inclined his head at the weight bench. "How about you show me how much an Oni demon can lift?"

Maine smirked. "You're on."

"Yeah, I'd like to see that," Noff squeaked from atop her shoulder. As he scanned all the inmates in the rec area, he looked like he was in paradise.

"You going to be okay?" Maine whispered to him as they walked.

"We're here. We're really in prison. This is better than sittin' first row at the IMAX theater."

"That's the worst seat in the theater. It kills your neck."

Noff narrowed his mouse eyes at her. "Woman, don't ruin my fantasy."

They meandered over to the weight bench, but there was already a line to use it so they got in the back of the line. While they waited, Maine wished she had the magic earmic to speak to her friends. That wasn't due to arrive until later that day. It would be good to get the scoop on the rest of the prisoners here from an outside source.

As in the lunchroom, she distinguished five different factions of mythical inmates. Each of the five gangs had a gang leader, and it was easy to tell them apart. At least, she assumed they were the gang leaders—they each had a shining crystal dangling over their chests.

"Hey, what do you know about the different gangs in here?"

The troll cocked an eye at her. "You really don't know? Or you just playing stupid?"

"I don't know. I might look like a thug, but I've lived a mostly straight life." Which was true. She, like her father, had always fought evil not joined them.

The troll rubbed his jaw, which Maine noticed had a scar on it. "You sure are one hell of a strange Oni demon. All right, I'll humor you. The Five Gangs of the Veil. You know anything about them?"

"All I know is that one of them is the Seeing Eye gang."

Hank nodded sourly. "Very good." He nodded toward some rigid, sharp-eyed inmates off to the side. They were huddled around a tall, lean redneck-looking guy with a short trimmed beard and a glowing crystal hanging from his chest. "That's the Eye gang. They're all about seeing things with their extra-sensory perceptions."

"You mean they're psychics?"

"No. They have innate enhanced eyesight, hearing, taste, smell, and touch. They're also all about using spies to infiltrate other gangs and organizations. They're real cutthroat and as devious as they come. They keep a low profile so they usually stay out of the limelight. They might not be the strongest gang in terms of magical ability or strength, but you do *not* want to cross them. I'm a little surprised that's the only gang out of the Five you know."

Maine did her best to deflect his suspicious glance at her.

Stay calm, the Mantle hissed. *This troll speaks true. There are those in this prison yard who can* hear *your quickening heartbeat. You must control the reactive functions of your body as completely as possible if you hope to evade notice.*

Maine gave a soft demonic chuckle to try to fit into her

guise and pointed a clawed finger toward some hippie-looking inmates. "Which gang do those prissies belong to?"

Finally, Hank stopped giving her the stink eye and continued. "That's the Light Burst gang."

"Light Burst?" Maine asked.

They stepped up a spot in the weight bench line as an inmate finished his repetitions. "Don't let their loose physiques distract you. They are the most powerful gang of the Five in terms of sheer magic power."

"But they look like hippies," Maine said.

The troll gave her a look that said So? "What does that matter? They have the strongest magic."

"Doesn't help them inside this prison, though does it?" Maine asked. "You know, because of the magic dampeners."

"You are correct," the troll said. "But if the dampeners ever come down, you had better watch your ass, demon. Because they will incinerate the place with their magical destructive power."

"What about the Seeing Eye gang? Can they use their extra senses powers with the magic dampeners?"

"Yes, they can. Because their extra senses are 'innate' magical abilities." Hank flexed his bicep. "You know, like innate troll strength and agility. You can't dampen that shit. Of course, my agility isn't what it used to be now that I'm older."

Maine considered all she was learning. This was important information. Hopefully, she'd never have to make use of it since she was going to get Noolie's information and get out, but Sage would want her to have a plan for dealing with the other gangs if something went awry.

"Okay, we've got the Seeing Eye gang and the Light Burst

gang. What about the other three gangs?" Maine gazed at the other three gangs gathered on the hot asphalt rec area.

The troll nodded at a group of five burly, thick-necked thugs arrayed around the basketball court. Opposing this gang was a group of five average-Joe-looking gang members with normal-proportioned muscles and bodies.

"The gang that looks like they're all on steroids—that's the Brick gang. They are all about their innate strength and fighting. Word to the wise, don't pick a fight with them and you should be good. Although they're the toughest bastards in the joint, they usually only fight when one of their members has been disrespected."

"Got it," Maine said.

"The team playing against them, the normal-looking guys, are the Triangle gang." The two advanced in line again as another inmate finished with the weight bench. "They're the most balanced of the Five Gangs in terms of magical ability, physical strength, and extra senses."

"So they're pushovers?" Maine asked.

"Quite the contrary. While they might be the weakest categorically, their combined prowess makes them formidable foes. Like the Brick gang, they rarely seek a fight so stay out of their way, and you'll be good." He sighed. "That only leaves one last gang."

Maine eyed some members of the final gang. They all seemed to wear permanent all-knowing sneers. "They're kinda creepy. What can they do?"

"Ah, the Parchment gang. Stay clear of them at all costs."

"Why?" Maine asked.

Hank rolled his massive shoulders. "They're all about binding and magical contracts."

"Such as?"

The troll rubbed his jaw again. "For example, they can bind two of their members' strength and temporarily imbue it into a third member to make him an overpowered goliath. Or, they can bind two people so if one of them dies, they both die, that sort of thing. You don't have to worry about them being able to do any of that inside the prison, though. It isn't innate magic. They have to use rituals and sigils, which are blocked by the magic dampeners."

"Good to know, but what's up with the names of the gangs? They make sense, but they're kind of random."

Off to the side of the weight bench line was a patch of exposed dirt with some weeds growing up in places. The troll squatted and smoothed some dirt with his hand. Then he traced five symbols: an eye, a light burst, a brick, a triangle, and an unfurled horizontal parchment banner. Then he looked up at her. "These symbols have grave power. Do they look familiar from anywhere?"

Maine thought about it, trying to find the answer in her head. They didn't seem to be related to each other, but Hank said they were symbols of great power. What if when incorporated into one unified symbol, they resembled something she knew? She overlayed the symbols in her mind until they made sense.

Yes! There was a symbol. However, it was a human symbol.

She squatted beside him and traced the same five symbols in the dirt. This time she drew the eye, then surrounded it with a light burst. After this, she drew a large triangle below it and filled the triangle in with bricks to form a pyramid. Below the pyramid, she added the thin horizontal parchment banner.

It was a symbol on the back of the United States dollar bill.

Very perceptive, the Mantle hissed.

Maine glanced at the troll, who was semi-smirking. "Good job," he said.

"I don't get it," Maine said. "How can the US dollar have the symbols of the Five Gangs of the Veil on it? It's a human currency."

Hank rolled his shoulders dismissively, then stood. "Humans unwittingly steal a lot of things from the Veil."

"Oh, right." Maine stood and tried to sound gruff like an Oni demon. "Damn humans."

Hank saw that it was their time to bench press. He waved her toward the available weight bench and grinned. "Time to see how much an Oni demon can lift."

CHAPTER TWELVE

As Maine wriggled onto her back on the weight bench, she felt the growing pairs of eyes on her. Some of the members of the Five Gangs and some of the oddball no-gang inmates she had sat with at lunch were gathering around her.

Maine wondered why.

Because you're the only Oni demon here, the Mantle hissed. *Correction, one of only two Oni demons here.*

Noff sat atop her leg, cheering her on. Maine had to remind herself that as long as Noff remained close to her, he was invisible to everyone else. If he moved away, he would appear to them as a mouse.

Maine glanced at the growing crowd around her as she wrapped her palms and fingers around the metal barbell. One of the Brick gang members, an Oni demon, watched with folded arms.

Maine knew that Oni demons were strong, and so were trolls. With her guise in addition to her troll strength, she figured she'd be able to bench press more than an ordinary Oni demon. But should she? Would that draw unwanted attention to her? If so, would it be in a bad way or a good way? Would it be seen as a threat to their strength or would it make her look like a shot-caller to give space to?

Half of the inmates hated her for sticking up for Hank when he had denounced the Corruptor earlier, so Maine figured it didn't matter what she did here. She decided to hold nothing back and display her full strength to everyone. After all, she had to get Noolie's attention. How better to do that than to make a quick name for herself?

I would advise against your idea, the Mantle hissed. *Better not to reveal all your cards all at once.*

She wasn't revealing all her cards to her fellow inmates. She was only showing off her strength. They knew nothing about her guise, the Mantle, or her friends watching over her via the security cameras. She had plenty of cards. Displaying her strength should only dissuade further violence toward Hank or her.

Right?

Hank stepped up to the head of the bench to spot her and glanced down at her. "You ready?"

"Born ready," she said, trying to fit in with the prison vibe. Then with a barely audible grunt, she hefted the barbell up off the bench and lowered it to her chest. After touching the bar against her chest, she lifted it and set it back in its holder. It was too easy. "More weight, please."

"How much more weight you want?" Hank asked as he prepared to add more circular weights to the ends of the barbell.

"How much weight you got?" she asked.

That elicited some chuckles and sneers from the crowd of onlooking inmates. Most of them were standing with their arms crossed.

Maine rubbed her hands together while Hank added a pair of the largest weights to each side. When he stood back over her to spot her, she said, "Is that all?"

"Don't get cocky, Oni. Overdo it and pull a muscle, then you're in real trouble."

She laughed, a great big grating sound while she surveyed the crowd, pretending to check out the competition while searching for Noolie. He still wasn't here. Damn, did he maybe not go to the cafeteria or the rec area? Did he stay in his cell all day long?

"Ready?" Hank asked.

Maine nodded and lifted the barbell off its holders. She pressed it a few times, sweat starting to form at her temples, then replaced it on its holders. She sat up on the bench.

Noff cupped his mouse hands in front of his mouth. "Baller!"

"Done?" Hank asked.

"Hardly." She interlocked her fingers and stretched out her elbows and shoulders. That's when she finally saw Noolie.

Once a hideous mythical creature separated cleanly down the middle with his rank-smelling insides visible to all, the former NasNas was now the most ordinary bald man she had ever seen. When she had solved her father's murder over a year ago and un-Mythed Noolie, he lost his magical powers. Maki-Mae had said that he could still see beyond the Veil. He just couldn't use magic anymore, which had to suck for a magical creature.

Noolie ambled across the rec area to join some Seeing Eye gang members who watched Maine's weightlifting exhibition. When Noolie tried to get a better look by stepping in front of them, one of his gang members elbowed him surreptitiously in the gut. Another grabbed him around the neck like an old buddy and gave him a noogie.

Noolie did not look pleased with the treatment.

That's weird, Maine thought. According to Maki-Mae's intel, Noolie was a high-ranking member of the Seeing Eye gang. Why would he be getting disrespected like this? Maybe because he was half the size of most of his fellow gang members or maybe because of his ruined reputation outside prison when Maine un-Mythed him? Either way, Maine tucked this away into her memory.

"Well?" Hank was saying. "You gonna lift or you gonna get off the bench?"

Blinking, Maine cupped her hands over her mouth and shouted, "What's the prison bench press record?"

The Oni demon from the Brick gang threw his head back and roared with laughter. Addressing Maine as "brother," he informed her of the weight, proudly stating that he was the one who had set it.

Don't try to beat his weight, the Mantle hissed. *You're drawing too much attention.*

Maine turned to Hank. "You heard the guy. Load it up. But add fifty extra pounds."

Hank gave her a tight look, then heaved a sigh with the hint of a smirk. Maine's gaze flicked back to Noolie in the crowd. He was gingerly rubbing his side and the top of his head and stood a little to the side of his gang mates. At least Noolie was seeing her so he would know her when she approached him later to try to extract information from him on her father in the painting.

However, a big part of her wanted to sock Noolie in the jaw and gut. He had, after all, murdered her father. Could she control herself when the time came to talk to him? Would she

RAMY VANCE & MICHAEL ANDERLE

be able to get him to talk on his own or would she have to use force? She hoped she wouldn't unwittingly kill him if it came down to the latter.

She gritted her teeth and seethed. She thought she had put this anger away in the past. But seeing her father in the painting and now having to relive grieving her father's death after she learned he wasn't the town asshole brought up hard emotions.

You need to reduce your heartbeat, the Mantle hissed. *You are showing weakness to those who can sense it.*

He meant the Seeing Eye gang, which was also the gang Noolie belonged to.

She shoved down all her feelings regarding Noolie and her father and laid back on the weight bench. Hank had finished loading up all the weight except for the extra fifty pounds. He was looking down at her, asking with his eyes if she intended him to add the extra weight. She nodded.

Hank did as instructed. Then Maine summoned all her energy reserves and gripped the bar above her.

At first, she couldn't budge the bar from the bench. It was damn heavy!

Sweat trickled from her forehead. Looming over her, Hank frowned down at her. She shook her head and grunted as she lifted the bar off the holders and held it at full extension above her. She was utilizing all of her combined troll and guise strength and wasn't sure she could bench this much weight. But she had to in order to build her reputation among the inmates.

She could do this. She knew she could.

With bulging, quivering arms, she lowered the bar to her chest. Gravity fought her every muscle impulse. Just a little farther...

66

Just had to tack on fifty extra pounds, didn't you? the Mantle hissed. *Couldn't have made it twenty or ten or even five more pounds?*

"Shut up, rag," she muttered, every muscle in her body feeling like it was suddenly drawn tighter than ever in her life, even the muscles she wasn't actively using to bench press the bar.

"What?" Hank asked, staring down at the bar and her shaky arms, ready to intervene and grab the bar at a moment's notice. "You tapping out?"

"N-never," she muttered, lowering the bar another inch and tapping her chest, then beginning the slow ascent up to the bench holders.

"Ya got this!" Noff squeaked.

Some in the crowd gasped while others cursed. She heard the Brick gang Oni demon give a proud demonic laugh as he watched. Even the nearby guards were watching with curious intent.

"He's going to do it," someone gasped from the crowd of inmates.

That's right. I am, she told herself as the bar neared the holders.

She managed to get one side of the barbell in its holder when a loud whip-cracking *whoosh!* split the air.

Maine took her eye off the barbell to see what or who had caused that sound. But she had already known as soon as she'd heard that *whoosh.*

"Not you." She groaned.

She tried to get the barbell in the other holder, but that's when her strength failed her. With her balance thrown off, the bar came free, slashing diagonally down at her waist.

CHAPTER THIRTEEN

Hank edged around the weight bench and caught the barbell before it could injure Maine. But it was too heavy for him to lift back to the holder and Maine was utterly spent. The Oni demon Brick gang member stepped up and helped Hank ease the barbell back on its perch.

Maine tried to catch her breath. "What's he doing here?" She gasped, her arms and core burning from the previous weight of the bar.

"Best to shut up," the Brick gang Oni demon hissed at her.

Agreed, chimed the Mantle.

With gritted teeth, Maine glared at the newly arrived angel who had touched down in the rec area. It was no ordinary angel.

It was the Guardian.

"Shit shit shit…" she muttered as she focused on the leader of the Angel Guard. What was he doing here? It couldn't be good. Was he onto her game? Was he here to sniff her out? Was he going to blow her cover?

"Form up." The verbal beckon was casual, but it came out

like a booming decree from the Guardian. Almost instantly, all the prisoners in the rec area stood ramrod straight and backed up, forming a long line.

While they did so, Hank helped Maine up from the weight bench, and together they got into the line of inmates establishing around them.

"Is this normal?" Maine whispered to Hank, who shrugged. Her heartbeat started to hike.

Calm yourself—you're going to give yourself away! the Mantle hissed.

She forced herself to take long slow breaths while the Guardian inspected the row of inmates. Even the hardest of criminals seemed small next to the Guardian, decked out in his Angel Guard armor.

What was he here for? What was he looking for? Her?

Do you know what 'calm yourself' means? the Mantle hissed.

Do you know how easy it is to say that but how hard it is to do? she mentally projected back.

No, because I do not have a heart.

Maine mentally rolled her eyes. The Mantle was right about keeping her calm so she forced herself to change her perspective. Maybe the Guardian was here for a routine prison inspection, not for her. She didn't know all that much about the angel's life except that he tended to be an asshole.

Swallowing her fear, she stood even straighter, imitating pure confidence.

The Guardian inspected the inmates, stopping to scrutinize some and skipping others. When he reached the leader of the Seeing Eye gang, he stopped and craned his head forward until his face was only inches from the gang leader's. Then the angel reached out and grabbed the gang leader's glowing crystal hanging from his neck. He hefted the object in his hand as if reading it like a crystal ball.

"I ain't done nothing," the gang leader said.

The Guardian's nose twitched in irritation, and the gang leader didn't risk saying anything else. Eventually, the Guardian let the crystal fall back to its wearer's chest. With a disgusted shake of his head, the Guardian moved on down the line repeating the act with the other four gang leaders.

He is searching for something, the Mantle hissed.

When he kept inspecting the inmates after he finished with the last gang leader, Maine started to worry that he was looking for her again. Could he sense a guise spell and try to see who was wearing it? The Guardian was more powerful than most mythical creatures.

After what seemed like an eternity, the Guardian neared her spot in the line. He skipped Hank and stopped right in front of her.

Maine managed to keep her heart rate mostly even by then.

The Guardian's eyes seemed to bore right through her forehead, but she kept her eyes averted and on the ground like the rest of the prisoners seemed to be doing. The Guardian sniffed. Waited. Shook his head with scorn. As he stepped away from her, he casually said, "You almost had that bench press, Oni demon. Almost." Then he continued down the line.

After he finished inspecting the inmates, the Guardian addressed one of the guards. Then he *whooshed* up and into the sky like Superman.

An uneasiness lifted from the rec yard with his departure and soon the chatter of the inmates returned.

The Oni demon stepped up to Maine. "What is up with you? You never seen a routine prison inspection before?"

Maine rubbed the back of her neck. "That's what that was?"

"Yeah, don't think you're special. One of the Angel Guards usually comes to check out the fresh meat when new deliveries come. Usually it's not the Guardian, but he checks in now and then. The Guardian is the unofficial warden of this prison."

"Really?" Maine was glad she knew who the warden was.

The Oni demon nodded.

"What's up with the crystals on the gang leaders' chests?" Maine asked.

"You really don't know?" the Oni demon said.

Hank slapped Maine's shoulder. "He's new to the prison system. Surprisingly," he added.

The Oni demon narrowed his eyes at Maine, then answered. "The crystals are what grant the entire Five Gangs their special abilities. It flows through the leader and the gang members receive its essence through them."

"Why doesn't the Guardian destroy the crystals?" Maine asked.

Both the Oni demon and Hank scoffed.

"They are next to impossible to destroy," the Oni demon explained.

"Then why doesn't the Guardian take the crystals?"

"He can take away the crystals, but they will always find their way back into someone else's possession."

"Oh, the crystals want to be found. Sort of like the One Ring in *Lord of the Rings*?"

The Oni demon nodded. "Lock them up in a magical vault, and they will teleport out. An ancient evil powers those crystals. Better to know who is wearing them so the Angel Guard can keep tabs on them."

Hank piped up. "Taking out gang leaders or trying to confiscate the crystals would only create a power vacuum among the gangs. That can be very unpredictable and dangerous for gang members and civilians alike."

Magical law enforcement was pretty interesting. At least now she was more informed about how things worked with the Five Gangs.

Suddenly the Mantle hissed, *Move!*

Before she could, a sharp-eyed Seeing Eye gang centaur bumped roughly into her. As she staggered, she recognized him as the gang member who gave Noolie the noogie.

The centaur laughed harshly at her. "Just couldn't get it up. So close and yet so far, Oni demon."

At first, Maine didn't know what he was talking about. Then she realized it was about her not getting the barbell on the rack.

Noff squeaked menacingly atop Maine's shoulder. "Ain't no disrepectin' a troll—whup his ass!"

When the centaur stepped in close to her again, rather threateningly, the Mantle hissed, *Frail front left leg due to a skiing accident.*

Skiing accident? Centaurs could ski?

The centaur moved to jab her in the gut, but Maine side-stepped and performed a quick side kick to the centaur's front leg. With a squeal, the mythical creature went down, rolling onto his side and clutching his leg.

Nicely done. That will earn you some respect.

When a guard stepped unhurriedly up to them, he gave Maine a fleeting, uninterested look, then lightly kicked the injured inmate. "Get up."

The centaur gritted his teeth. "That Oni demon hurt me."

The guard shook his head. "Quit making a scene and get up."

The centaur tried, but his leg gave out beneath him. Luckily he had three other legs and could stand with some effort.

Hank smacked Maine's arm and nodded for them to meander away from the centaur. Maine followed Hank with the Oni demon behind her.

"Nice work defusing that situation," Hank casually observed as they walked. "I'm impressed. It's like you knew his weak spot."

"Yeah," the Oni demon agreed. "But what was up with you and the Guardian?"

"The Guardian and I have history," Maine said diffidently, and the Oni demon and troll left it at that.

When they had to stop walking to let a group of inmates pass, the Oni demon extended his hand to Maine. She shook it, and he said, "I guess I ought to introduce myself. I'm Owen."

"Owen the Oni demon?" Maine asked.

He growled. "Yeah, what of it?"

"Oh, nothing. My name's uh, Mantle."

"What an odd name." Owen shook her hand again. "Pleasure meeting another brother in the joint." He held the grip longer than necessary as he appraised her.

Social distance! the Mantle hissed. *He's going to see through your guise.*

"Look, I know you didn't officially complete your bench press rep to beat my record, but if the Guardian hadn't shown up, you'd have had it."

Maine nodded, not saying anything as she waited for the right moment to remove her hand from his grip.

RAMY VANCE & MICHAEL ANDERLE

"What I'm trying to say is, do you want to join the Brick gang?"

Maine's eyebrows arched. "Really?"

Congrats, the Mantle hissed. *You've proved you're a badass to a real badass.*

The Oni demon glanced at Hank. "I can't offer the same to him since I don't know him. But you're a fellow Oni. I can vouch for you."

Maine glanced Hank's way. The troll had his hands in his pockets, his head and shoulders sagging as usual as if he didn't give a damn.

"No skin off my back," he said. "I don't want to be in a gang."

Owen smirked. "Your funeral."

"I guess we'll see," Hank said, continuing onward, leaving Maine with the Oni demon.

She met his gaze and succeeded in slipping her hand from his grip. Luckily, her guise hadn't faded. "I'll think about it, okay?"

Owen grinned. "Don't think too long." He turned and headed back inside the prison.

Maine started walking toward where she had last seen Noolie. Now was as good a time as any to introduce herself to him.

She found him in a heated discussion with three other Seeing Eye members. They started laughing, and when Noolie protested, one of them shoved him backward to the ground. Then they walked off.

"Damn," Noff squeaked. "With friends like that, who needs enemies?"

"Yeah," Maine said flatly. "Almost makes you feel sorry for him."

CHAPTER FOURTEEN

Maine ambled over to where Noolie was picking himself up. She offered her hand to him, but he shook his head and rose wearily to his feet.

"You okay, man?" she asked in her gruffest voice.

"What's wrong with you?" he muttered, patting himself off. "Huh?"

"I can take care of myself," Noolie grumbled. "I don't need some new fresh meat watching out for my back."

Act casual, the Mantle hissed.

Maine shoved one hand in her pocket. "Hey, don't I know you from somewhere?"

Noolie squinted at her. "You don't look familiar to me."

Maine rubbed two of her claws together in mock introspection. "Yeah, didn't I see you on the news or something?"

Noolie gestured at the whole prison yard. "Weren't we all probably on the news when we got arrested? Anyway, I've never been one to watch TV."

"He's missing out," Noff squeaked as he scampered around on the ground.

"What the hell?" Noolie said. "You got a pet mouse or something?"

"Something like that."

"Ugly little thing."

"Hey, watch it, asshole!" Noff squeaked. He reared up on his hind legs and flipped Noolie the bird.

Noolie's eyes narrowed first in amusement, then suspicion. "You know what, it's almost as if your pet mouse is talking to us. Is it a mythical creature?"

"Nope, just a mouse. And it can't talk."

"I always liked mice," Noolie said. "You mind if I hold it?"

Social distance! the Mantle reminded her for the umpteenth time. Noff was under a guise spell too, which meant no one could hold him.

"Yeah, lemme," Noff squeaked. "I'll bite his damn pinky finger off."

"Sorry, he might run off," Maine said. "I've grown attached to him."

"Aww," Noff squeaked.

"Yeah whatever," Noolie said. "Although it is kinda odd you getting attached to a prison rat on your first day in the slammer."

"Animals like me," she said.

"What's his name?"

Noff squeaked. "Tell him my prison name is Tiny!"

"He doesn't have a name." Maine eyed Noolie's tattooed neck, arms, and fingers. She was ready to change the subject. "Let me guess? Tattoo aficionado?"

For the first time in their conversation, he looked proud and able. He nodded, eyeballing her tattoos. "Yours aren't too bad either." He folded his scrawny arms. "I could do better, though."

"You're a tattoo artist?" Maine asked interestedly. Already she felt a rapport establishing between them.

"Best damn one in the joint. All the Five Gangs use my skills."

"But you're in the Seeing Eye gang, right? What's your most requested tattoo?"

Noolie sighed as if any respect she had earned with him had shriveled. "You really are fresh meat. I'm the guy who gets called when a new person gets inducted into a gang. I give them their symbol." He pulled up his orange shirt sleeve to reveal an elaborate "seeing eye" tattoo on his shoulder.

"Nice," Maine said. "Is it just a tattoo or does it have some other purpose?"

Noolie recrossed his arms. "I shouldn't even answer such a stupid question. But you did help me out." He cocked an eye at her. "Although I didn't need your help and didn't ask for it. The tattoo syncs to the respective power crystal dangling from the neck of the gang leader. It's what enables each gang member to tap into their special ability. No tattoo, no ability."

"Makes sense," Maine said.

Noolie unfolded his arms and rubbed his cheek. "Now, you want me to answer any more stupid questions, don't even think about asking them unless you're a member of the Seeing Eye gang. Got it? Good. Now I'm going back to my cell." He sighed. "Lots of new fresh meat to be inducted soon. Got to prepare."

Maine nodded, watching him leave the rec area and go back inside the prison. As she did so, Hank strolled up to her.

"You really do like to make the oddest acquaintances."

"You should see my team back home," she said, catching herself when she saw Hank's suspicious look. "Oh, you know, my gang. Back home. Running them streets."

The troll stared at her for a while, then snorted. "You are one odd Oni demon. If I didn't know better, I'd say you've never been in a gang."

They stood together observing the other inmates in the rec area. The basketball game between the Brick gang and Triangle gang was heating up. The weight bench had plenty of inmates still lined up for their turn at it. Off to one side, some Parchment gang members were sitting on the hot asphalt playing poker.

Although some of the inmates' symbol tattoos stayed concealed, others were displayed. It was interesting to imagine all of them magically linked to their respective gang leader's power crystal like Bluetooth.

"What's on your mind, Oni?" Hank asked without looking at her.

"Magic tattoos."

"You've got a lot to learn about prison life so my first lesson to you is tattoos and symbols have much meaning in prison. Mythical prisons more so."

"I get that. Hey, can someone's allegiance to a gang be erased or canceled? Say I join a gang, get a tattoo, then want out."

"Sure. Symbol tattoo removal is possible. Then the former gang will track you down and kill you."

"Oh."

"So make damn sure you're picking the right gang before you get your tattoo. Why you asking? You already have a gang in mind?"

She smirked at him. "I have an open invitation to join the Brick gang."

The troll looked unimpressed.

"What? You think I could choose better?"

"I didn't say that. As a troll, I value strength and abhor weakness."

"Then what?"

The troll eyed her bulging arm muscles. "You already have strength. You could bench the heaviest out of all of us. Wouldn't you want to balance your skills by joining another gang?"

In truth, she wasn't planning on joining any gang. The prospect of removing a symbol tattoo afterward and dealing with gang members trying to kill her for the rest of her life wasn't appealing. She was tired of assassins trying to kill her.

She also realized that she might need to join the Seeing Eye gang to get Noolie to open up to her. She considered that for a moment. Sage would be completely against that idea. But it might be her only way to get the information she needed. What else was she supposed to do, call off the mission now? Ask Maki-Mae to use her contact to pull her from prison?

No, that wasn't an option. She wasn't leaving until she figured out what was going on with her father in the living painting.

"You don't have a symbol tattoo, right?" Maine asked Hank.

"Nope. Never been in a Five Gang. Never plan to."

"Never say never," Maine said jokingly. "You said you've been in and out of prison. Why not join a gang? Get some peeps on your side?"

"It would be safer, but I can't. The Five Gangs support the Corruptor. That, I can't abide."

"Because you fought against him in Troll War II?"

"Exactly."

Maine was about to ask him for more information since

he seemed like he wanted to talk now, but then an elbow flew out of nowhere, catching her in the chin. She cartwheeled to the ground, and when she picked herself up, she saw the centaur.

Oops, sorry, the Mantle hissed.

"You." Maine wiped her lip and eyed the centaur. He was hobbling on his wounded leg but moving well enough to fight.

A pair of Seeing Eye inmates stepped in behind her. They cracked their knuckles, glancing at the nearest guards who had suddenly and curiously turned their backs to the commotion.

"You're really going to make me kick your ass again?" Maine asked the centaur.

The centaur grinned. "Oh, this time is going to be different —I got friends. Don't you even think about calling out to the guards. I bought them off for this little fight. Course, it's not going to be just some little fight." He ground his fist into his palm. "It's going to be your gods damned grave."

Noff hopped into Maine's pants pocket and peered out with his mouse hands clasped together with glee. "This is gettin' good!"

Maine tilted her head from side to side to pop her neck. With an eager semi-smirk, Hank stepped up to join Maine at her side and popped his shoulders. The guards still weren't looking. It was going to be the two of them versus the centaur and his buddies.

"You're going to put me in my grave?" Maine asked. "We'll see about that."

CHAPTER FIFTEEN

Six inmates charged Maine and Hank, who shifted their positions so they were back-to-back.

"Three for me, three for you," Hank called, throwing a right hook at his first attacker.

"This is awesome!" Noff squeaked. "Prison fight!"

Using the Mantle's suggestions, Maine quick-stepped out of range of all three of her attackers. Then she darted in, dealing two quick kicks behind the knees. One fell to his face with a groan, but the other swept back at her with unfurled claws.

Back! the Mantle hissed.

Maine backstepped but was a moment too slow. The inmate's claws tore open part of her uniform shirt, revealing glimpses of her chiseled Oni demon *male* chest to all gathered.

Maine's cheeks reddened. *Thank troll for guises!*

This is no time to worry about modesty, the Mantle hissed. *Crush your foes with utmost efficiency or else more will keep coming for you!*

The third inmate lunged for her, anticipating her to evade at the last moment as she had before. Instead, she leaned back on the soles of her feet and sprang at him, tackling him head-on and throwing him up against the chain-link fencing.

He bounced off the fence and fell to the ground. Then Maine was atop the inmate, straddling him. She punched him hard across the jaw to make sure he wouldn't get up anytime soon.

Watch out!

Before Maine could react, the second inmate she'd kicked behind the knee sprang at her from behind, catching her by the shoulder. He twisted her around, and she shoved him off her. As she did so, her prison uniform shirt tore further, revealing more of her chest.

Murmurs of awe rose among some of the inmates.

"They're so big!"

"Like Arnold Schwarzenegger in his prime!"

"So jealous…"

Maine was about to cover her frontside with her hands when the sight of her Oni demon claws reminded her that oh yeah, she had a guise.

"This fight sure is gettin' spicy," Noff squeaked, peeking out from her pants pocket. "Too bad nobody can see the real show."

"If you're not going to help me, shut that Mickey Mouse yapper of yours."

"Hey now, partner…"

The clawed inmate leapt at Maine again. This time she fell to the side while extending her arm, clotheslining him so hard in the chest that she felt the air get knocked from his lungs. Before he could land on the ground in a daze, a voice roared, "Get him!"

Maine pinpointed the speaker as five new inmates came her way. It was the leshy, and he looked like he was in a berserker rage.

Warning, the Mantle hissed. *This leshy has unleashed his innate 'leshy rage.'*

"What does that mean?" Maine muttered as she tried to anticipate her new attacking order.

He will feel little to no pain so he's going to put up a bigger fight than last time.

The centaur tried to intervene, but the leshy spun and knocked out the centaur with a single punch. With that done, the leshy turned his attention to Maine. He looked ready to murder her.

Maine turned to the nearest guards and shouted, "Guards!"

The two guards standing only five yards away continued to stand with their backs to the fight as if oblivious to the whole thing.

"The guards have nothing to do with this," the leshy shouted. "If you're worthy, prove it."

"This is gonna be interestin'," Noff squeaked as five new inmates closed in on her.

Maine threw herself forward into the midst of them, knocking three of them out of the way while the other two circled her and began to pummel her backside.

The Mantle helped absorb the brunt of the blows so the two attackers were surprised when she had the energy and strength to round on them, socking them both in the jaws in a tornadic fury.

Noff squeaked in awe. "Your prison name oughta be Hurricane Maine 'cause that was an awesome takedown."

Maine's flapping shirt was a distraction, but she figured she'd be all right as long as she made sure no one grabbed her for an extended period. If they did, her guise would start to fade.

The three inmates she'd thrown back had now nearly recovered.

Strike swiftly—take them out quick and dirty!

"Tell me how," she muttered as she rushed at the three.

Left attacker: right shoulder. Middle attacker: left hip. Right attacker: broken nose.

Maine fell through them like a scythe through a wheat field. With each weak spot she targeted, a new groan or yelp split the air.

The two prison guards' radios squawked, and a guard's voice asked, "Everything all right in the rec yard?"

One of the guards calmly raised his walkie to his mouth. "Affirmative." He didn't look back at the fight.

The three inmates were squealing on the ground in pain, but they'd all live. Maine turned to Hank as he finished his original three attackers. The troll wore a victorious half-grin even though his face sported multiple bruises.

"Nice fighting," he said. Then his eyes widened. "Watch out!"

Suddenly the leshy was on Maine, reaching out for her with a daring quickness. The next thing Maine knew, she was in the air, held at the throat by the leshy.

Inmates gasped. The two guards continued not to intervene.

"You," the leshy growled, his face strained to the max with tension. "Think you're so tough, huh?"

Hank rushed up to deliver a stiff hook, but the leshy was quicker, backstepping and slinging Maine's body at the troll. Her feet struck Hank in the lower jaw with such force that she feared it had broken Hank's face. The troll was flipped end over end to the asphalt while the leshy continued to throttle Maine.

"You're just an ordinary inmate, nothing special about you," the leshy grunted, applying more force.

Maine was distantly aware of Noff squeaking at her and the Mantle hissing in her mind, but the words were all fuzzy.

"You're pathetic." He raised his eyes to hers as her chest and legs hung limp in front of him.

She was starting to fade out of consciousness when her blurring gaze fell to her darkened Oni demon skin. For the briefest moment, her normal skin showed through.

Social distance, woman! the Mantle hissed.

She didn't know what the leshy had seen but he must have seen something because his grip had loosened. Seizing the opportunity, she kneed him under the chin.

He staggered backward, dropping her as he reached up to cover his mouth. He must have bitten his tongue or cheek because he spat some blood to the side. He glowered at her, full of hate. "I am going to tear you apart!"

He lunged at her, but he was off-balance, and she hit him from the side. He fell to his hands, and she delivered a kick to the back of the head. None of the other inmates rushed to the leshy's aid. Many were gaping at her in astonishment.

Maine maneuvered around the leshy and wrapped an arm over his throat. Applying every ounce of troll strength she had left to the squeeze, she said, "Yield."

The leshy didn't yield. He thrashed and continued to fight while spitting, "What are you? Who are you? I saw…"

Do you know what social distancing even means? the Mantle hissed in irritation.

Maine chopped the leshy on the side of the neck and climbed off him before her guise spell could fade out again. "What you saw must have been a hallucination. Because I just kicked your ass."

The leshy rubbed his neck and clambered to his feet. He had a black eye and bruised chin, but by the look of him, he still didn't feel any pain. He beat his chest with a fist. "You have not beaten me."

"Yield," Maine repeated.

"Never!" The leshy charged her with more caution this time. Still the two guards paid them no attention.

He is not lying, the Mantle hissed. *The leshy will die before he yields to anyone. He wants to prove himself in martial combat so a gang leader will ask him to join their gang.*

Maine wondered how she was going to end this fight. Beat on him until he passed out? Damn leshies and their super-endurance and leshy rage. "Any help?" Maine muttered so only the Mantle could hear her.

I have enough energy for you to take one more heavy blow. Make it count. His rage is waning.

That's all she needed to hear.

She and the leshy circled each other for five or ten seconds, then the leshy lunged at her, raising a fist. He drove it at her with incredible force, but with the Mantle's help, she caught the fist and twisted. The leshy let out a seething hiss, then Maine was on top of him, throwing punch after punch at his exposed face.

"Ya got him now!" Noff squeaked. "Keep it up!"

Yes, yes, his leshy rage is almost depleted, the Mantle hissed.

Maine didn't know for how long she rained down blows. It couldn't have been too long because her guise was still holding when a sudden *whoosh* split the air, and a torrent of wind gusted over all those gathered in the rec area.

"Enough!" the Guardian's voice boomed over the rec area.

Thank troll, Maine thought, about to collapse in exhaustion. She never thought she'd ever be grateful for the Guardian to show up.

CHAPTER SIXTEEN

As two guards escorted Maine through a part of the prison she hadn't seen before, she heard some inmates shout and howl as if mortally afraid.

"What the hell are the guards doing to them?" Maine muttered so the guard ahead and behind her couldn't hear.

Perhaps they are being drawn and quartered, the Mantle offered in an evil hiss. *Or maybe they're being waterboarded. That form of torture is hip these days.*

Was that where these two were taking Maine? To be tortured?

This was not part of the plan. She was to infiltrate the prison as an inmate, get Noolie to spill the secret of the living painting, and escape, all while lying low.

Oops.

Noff gasped inside her pants pocket. "They're prob'ly throwin' ya in the hole."

"The hole? What's that?"

Her guards looked at her like she was a crazy person talking to herself.

"Well, in the human world, it's solitary confinement. In the mythical world, it's being cast into a black hole for twenty-four hours."

"An actual black hole?"

"Well, a magical black hole."

The guard walking behind her smacked her in the back with his baton. "Enough talking to yourself."

"Are you throwing me in the hole?" she asked, her voice losing its confident Oni demon tone and coming off as semi-concerned.

The guard scoffed. "You'll find out soon enough. You break the rules, you pay the price."

Worry gripped her throat and heart. If she was locked away in a magical black hole for twenty-four hours, her friends would worry when she didn't receive her magical earmic right away. She couldn't let these two throw her into a black hole. "I didn't start that fight. And two guards were standing a few yards away the whole time!"

"That's what they all say."

"But I didn't—"

"Shut up!" the guard in front of her shouted. "If you ask me, all you inmates deserve to be shoved into the hole and forgotten about."

Maine did shut up, for the moment. *Mantle, if these guards do decide to throw me in the hole for longer than twenty-four hours, I might need your help to escape.*

Certainly. My energy is recharging. Soon I shall be ready for you to bathe in the blood of your enemies.

Eww. Never mind.

The two guards stopped abruptly, turning to face a plain looking office door. The blinds in the office were all drawn shut so that not even a speck of light showed through from inside.

"The dark hole is inside a conference room?" Maine asked the guards.

The Mantle hissed. *Some say office work is hell.*

One of the guards opened the door, and the other pushed her inside, shutting the door behind her. The office was sparse, with only a big desk, two chairs, and a clock on the wall.

No black hole.

She glanced up and saw who was sitting behind the desk. "Should have known it would be you."

The Guardian rapped his fingertips on the desktop. "Why?"

"Because things couldn't get worse. I thought I was going to be thrown into a magical black hole. Instead I get to talk to you."

The Guardian cocked one eyebrow at her. "Do you *want* to be thrown into a black hole?"

She tried to put on her tough guy Oni demon tone again and shrugged. "All the other inmates are getting the black hole treatment."

The angel leader stared at her for a long time. Then he stroked his chin. "They are. But you and I are going to have a little chat instead."

"Oh." That was at least a relief. The hole sounded like awful torture, although Maine was vague on why it was so bad.

"Do you know who I am?" the Guardian asked.

She briefly considered playing dumb but decided against it. She wished she knew if he knew she was Maine or some Oni demon convict. According to Maki-Mae, the Guardian shouldn't be able to see through her guise, but he was one of the most powerful mythical beings alive.

"Is there anything you wish to confess?" the Guardian asked with a hint of impatience.

"Like what?" Maine asked.

"Anything you're hiding from me, Mr. Johnny *Mantle?* I am very good at finding out information, and it's best if you come clean yourself."

Crap. Did he know?

The Guardian stared at her impassively.

Maine was starting to sweat. Maybe if she came clean to him about her identity and mission, he wouldn't do something douchy to her. Maybe he'd even understand.

The Guardian rapped his fingers once more against the desktop. "Last chance."

Be careful, the Mantle warned.

"Fine. This isn't really me. I'm not an Oni demon—this is a guise spell. I'm really Maine Half-Troll."

The Guardian's steely gaze never lifted from her face. "I've heard crazier confessions." He crossed his arms. "Say I don't believe you?"

Maine extended her hands across the table, probably faster than she should have for an interrogated prisoner. "Touch me."

"Sounds dirty," Noff squeaked from her pants pocket.

"Touch you?" The Guardian didn't look convinced.

"Touch my arm. My guise spell will begin to fade."

This is a stupid idea, the Mantle hissed. *Unless you plan to catch him unaware... Yes, rip his arm out of its socket as he reaches over the table, then flip him onto his back and elbow-chop him in the throat. Yes, this could work. Troll woman, you are a bloody genius.*

Finally, the Guardian nodded slowly and placed a wide, warm palm on her wrist. At first, nothing happened, then the demon skin faltered and was replaced by her skin. The demon claws on her fingernails disappeared, her bulging muscles melted away. When she glanced down at her frontside, she saw her partially covered front. She tore her hand away from the angel leader's grasp. "There, convinced it's me?"

For a moment, the Guardian showed no reaction to her lifted guise spell or her words. But then, as her Oni demon guise returned to cloak her half-human, half-troll body, the Guardian broke out in a hearty chuckle.

"What's up with you?" Maine asked after he'd gone on for half a minute.

The Guardian wiped the smirk off his face. "Oh. Only that I knew it was you the whole time."

"What? Are you serious?"

"Very."

"Then why did you… How did you… You're not supposed to be able to see through a guise spell."

"I didn't," the Guardian said. "Until just now. Let's just say I had some inside information about your true identity."

"What do you mean?" Maine was frantically trying to figure out how the Guardian had known it was her the whole time. Was he bluffing? No, he didn't lie or joke around. Ever.

Suddenly, she realized he had seen her partially revealed frontside through her torn shirt. "Hey, you perv, how about a new prison uniform? Or something to cover up with? You're such a jerk."

"My apologies." The Guardian snapped his fingers, and an orange prison shirt appeared in his hand. He tossed it to her.

The Mantle hissed. *Pretend to don the shirt, then leap over the desk and throttle your opponent with it.*

She turned away from the Guardian, removed what remained of her tattered shirt, then pulled the new one over her head. When she finished, she pivoted to face him again. "Tell me how you knew it was me."

"I didn't see through your guise spell if that's what you're thinking. Guise spells hold up even to gods. The guise spell you have is quite good. Maki-Mae and her rituals."

"Wait, what?" Maine said. "How did you know…"

"Because I paid them a visit at your mansion."

"You what? This isn't making any sense. Why?"

The Guardian peered at her. "Because I need your help."

CHAPTER SEVENTEEN

"You need *my* help?" Maine asked.

"Did I stutter?"

"If you knew who I was all along, why didn't you pull me into an office right away?"

"Because I had to sell it and pretend to inspect the gang leaders. I couldn't betray your identity or look suspicious."

"Okay, fine, then what's this all about?" She plopped down in the chair facing the Guardian.

"There's something big and sinister about to go down with the Five Gangs of the Veil. I've been tracking them for years and now time is running out. I've tried interrogating gang members, but they won't talk to me."

"Oh really? You're super powerful."

"They have ways of resisting my interrogation techniques."

"Oh, you mean when you drag them into a bland office room and ask them questions nicely, they don't answer you?"

"It's those power crystals they wear around their necks. It protects the leaders and the members."

"I've heard a little about these crystals. Anything else you can explain about them?"

"The five gangs draw their power from five ancient evil symbols. These symbols manifest in the power crystals."

Maine kicked her legs up onto the desktop. "So it's like *Lord of the Rings*. The gang leaders all get a ring of power."

"No, they get a crystal."

"Like an All-Spark in *Transformers*?" Noff squeaked.

"Like an All-Spark?" Maine asked.

"Kind of, I guess, but with magic."

"Like Harry Potter?"

The Guardian scratched his temple. "Look, whatever helps your puny mortal mind understand the situation. The crystals are embedded with a symbol of evil power."

"Rude. Okay, I get that the Five Gangs are bad news. Also that you can't take out the leaders because the power crystals will escape and be drawn to new leaders. Where do I come into this equation?

"If you spoke to Sage and Maki-Mae, you know that my mission is to talk to Noolie and get out. I'm not getting involved in the matters of the Five Gangs. I want to finish, then get out. I don't need gang assassins after me for the rest of my life."

"There is something up with the Seeing Eye gang. They're planning something, and I need you to infiltrate them and figure it out."

"That doesn't sound too world-ending to me."

"Not everything has cosmic repercussions. This isn't life and death, but I need to get a handle on this before it escalates and we have a major issue on our hands. The Five Gangs of the Veil operate all over the world."

"You have any ideas about what the Seeing Eye gang might be planning?" Maine asked.

"The only clue I have is the prophecy that one day all the gangs will be united."

"That's a bit weird. Can you explain?"

"Those with tattoos will follow whoever bears the crystal with the same symbol. If one gang leader managed to unite all five gangs under one leader, they could become immensely powerful. For the first time, all the Five Gang leaders are in the same place at the same time."

"In a magical supermax prison," Maine added. "Yeah, I guess if one gang were to make a power play, now would be the time to do it. How would they manage it with the magic dampeners all over the place? Are you protecting the dampeners? That's the first thing I would take out if I was an evil overlord wannabe."

Says the troll woman wearing a demonic Mantle, the Mantle hissed. *I am quite pleased by your turn to the dark side.*

"I can assure you the magic dampeners are fully protected. They even have a backup power source in case of a power outage. The only way they could fail is if it were an inside job."

Maine thought about this. "Two of the prison guards turned a blind eye to my fight earlier. They might be on the gang's payroll."

The Guardian sighed. "I would not be surprised. If they are, they will be promptly fired. It is extremely difficult to weed out any likely traitors. The Seeing Eye gang specializes in infiltrating organizations such as law enforcement."

"So this is an important mission then?" Maine asked.

"I don't believe in their prophecy, nor do I think one of the gangs will pull it off and become grand dictator beyond the Veil. But the threat must be dealt with as soon as possible and before it can progress." He cleared his throat. "To that end, I've altered your made-up prison record to make it more...befitting to attract the kind of attention you will need."

"Really?" Maine asked. "What's on my record now?"

"Mythical creature trafficking, a couple of violent bank robberies, and you're a card-holding member of the Corruptor's inner circle."

Your new identity keeps getting better, the Mantle hissed.

"This should get you in good with the Seeing Eye gang," the Guardian said.

"That won't work. I've already pissed off all five gangs for speaking against the Corruptor."

The Guardian raised his hands in an unconcerned manner. "That's your problem. I'm sure you'll figure something out. You're quite ingenious when you need to be."

Maine narrowed her eyes and gave a low Oni demon growl. She sensed that her time was just about up with the Guardian.

"Wait, fine, I'll do what you want. But I need something in return."

"What?" The Guardian's tone was dismissive and unconcerned.

"In order for me to get the scoop on the Seeing Eye gang, I'll have to become one of them. That means I'll have to get a magic tattoo, which means I will never be able to leave the gang, or else they'll hunt me down." Maine paused. "I don't want to constantly look over my shoulder for the rest of my life. What can you do about that?"

"I see," the Guardian said. "You wish to be put in witness protection after this is all over."

"No, I do not. I'm starting a life in Rainwater. I'm not leaving. I need you to magically erase the gang tattoo or whatever after this is all over with. Can you do that?"

The Guardian nodded. "It shall be done. The gangs only know you as your guise, so as long as you maintain it, they will never know your true identity."

"What if they come looking for me after I disappear from prison?"

The Guardian rapped his fingers upon the desktop. "Then I guess we'll have to kill you."

"Kill me?" Maine put her feet down from the desk. "I don't think you're hearing me."

"Kill your prison identity," the Guardian clarified. "It will have to be public. Whenever you're ready to be extracted from prison, we'll arrange for you to be 'shivved' in your cell. Then we'll smuggle your body out through the infirmary. No one will ever know your true identity and your old identity will stay dead."

"Woohoo!" Noff squeaked.

Very cunning, the Mantle hissed. *I approve.*

"And you'll be able to remove my gang tattoo?" Maine asked.

"There might be no need to," the Guardian said. "You will still be able to receive Seeing Eye abilities, but there will be no way for the gang to track you down."

"Okay, we can deal with the tattoo later." Maine felt better. "Maki-Mae was supposed to have a way for me to get out of prison. Do you promise you'll keep your word?"

"Yes. Do not insult my honor."

"Okay, fine, I'll just have to update my friends on my new escape plan. It'll be more exciting at least."

"Anything else you'd like to know or request?" the Guardian asked rather grumpily.

She considered asking him about living paintings or her father, but she didn't want to tip him off to what they were investigating. She decided to inquire about the state of the Veil in general. "Um, have you noticed anything odd lately beyond the Veil?"

The Guardian tapped on the desktop again. "If this is about you and your friends sealing that Chaos leak, I already gave my thanks." He seemed perturbed.

"Are you grumpy because Chaos almost got through and you didn't detect it?"

The Guardian leaned over the desk so his face was close to hers. "I don't have to explain myself to you, mortal. If you must know, I detected a slight anomaly with the Nexus during the 'Mist situation.' It was very much like an anomaly that occurred with the Nexus right after Troll War II ended. I did not intervene that time, and the anomaly corrected itself. So I decided not to intervene this time."

Wow, that was interesting. The timing suggested that maybe her father was involved in fixing the "Chaos anomaly" that occurred after Troll War II. She tucked this into her memory so she wouldn't forget.

"Anomalies don't always spell world-ending catastrophe," the Guardian said. "Now, I've got another appointment to attend to. If you would like more information, perhaps Noolie can help you. He was involved with Chaos behind the Corruptor's back."

"Thanks for nothing," Maine said. "I already knew that."

"Hey, I gave you a shirt. Don't you forget that."

Maine glanced down at her new prison shirt, then back at the Guardian. "Was that a joke?"

Instead of answering, the angel leader turned and checked the clock on the wall. "Ah, look at the time. You won't get exactly twenty-four hours, but at least you'll get enough for the full experience."

"Full experience?" Maine asked. "What are you talking about?"

The Guardian's granite face lightened. "You didn't think you weren't going to be punished for fighting in my prison, did you? You're going in the hole."

CHAPTER EIGHTEEN

"My head still hurts." Maine groaned as she agonizingly rolled over on the floor of a padded cell. She had just been let out of her black hole punishment and deposited here alone. Her hair stood on end as if still weightless in the void and her stomach felt like it was turned inside out. She blinked to try to orient herself. Noff lay beside her, his eyes crossed, his tongue lolling, and his mousy feet straight up in the air.

"Worst. Hangover. Ever," he squeaked weakly. "Black holin' really is worse than waterboardin'."

Another groan escaped Maine's throat. "The Guardian is a real bastard. He was probably over the moon when I gave him a reason to put me in a black hole."

Oh, stop your whining and take it as a mark of pride, the Mantle hissed. *Only the toughest survive black hole therapy without losing their marbles. I think you still have one or two left in your thick troll skull.*

"Shut up, rag," she muttered with eyes scrunched shut. This was worse than a hangover.

"At least we got some useful info," Noff squeaked hoarsely.

Maine moaned. "Remind me what that was again. Because I can't hear over the pain in my eyes."

Noff shook himself off and rolled onto his feet. He stood there woozily for a few moments, then tottered onto his side with a soft squeak. "We learned more 'bout the power crystals and the Five Gangs. That was pretty excitin'. Even more excitin' is havin' to join the Seein' Eye gang to figure out how to stop a mythical gang war."

Maine kicked at Noff with her eyes closed but missed. "You make it seem so easy."

"Uh, after all we've done together, this mission *is* pretty easy. Sure, we ain't got no magic, we're surrounded by hundreds of hardened inmates, and we ain't got no means of communicatin' with the outside world yet, but we've faced worse odds. We've saved the world from an apocalypse. We can save it from crime."

With her eyes still closed, Maine rubbed her forehead. "I guess so. But all I want to do is get Noolie's info and get out."

"Partner, Noolie is in the gang the Guardian wants you to infiltrate. It's like Fate is guidin' your path."

She forced one eyelid open. "Let's not talk about the Fates, okay?"

"Yeah, sore subject, I forgot. Thing is, with you watchin' my back and me watchin' your back and the Mantle watchin' both our backs, we got this."

Maine managed to roll onto her hands and knees. She couldn't stand yet so she crawled around to work out her muscles. Now she knew what it felt like to be a toddler trying to learn how to walk.

Gravity was such a bitch.

Noff stood and shook himself out. This time he didn't fall over like a drunk domino.

Maine glanced at him and lost her balance. "How did you get to your feet first?"

"Heh, heh. Maybe 'cause I've got the ancient Noff bloodline runnin' through my veins."

"Yeah, that's got to be it." Maine groaned as she fought back to her hands and knees. It took a herculean amount of effort to balance like that. "Look, getting thrown in the hole for bad behavior wasn't in the plan. Now we've missed the agreed-upon time to contact Sage and Maki-Mae. They're probably worried sick about us."

"Yeah, prob'ly." Noff stretched out his body, then pranced about in a tight circle. He didn't fall over. "Hey, I think I'm ready for my part of the mission. I'll take the 'mouse holes' the Guardian mentioned and sneak outside the prison to get the magic earmic Blue Dots left outside the perimeter fence."

"You sure you're ready?" Maine felt some strength return but not enough to stand yet. "Don't want you to get caught."

"You worry too much. Don't forget, I am the Noff, and I'm…"

"Small like a mouse?" Maine finished.

He flashed her a dirty look. "Nah. I'm the Noff, and I'm quicker than a shadow."

"Shadows aren't quick, though."

"You're ruinin' my heroic moment. I'll hurry up and get the earmic."

"I might be back in my cell by then."

"Don't sweat it, partner. I'll find ya."

Noff twitched his mousy whiskers, then spun and darted into a mouse hole in the padded room's corner.

"I hope he'll be all right," Maine muttered, then collapsed to the padded floor to sleep off the effects of the black hole treatment.

Two guards ushered Maine back to her cell a couple of hours later. She stumbled, but overall the guards seemed surprised that she didn't need more help making the long walk.

They unlocked her cell, which was empty, and shoved her inside.

"Where's Hank?" Maine asked.

"Still in a padded room," one of the guards said. "You recovered quickly."

"Well, relatively quickly," the other said. Then they closed the cell door behind her and strolled off while they whistled.

It would be nice if Noff got back soon. Since she had the cell to herself, she wouldn't have to worry about Hank overhearing anything he shouldn't.

She stumbled across the cell and plunked down on the lower bunk bed, which was Hank's, but he wasn't here. He wouldn't mind, and she didn't feel like climbing up to the top bunk right now. Instead, she lowered her elbows to her knees and rested her palms over her eyes as she drew some deep, calming breaths. It was good to relax and not have to worry about someone else in the room watching her—

"Hey, partner!" Noff squeaked from directly above her.

Startled, she nearly fell off the lower bunk. When she twisted her head up at the top bunk, Noff was peering over the bed with a magical earbud hooked around his buck teeth.

"Got somethin' for ya."

Maine reached up for the earmic, but Noff bobbed out of the way in a tease. "I can't believe you beat me back here." She reached out again but missed the earmic as Noff pulled it back out of range.

"Gotta be quicker," he squeaked.

"I've got a migraine that could split a mountain." She groaned and snatched at the earmic again. This time she feinted to the side first and reached out with her other hand. Her fingers latched onto the earmic and Noff let it go.

She sat back, and Noff hopped down beside her. He sat back on his pink hind legs and twitched his whiskers as Maine inserted the tiny device into her ear. It was so small that no one would see it, and somehow it worked on a frequency that the magic dampeners or walls didn't block. Thank troll for magic technology and her friend Blue Dots.

"Press your earlobe once to call them," Noff squeaked.

She did so and felt overjoyed as a ringtone flooded her ear.

"Hello?" Sage answered almost immediately.

"Sage, I miss you guys!"

"Are you okay? Are you hurt?"

"I'm fine."

"You missed your first check-in. What happened?"

"Oh, not too much. Just got in a prison fight, then thrown into the hole."

"What! You got thrown in a black hole?"

"Yup. It's about as bad as you can imagine. Worse."

"Dear," Maki-Mae's voice came across the earmic. "Did I hear you correctly, a magic black hole?"

"Yep, they should give you a shirt that says, 'I survived a black hole' afterward. I'm feeling much better now, though." She rubbed her throbbing head. "At least I can walk a straight line now."

"Must have been a hell of a prison fight," Sage commented. "I hope it was worth it."

"You know me. Trolls and their fists." She laughed. "No one got seriously hurt except for the inmates who tried to hurt me. Let's just say that I went full troll and exploited some weaknesses with some help from the Mantle."

"That's good to hear." Maki-Mae was obviously tense after hearing her stepdaughter was involved in a prison fight. "How is prison life?"

"The food is awful!" she shouted. As she did, her stomach rumbled to show its irritation and hunger. She rubbed her belly. "But after a day without food, I'm famished. I'm kind of looking forward to that yellow lumpy slop now."

Noff squeaked. "Ew. That's just wrong."

"Agreed," Sage said. "It looked disgusting on the surveillance footage. I wish I could smuggle in some bits of sourdough bread or something for you."

"I'll be your smuggler, chef boy," Noff squeaked. "Heh, as long as there's some food in it for me."

Maki-Mae cleared her throat. "Dear, before we continue, I must give you some grave news. My contact is unable to get you out of prison. I'm so sorry. We'll have to figure out—"

"It's all good." Maine grinned. "I've got a new way out. The Guardian promised to get me out in exchange for me helping him prevent gang war Armageddon."

"Really?" Sage did a verbal double-take. "What did you say?"

Maine filled them in briefly on what the Guardian had told her about the Seeing Eye gang, global mythical war, and her having to infiltrate the gang.

"I knew it was too much of a coincidence, the leaders of the Five Gangs being together for the first time." Maki-Mae sounded concerned. "I'm afraid you're in a very dangerous position."

"Yeah," Sage said. "That prison is like a pressure cooker for violence. You're not going to take the Guardian up on this, are you?"

Maine knew he was going to freak out. "It aligns with my mission of speaking to Noolie. He already told me he wouldn't speak to me again unless I was a member of his gang. Who knows, joining a gang might be fun."

"Fun? Fun!" Sage was about to lose his shit.

"I've got this handled," Maine said soothingly. "I've got Noff and the Mantle on the inside with me. Now the Guardian is here to maybe watch my back. He sure did take joy in seeing me thrown in the hole."

"Be careful, dear," Maki-Mae cautioned. "The Guardian can only do so much to protect you. How exactly did he say he would extract you from the prison?"

"By killing me," Maine said simply.

"What?" Sage croaked.

"Killing my Oni demon guise," Maine clarified. "He'll fake my death and smuggle me out through the infirmary."

"Well, what could go wrong with that plan?" Sage's sarcasm was biting. "Anything else non-life-threatening worth mentioning?"

"Oh, I met Hank."

"Hank?" There was a tinge of jealousy in Sage's voice.

"Yeah, he's super cool. He's been in and out of the system for a while now. Did I mention he's a troll?"

She heard the sound of Sage slapping his forehead. "You've been in prison for over a day, and you're already falling for some bad boy inmate?"

"He's my cellmate."

"I can't believe this." Sage groaned.

"He thinks I'm a guy because, hey, supercharged guise spell."

Sage audibly exhaled. "So you're not in some sordid affair with this troll?"

"Um, not yet."

"What?"

"Just kidding. Hank's my father's age. That would be like dating my dad, gross."

"Whew." Sage didn't try to conceal his relief.

"Can you believe he fought in Troll War II with my dad?"

Maki-Mae cut in. "It isn't that much of a coincidence. Many trolls joined your father in rallying against the Corruptor."

"Oh. Well, I think he knows some cool stuff about my dad. He keeps his mouth closed tighter than a garbage clam so it's been tough getting him to talk about the war days, but I think I'm growing on him. When he gets back from the hole, I bet he'll spill all, considering it was him and me fighting against like twenty Corruptor-loving inmates."

"That's great," Maki-Mae said. "I'm sure he'll be able to help you to get to know your father more, at least how he was back during the war."

"Yeah, he even gave me the same salute Dad would give me when I was a kid and we played soldier. Do you remember that salute?"

"I remember him giving that salute to other trolls he met," Maki-Mae said. "I'm glad you're getting to be closer to your father if only in memory."

"I plan to get to know my father in person," Maine said confidently. "Once Noolie tells me what's up with that living painting." She drew a deep breath, having gotten caught up in the excitement. "Have you guys found anything interesting from your side?"

"Yeah, and it's a doozy." Sage was glad to be off the topic of prison and Maine's welfare. "Not something we told the Guardian when he visited us."

"What?" Noff squeaked. "Enough with the suspense."

Sage chuckled. "It concerns the Nexus. By using advanced weather applications and a few complex spells, we found a big anomaly with the Nexus. It seems the Nexus doubled in size after the Maine-Corruptor Conflict, then shrank again. I checked historical records, and it looks like the same happened after Troll War II."

"The Guardian mentioned an anomaly with the Nexus, but he shrugged it off," Maine offered. "Do you think Chaos was trying to make a power play both times?"

Maki-Mae took over. "It is possible Chaos was trying to do something to disrupt the balance. Or, maybe each instance was linked to the usage of a Wish Card, which Chaos is involved in. You said your father used a Wish Card. Maybe that's the key to this."

"Too bad we can't talk to Valkious," Sage said.

"We can't *yet,* not until we solve the mystery of the painting."

Sage's words were careful. "Maine, I don't want you to get your hopes up too high. That isn't your dad. It can't be."

"Even if it's just a memory of him or something… Look, this is really important to me."

"So is our wedding," Sage countered. "I love you and don't like you being in a supermax prison where we can't help you as much."

"I love you too," Maine replied. "You're watching me through the surveillance cameras, aren't you?"

"Yeah, but I can't touch you through a camera."

Maki-Mae broke in. "However, you could touch each other if you had a conjugal visit."

"Good luck with that." Maine sighed. "I don't think the Guardian would approve of that. Not for me."

"Good thing I didn't go through the Guardian." Maki-Mae sounded satisfied. "I worked my persuasive and balancing powers on the prison's next in command. I got a conjugal visit with Sage scheduled in a couple of days."

"Woohoo!" Sage shouted. "Maki-Mae, that's awesome!"

"Consider it an early wedding gift," Maki-Mae suggested.

"Best gift ever," Maine agreed. "With that thought on my mind, prison won't be that bad."

CHAPTER NINETEEN

The dinner bell sounded, and Hank still hadn't returned to their cell. His older body must've needed longer to recover from the black hole.

"Wonder what we're eatin' today," Noff squeaked as he hopped into her shirt pocket. "Yellow gloop or orange gloop?"

Maine got up and left the cell. As she made her way to the cafeteria, a minotaur inmate approached her. His symbol tattoo showed he was in the Parchment gang. That couldn't be good news.

Prepare to gouge out his eyeballs! the Mantle hissed.

Instead of attacking, the minotaur clapped her back. "Dude, you are awesome."

Maine kept her guard up in case this was a Parchment gang trap.

The sloppy grin on his face showed he meant the compliment.

Maine raised her eyebrows at him in question.

"Your rap sheet. It's getting around to all the boys. You are one crazy Oni demon."

"Oh, that." Maine popped her knuckles and continued to the cafeteria.

A kappa with piercings on all his exposed webbed areas strolled up to her and nodded. He was a Triangle gang member. "All five gangs are going to want you in their gang. I hope you choose Triangle."

"No, Brick!" a blocky ogre inmate called to her. "You're one impressive Oni demon. No one is going to mess with you ever again. You're like, my hero."

"Why?" Maine asked. "I got into a fight my first day here over denouncing the Corruptor."

The Brick gang ogre shrugged it off. "You were testing us. We failed. But we truly had never heard of you and your exploits. You're a trickster, aren't you?"

"A little." *If they only knew...* she thought. "But I'm part of the reason some of you got thrown in the hole."

A Brick gang gargoyle chuckled. "Bet that black hole was a walk in the park for you. It toughened us up!"

The Brick gang ogre joined in. "Yeah, it was good for us! Makes us stronger to fight the guards one day. Being thrown in the hole is like tackling fuel!"

The Mantle hissed in delight. *If these simpletons only knew you were a troll woman in a guise... These inmates are dumber than bricks—pun intended.*

A Triangle gang gnome skipped up to her, peering up at her like she was his savior. "Is it true what they say?"

"What?" Maine asked.

The gnome's eyes glistened. "That you have personally spoken with the Corruptor."

Crush his dreams and tell him, No. Then crush him under your heel.

"Yeah," Maine answered gruffly. "What of it?"

Several more inmates approached her as she neared the cafeteria. Many of them bowed or knelt to her as she passed them.

"Blessed by the Corruptor," a gargoyle cried with joy.

Noff squeaked from her chest pocket. "You're a damn hero, congrats!"

Maine did a mental facepalm. The Guardian had outdone himself when mocking up her fake rap sheet. She wouldn't have believed it had she not seen it. This would probably make her job of infiltrating the Seeing Eye gang and getting Noolie to open up to her much easier. But so far, every gang but the Seeing Eye gang was fawning over her. The Eye gang members seemed to be avoiding her for the moment.

The satyr from the prison bus jumped in front of her, blocking her way. He wasn't committed to a gang yet. "Is it true that the Corruptor will rise again one day soon?" His eyes glowed like a child about to receive the best birthday present ever.

Crush his dreams and life mission and tell the truth. The Corruptor is finished. He will never rise in a thousand lifetimes. No, tell him the Corruptor has given up on world domination. Tell him he's joined clown school. Or become a monk...

Placing her fists on her hips, Maine flashed her wickedest Oni demon grin. "Rumors of the Corruptor's demise have been greatly exaggerated."

The growing crowd of inmates gave a collective gasp, then cheered with roaring cries of victory.

"I knew it!"

"He will rise!"

"The apocalypse is back on, baby!"

Maine smiled awkwardly, then pushed through them into the cafeteria. Everyone in the lunch line stepped aside so she could move to the front. The inmates volunteering at the lunch line even gave her extra scoops of food.

"Bein' a hero sure comes with perks, heh," Noff squeaked.

With her plate loaded, she turned to find a table to sit at. Gang members from all the Five Gangs except the Seeing Eye gang called for her to sit with them.

Instead of choosing a gang, she sat with the sixth group reserved for the oddballs.

"The Oni demon is testing us," a gang member called.

"Pick our gang!" another shouted.

"He's so cool," someone said.

"Smart," Noff squeaked. "Way to make 'em jealous. Now how 'bout ya try to make some friends at this table?"

Maine turned to the oddball inmates sitting around her, but they all moved down the table away from her as if she had a communicable disease. All of them except for a spider shifter sitting next to her.

I suggest not interacting with the spider shifter inmate, the Mantle hissed.

"Why not?" Maine asked.

The spider shifter waved at her with a long slender finger. "Hey, new guy. You smell delicious."

"Got it," Maine said and got up to find an empty table.

"Good move," Noff squeaked. "Forget what I said about makin' friends."

The spider shifter called to her. "Hey, gorgeous, how about you come visit my parlor later tonight?"

Gulping, Maine turned her attention to her plate and started eating her meal. With the extra food portions, it took longer than usual. Fortunately, the spider shifter didn't follow her. She dumped her plate when she finished.

She headed back to her cell afterward, a pep in her step as the other inmates cheered her, shook her hand, or asked for her autograph etched into their skin with her claws, which she declined. She was still disturbed that none of the inmates fawning over her were from the Seeing Eye gang. According to what she knew about them, they were more distrusting than the other gangs and liked to spy and gather intel with their enhanced senses. So maybe they were still investigating her. If she had somehow ended up on their blacklist, she wondered why.

When she got back, she found Hank waiting for her, sitting on his bunk. He was giving her a sour look like she'd punched his kitten or something.

"Hello to you too," she said when it was clear he wasn't going to speak first.

He didn't say anything, wouldn't even meet her eyes.

"Did I do something to piss you off?" Maine asked.

The troll just grunted.

I sense antagonism—he's a threat. Beat him to the punch by drop-kicking him in the face!

Maine softened her gaze at Hank. "Did the black hole mess you up that bad?"

"Not nearly as bad as me finding out about your real identity."

Maine barely heard the troll's words they were so low and gravelly. But which identity did he mean? That she was a half-troll girl? Or the one on the rap sheet the Guardian had enhanced...

"I can't believe it," Hank said finally. "You denounced the Corruptor. Now you're his biggest fan? You're a lying piece of shit. You know that?"

Maine wasn't sure what to say. She wanted to keep Hank's

support, but she needed to join the Seeing Eye gang even more. "You don't know the real me."

"No, I guess I don't." Hank laid on his bed and turned away from her.

"You going to eat dinner?"

"No."

"I can get you some food."

"I said no."

His guard is down, and his back is to you. Punch him in the spine and then smother him with his pillow...

"Whatever," Maine said. "I wish I could tell you what's really going on. But I can't—"

From out of nowhere, Hank twisted on the bed and leapt at her. Then the two of them were locked in a wrestling match, trying to throw the other to the floor.

Social distance! Social distance!

"Get out of my sight!" Hank roared. He threw a punch at her, but it was easy to dodge. He was still woozy from the black hole.

Noff blasted out of Maine's pocket and bit the troll's ankle. "Hey—ow!"

Hank's balance was thrown off. Maine easily broke free of his grasp, then shoved him backward with a palm to the chest. He stumbled and crashed to the floor, bumping his head on the toilet. "You're going to pay for that, Oni demon!"

The troll was pushing himself up with a hand on the toilet when an inmate cleared his throat from the other side of the open cell door.

A Seeing Eye gang member stood watching her carefully. "Mr. Mantle?" the inmate asked softly.

"Who's asking?" Maine tried to read the inmate's manner.

Non-threatening, the Mantle informed her.

"My gang leader," the Seeing Eye member said. "He seeks a private audience with you. Will you come with me?"

Maine glanced over her shoulder at Hank, who was stooped over and leaning against the toilet, exhausted from their brief scuffle. She didn't want to leave him on these terms, but she was about to chat with the Seeing Eye gang leader. This was part of her objective. She couldn't pass it up.

She pushed her shoulders back and growled pleasantly. "Lead the way."

CHAPTER TWENTY

The gang member led Maine to a cell block on the other side of the prison. He stopped beside an open cell and waved for Maine to go in.

The Seeing Eye gang leader's cell was nothing like hers. It was five times bigger with a larger bed, toilet, and sink. Also, various tapestries covered the three cell walls. It seemed that being a gang leader came with extra amenities.

The gang leader was sitting on a yoga mat on the floor, deep in meditation when she arrived. A glass of iced tea sat next to him. He opened his eyes and nodded for her to sit across from him.

Seeing a lean redneck-looking gang leader sitting in meditation was odd, and it was difficult for Maine to keep from laughing. The hardness in the gang leader's face and the teardrops tattooed beneath his eyes made it easier to act serious.

"Fresh Meat, I've heard a lot about you. Any of it true?" His words were soft and balanced.

Warning, the Mantle hissed. *As a Seeing Eye gang member, he possesses enhanced sensory perception. He can hear your heartbeat and see each flutter of your eyelid. Answer with caution.*

"Yeah, some of it," Maine said simply.

The gang leader scoffed. "Even if only half of your rap sheet is true, it's quite impressive. For an Oni demon."

Maine focused on the gang leader, waiting for the Mantle to tell her what type of mythical creature she was up against.

Daywalker. A creature 'born' a vampire that is immune to daylight. Only a handful of daywalkers in existence. Don't let their human appearance fool you. Possesses incredible speed, power, and agility, the perfect match for a troll. Reminder: his sensory abilities are enhanced further by the power crystal around his neck.

It had been a while since she'd faced off against a vampire. This guy was much more intimidating than a normal vampire, though.

The daywalker grabbed the glass beside him and lifted it to his lips. He took a sip. "Ginger tea. It clears the mind."

Maine nodded.

"How was your experience in the hole?"

"It was quite the experience," Maine said casually. "But I recovered quickly."

The daywalker regarded her coolly as he set his tea glass back on the floor. "Yes, that's what I hear. You're an interesting character."

Maine shrugged. "Thanks?"

"Got any skeletons in the closet?" The daywalker's words were like the hiss of a trickling stream.

"Don't we all?"

The daywalker's stiff face relaxed. He chuckled. "Fresh Meat, I like you. There's only one thing that concerns me."

"Yeah?"

The daywalker paused for an abnormally long time. "How is this the first time I've heard about you?"

Maine didn't know what to say, but she couldn't show fear or anxiety. She kept as close to the truth as possible. "I keep a low profile."

"How did you get caught? Prolonged car chase? Tense bank standoff? Betrayed by a crew mate?"

"I, uh, threw some green juice on a cop."

The Mantle groaned. *Anything would have been better than that.*

"Lame," the daywalker said. "But I can sense it's the truth. It's all good. We all mess up. But green juice? Gross."

Maine nodded, unsure what was expected of her to say. Had she blown it?

The gang leader tilted his head from side to side, relishing each crack and pop of his spine. "I'll be frank with you. I want you in my gang."

Yes! Maine thought.

"Do you accept?" the daywalker asked.

Draw it out, the Mantle hissed. *Make him sweat.*

"Yes," Maine said before her emotions could go unchecked and give her away.

The gang leader gave a blood-curdling smile, displaying a mouth filled with sharpened teeth. "Then rise."

Maine stood. Before she was fully up, the gang leader was behind her, pulling up her shirt sleeve to reveal her shoulder. But why? To bite her?

Social distance!

Maine swatted the gang leader's hand away. When he flashed her a death look, she said, "Skin condition. Wouldn't want you to catch it."

"I see. Noolie!"

Maine nearly jumped at the suddenness of the command. The next thing she knew, Noolie was standing next to her, having slinked in through the open cell door. "Give her the tattoo."

"Yes, sir." Noolie lifted a wicked-looking tool that resembled an evil version of an archaic ink quill.

"Whoa, right now?" Maine asked in a faltering tough guy voice.

"That a problem, Fresh Meat?"

"No."

"Good." The gang leader stepped away, sat on his mat, and resumed his meditative pose. "Noolie," he called with his eyes closed.

"Yes, sir?"

"Avoid touching the Oni demon's shoulder with your hand. Skin condition."

"Certainly." Noolie flashed Maine a look of startled recognition. Maine grinned at him.

"Oh," the leader added. "Try not to smudge the iris of the eye. I've seen some of your latest work, and you're getting a bit sloppy."

"Yes, sir."

"You won't disappoint me, will you?" the leader asked.

"No, sir."

"Then proceed."

Gritting back his frustration, Noolie flexed his wrist and fingers. Then he brought the magic tattoo needle to her shoulder and began to apply the ink.

The pain of getting the tattoo was like nothing she'd ever experienced. It was no ordinary tattoo needle Noolie was using. The ink itched and tore at her soul as it formed the ominous "seeing eye" of the Seeing Eye gang beneath her top layer of skin.

"You didn't scream," the gang leader said in a conversational tone when Noolie had finished. "Usually they scream. Impressive."

The truth was, she would have screamed had the Mantle not been suffusing her with its energy.

"Oftentimes, they pass out from the pain," the gang leader remarked casually. "Sometimes, they die. But you survived, so congratulations on passing the entrance test."

"Thanks?" Maine rotated her shoulder and studied her new tattoo.

The leader gave her a cursory look. "Your Seeing Eye abilities should begin to manifest shortly. Enjoy them and honor our gang through their use."

Maine gave a quick half-bow. "Thanks, leader."

"Now leave me," the gang leader ordered. "I will see you at the formal initiation tomorrow. I currently have much work to do."

"You mean you have to meditate?" Maine asked.

"Something like that. I must listen to the heartbeat of the prison. I must check its pulse. Plant my seeds. Root out potential spies."

Maine didn't know if the gang leader was speaking metaphorically or not. She nodded politely, first at him, then at Noolie, who only gave her a confused look.

The tattoo ached and burned as she returned to her cell. She had hoped for a chance to speak to Noolie or an extended chat with the gang leader to see what he was planning, if anything, to make good on her deal with the Guardian.

Oh well. According to the gang leader, she'd see them both at the "formal initiation," whatever that was. Was she going to be put through another test? She hoped not. It sounded ominous, but it couldn't be nearly as bad as getting that tattoo.

As she walked back to her room, she glanced at the seeing eye on her shoulder. Was it just her or did its gaze follow her eyes? Had she made an awful mistake?

Lights out was called right before she reached her cell. A guard led her the rest of the way and slammed her cell door behind her.

The lights were off, but oddly enough, Maine could see Hank sitting on his bed facing the cell door.

That would be the power of the Seeing Eye augmenting your eyesight, the Mantle explained.

Night vision? *Now, this I could get used to,* she thought as she stepped farther into her cell.

"I see you're still alive." Hank's voice drifted to her through the darkness. "So that means you're a Seeing Eye now?"

"Yeah. Got a problem with that?"

"No. Not at all. In fact, it was I who told you that you should join a gang." He scratched his beard stubble in the darkness. "Gotta say though, that was pretty fast. At least you picked a strong gang to join. The Seeing Eye gang will watch your back. Just don't double-cross them or they'll plant a knife in it."

Maine let the troll's words hang in the stillness for a few moments. "So we're all good then, you and me?"

"Hell no. We're sworn enemies. Now quit bothering me and get some damn sleep."

Maine cleaned up at the sink, then climbed onto the top bunk. She lay for what seemed like a while, staring up at the dark ceiling she could touch if she extended her hand.

This felt so wrong. Hank was a criminal, but he was also a good guy. He also had known her father back in Troll War II.

Mantle, she mentally projected. *I need to learn about my father and Hank can help with that.*

I have an idea. It is a good one.

What is it? If you say, 'Sneak down and throttle him 'til he talks,' don't waste my time.

The Mantle remained silent.

She lay a few more minutes in the darkness. She hadn't heard Hank move so he was presumably still sitting on his bed, awake. But why? Was he still reliving the days of the war, maybe?

That was it!

Mantle, you were there during Troll War II, right? When my father and his army stormed the keep and seized the demonic weapons.

I remember that day well, the Mantle hissed. *I gained a new master that day.*

Do you remember seeing Hank there?

Yes.

Then describe that day to me. Tell me about my father. And Hank. I need to get through to him.

What do you wish to know? the Mantle hissed.

Details only Valkious and Hank would know.

The Mantle did, including the part where Hank stepped in front of a spear meant for Valkious. The spear had pierced Hank's chest, narrowly missing his vitals but wounding him before the final charge of the war. Was that why he was so down and out? Because he saw himself as a failure?

"Hank," she called to the darkness below. "I know what you did in the war. The way you stepped in front of that spear. I just want to say thanks for saving my father. Thanks for saving Valkious."

For the first time since she laid down, she heard Hank stir. When he spoke, there was no more animosity in his voice.

"Your father? Valkious was your father?"

"Yeah."

"But you're an Oni demon. Uh… You messing with me?"

"No."

"Shit. Then what the hell, Oni?"

Maine sighed. "It's a long story." She thought Hank might tell her to shut up again, but he exhaled a long sigh.

"We're in prison. We've got time."

Maine grinned in the darkness. She'd gotten through to Hank.

CHAPTER TWENTY-ONE

Even though it was nearly midnight, things were strewn out everywhere in the mansion's study. There were tables lined with equipment and tools, and all the sofas and coffee tables were pushed aside. Sage was wearing a lab coat and inspecting the living painting with a magnifying glass. Al stood behind him, his ghostly cyclops eye blinking.

"There has got to be something to learn from this painting." Sage strapped on a pair of safety goggles and adjusted his lab apron. He couldn't sleep so he might as well experiment some more on the painting.

Today he and Maki-Mae had been able to confirm one thing. This painting was an actual current place and not a memory. Where that place was, they had no clue. It looked like a quaint countryside on Earth, but all of the advanced location spells he and Maki-Mae had cast on it revealed nothing.

It was so frustrating.

Sage was glad they had moved Blue Dots' surveillance monitoring station into the foyer. Had it still been in here, he would have been tempted to stare at the footage all night in case he could detect some danger Maine and the Mantle couldn't see coming.

Zombie Icarus had moved the expensive computer equipment and desk, complaining about how Sage had better not make a mess with his "experimenting."

Sage thought *he* could be uptight at times. Zombie Icarus was the one who needed to loosen up. Sage didn't intend to make a mess tonight. He just wanted to run some more tests on the painting.

"Ice pick." Sage reached behind his back.

Ghost Al selected an ice pick from one of the tables arrayed with tools and placed it in Sage's palm.

"Thanks. Al, you're really getting the hang of being a ghost."

Al blinked. "Why, thank you. Yes, interacting with physical objects is becoming more natural to me. It takes less energy out of me too, so I don't have to fade out and recharge as often. It shan't be long until I can stay visible all the time if I wish to."

Sage prodded the painting with the ice pick. Oddly, the painting's fabric resisted the pointy tool. A tiny semi-liquid tentacle reached out from the painting and batted the ice pick aside. "Hmm, interesting." Sage wiped more sweat from his eyes, then turned back to Al. "You're working hard at building your ghost stamina. It's showing."

Al blinked and hovered a little taller and straighter. "Got to be ready for your and Master Maine's wedding. It will be simply splendid, and I want to see every moment of it."

Sage paused and dropped the ice pick onto his lap. "The wedding. Yes. It will be splendid if it ever happens."

"You have doubts, Master Sage?"

"What? No, of course not. It's just Maine's always rushing into danger. The Veil isn't the safest place. Maine has tangoed with so many powerful entities, and she doesn't have much of a clue about how magic works. I just hope there is a wedding."

Ghost Al patted Sage on the shoulder. "There there, she'll be all right. She always is."

"She's been pretty lucky so far. I hope that luck doesn't run out."

"I think her in-flux destiny helps more than it hinders." The ghost butler chuckled. "If anything, it makes life more interesting for the rest of us."

"It certainly does." Sage turned back to the painting and prodded it with the ice pick, but again the tiny liquid tentacle jutted out from the painting and pushed the ice pick aside. Hm. This was the first reaction he'd gotten from the painting. Was he onto something? "Hammer," Sage said.

Ghost Al floated over to the table with the hammer. He picked it up and glided back to Sage. "What are you going to do?"

"See if I can punch a hole through the painting."

Al blinked. "Are you sure that's a prudent idea? Sounds like something Maine would do."

Sage chuckled. "What can I say? I think she's rubbing off on me." He steadied the ice pick in one hand and poised the hammer above it. After a quick intake of breath, he struck the butt of the ice pick.

The painting didn't have time to knock it aside with a liquid tentacle this time. The ice pick pierced the painting's fabric, making a tiny ripping sound as it punched through.

"Uh-oh." Sage stooped closer to the painting as its sunny sky flashed dark. All of a sudden, the lights in the mansion's study flickered, then the painting emitted a piercing scream.

"Probably shouldn't have done that," he murmured as the painting's surface rippled. He withdrew the ice pick from the painting, leaving a small hole, and took a step back.

With the violent way the painting was rippling, he thought a hand might shoot out from the painting and clutch him by the throat and pull him inside the painting.

That didn't happen.

Instead, a tiny black batlike creature shot out of the tiny hole in the painting, flapping about in the study as if it couldn't find its way.

"A baby bat monster?" Sage asked aloud.

Then a second and a third creature flapped out of the painting.

Al hovered next to Sage. "I think you have angered them."

More baby bat creatures fluttered into the room from the painting. Soon they formed a black cloud of flapping wings. Their tiny teeth glimmered in the study's lighting. As terrifying as this was, he was glad the lights had only flickered and were still on.

"Looks like they are hungry too," Al said. "Not a bad time to fade out to recharge…"

"I'm not a ghost!" Sage shouted, frantically surveying the room around him. The doors to the study were closed so the bats couldn't escape that way. At the opposite end of the study, windows led out into the peaceful night.

Whatever these creatures were, they did not look friendly. They didn't belong in this realm and Sage couldn't let them escape outside where they could terrorize the world. He didn't know anything about them. What if they could reproduce at a speedy rate? If they got out, they could cause widespread ruin. All because he had to try to investigate the painting. Sheesh, Maine was rubbing off on him!

"Maybe they're friendly?" Al offered.

The bat creatures swarmed toward Sage with chomping mouths and flapping wings.

"Oh crap!" There was no time to get out of the way so Sage erected a magic shield around him. The bat horde ran into it, bounced off, and continued past him, smacking into one of the bookcases. With tiny wings flapping against ancient leather tomes, the swarm turned and prepared a second fly-by at Sage.

His magic forcefield was still functioning, but it was weakened from the first assault. This wasn't good.

"Hey, over here!" Ghost Al called, waving his translucent arms in wild circles above his head. The bat swarm locked in on him and swarmed him, passing right through Al's ghostly body and shredding a sofa that lay in the way. Couch stuffing wafted into the air like snow floating upward.

"That was my favorite sofa!" Sage shouted, casting a wide-radiused disorientation spell at the bat swarm. It had no effect, passing through their bodies. They opened their hundreds of tiny mouths and shrieked.

Al was gone, having been sent to wherever ghosts went when the bats had attacked him. It was up to Sage to stop this threat.

As the bats prepared a third fly-by, he cast a sleep spell at them. This time he concentrated it so it would strike only a small portion of them instead of a wide radius. As before, the spell passed through the bats' bodies with no effect.

"Seriously, what the hell?" He grimaced as the tiny dark bodies flapped against his magic forcefield, pressing him down to the floor with their weight. There were so many of them, and a frantic glance at the painting showed they were still pouring into the study.

The study was a large, long room, but if left unchecked, the swarm would grow to fill it within a few minutes. Then they'd burst out the window at the end and escape into the world. He had to find a way to close off their passage from the painting and then take care of all the bats. But how? His spells didn't faze them!

"Why am I always fighting tiny things that shouldn't hurt me but do?" he muttered.

His magic reserves shook to the core as the energy it took to sustain the forcefield took its toll on him. He rolled under a table lined with equipment as his shield gave out. Bat creatures followed him, shrieking with mad screeches and dislodging heavy tools to the floor in their attempt to get at him.

Sage army-crawled out from under the table, exclaiming when a crowbar smacked him on the lower back from the table above. With a stifled curse, he gripped the crowbar and swung in a mad gyration as he stood, the metal tool striking bat creatures and knocking them to the wall and floor.

His spells might not affect these hellish creatures, but physical weapons did. That meant he could kill these things. But where had they come from? Some magic realm? A hell dimension, maybe?

A few bat creatures detached from the swarm and beelined for Sage's face.

Sage set a defensive stance and swung at the first one, knocking it to the floor. He took out the second one too, sending it careening into the ceiling and flopping to the floor. The third bat creature got past his attack, striking him in the face where it latched onto him with splayed-out wings wrapping around his face.

"Ah!" he shouted in a garbled mess as he pinwheeled his

arms. He lost his balance while trying to pry the thing off his face and stumbled backward over a sofa. He tumbled over the padding as soft fur brushed his face. Tiny teeth chomped at his nose, and he managed to pry the bat creature off him. It hovered a foot away in front of him with glaring eyes. Sage swung the crowbar, sending the creature rocketing into a bookcase.

Over on the desk, a seemingly endless supply of bats continued to pour out of the painting.

The creatures were preparing to swarm him again. Sage didn't know if he had enough magic reserves to cast another shield spell. Was this the end? Was *his* death going to be the reason why the wedding wasn't going to happen?

If so, he was going to make his final moments count.

The bat creatures burst toward him, and he charged headlong at them.

The swarm engulfed him as he started swinging. Wings smacked his head and shoulders, hair brushed him, and teeth chomped on his skin and clothes.

He held his own, swinging the crowbar enough to part the swarm for him to have some breathing room. He was breathing hard, but he realized the bats were breathing even harder with each flap of their wings. It was almost like they were in such a mania they were having trouble breathing. They weren't from Earth. Were they having trouble because the air on Earth wasn't what they were used to?

He was trying to figure out if he could somehow use this idea when they swarmed him again, this time going low for his legs and out of the range of his crowbar.

He couldn't protect his bottom half and top half at the same time. Tiny teeth and claws shredded Sage's legs, arms, and chest as he did his best to fend them off, but it wasn't good enough. He was taking out a good number of the creatures, but for every one he knocked to the floor, five more flapped out of the painting.

If he'd been quicker, he might have been able to cast a forcefield spell around the painting to keep the bat creatures from entering the study, but it was too late for that. He'd done his best but had come up short.

He was about to charge them one last time when the door to the study burst open.

"What did you do?" Maki-Mae shouted.

Sage knocked down a bat creature flying at his throat. "The painting...sent these creatures..." More bats slammed into his back, knocking him to the floor. This was it. Not even Maki-Mae could help now.

Maki-Mae uttered an incantation, and suddenly all the bats flapped away from Sage and hovered near the ceiling. As they spread out, it looked like the ceiling had grown giant fuzzy mold spores.

"What did *you* do?" Sage sputtered, clambered to his feet, and rushed over to where Maki-Mae stood eyeing the bat creatures.

"These are creatures of chaos. I negated some of their chaos magic."

"What? Chaos? But how?" Sage wiped a trickle of blood out of his eyes from one of the cuts on his forehead.

"I don't know," Maki-Mae said, "but if Chaos is involved with this painting, it can't be good. Do the creatures have any weaknesses?"

Sage sucked in a breath. "Can't you just use your balancing powers to neutralize them?"

The harionago attorney shook her head. "It can only repel them."

Sage whipped his head toward the study's door, which was wide open from Maki-Mae entering. A small swarm shot for the door.

"The door!" Sage cried.

Maki-Mae flicked her wrist, and the door slammed shut.

"That was close," Sage said. Some bat creatures flew at him, and he knocked them out of the air with the crowbar.

More bats attacked Maki-Mae, and she karate-chopped them and kicked them out of the air with graceful hops and pirouettes. The bat creatures she missed with her hands and feet, her barbed hair attacked. Soon the floor surrounding Maki-Mae and Sage was littered with bat bodies.

"The painting!" Sage exclaimed. "We've got to shut the portal somehow."

Maki-Mae paused long enough from her fighting to utter an incantation. Suddenly, the painting glowed with white light, and the dark sky in the painting reverted to its former sunny self. The bats ceased pouring into the room. However, there were still a ton of bats already there. "They must have some kind of weakness." Maki-Mae assumed a defensive stance.

Sage smashed another little creature out of the air that was going for his ear. "They're breathing really fast. Maybe the air is too thin for them?"

"That's it," Maki-Mae agreed. "Don't you manipulate air when making magic sourdough bread?" When Sage nodded, she instructed, "Then do that now, but in reverse."

Sage set his face with grim determination. Yes, that might work *if* he had enough magic left in his reserves. He had to hope he did. "You trust me?"

"With my life."

"Okay, watch my back while I cast the spell."

Normally he cast a rising spell. The basic cooking spell made yeast bread and other dishes rise quicker than if he let nature run its course. He could augment it, though. Basically, he was going to suck out all the air in the room and see if the bat creatures died before he and Maki-Mae did.

"Ready?" he called as Maki-Mae karate-chopped a bat creature in half right in front of his face.

She nodded solemnly, her beautiful face speckled with chaos creature blood. Her barbed hair bobbed in ascent too.

"Hold your breath!" After inhaling, Sage cast the spell, using every last bit of magic he had left. The bats initially showed no sign of being affected. They rallied into a circular swarm, surrounding Sage and Maki-Mae.

The two of them backed up, butt to butt, and Maki-Mae cast a forcefield shield to surround them. Then the bats began to attack in earnest again, throwing themselves at the shield with wild abandon.

Twenty seconds passed. Then thirty. Still the bats came.

Damn. Would this work or was it going to be his and Maki-Mae's final stand? Why had he had to let in a bunch of chaos creatures?

Maki-Mae flashed him a look that said, This is going to work, right?

He hoped it did, but when forty seconds rolled around, he began to have major doubts. Maybe the bat creatures breathed fast. Perhaps they didn't breathe air as living creatures did. Maybe they were somehow breathing chaos from the chaos realm or something?

Fifty seconds and Sage started to feel the need to breathe. A glance at Maki-Mae showed that she was perfectly fine still. Her forcefield looked healthy too.

Damn her and her meditative prowess! he thought sourly.

Then the first bat creature dropped out of the air and landed on the floor, dead.

Yes! It was working!

Another bat creature fell, then another. It wasn't long before the swarm started to break apart, sagging to the floor. The piles grew and grew like dunes all around them. It was a lot of bat creatures!

Sage felt like he was about to pass out, but he held the spell for a bit longer until he did pass out.

When he came too, an angel was kissing his lips, breathing air into his lungs. He sat bolt upright, coughing, then sucking in a great intake of breath.

As his eyes adjusted to the room, tiny bat creature carcasses towered everywhere around him, stacked nearly as tall as some of the bookcases.

Maki-Mae leaned over him. She looked so gorgeous in her crimson kimono. Or was it a blue kimono drenched red by all the...

"Are you an angel?" he asked airily.

Maki-Mae smacked him lightly once on each cheek. "I'm your future stepmom-in-law. Now, are you all right? You blacked out and stopped breathing. I had to give you CPR."

"I'm good now." He was embarrassed as he rolled onto his hands and knees and drew long slow breaths. Their gambit had paid off, but if Maki-Mae hadn't been around to revive him, he might not have made it. "There are so many of those bat creatures..."

"I know. We must figure out why your interaction with the

painting allowed them to come here. And how Chaos is involved."

"You're right." Sage was still heaving in breaths. "Maybe we could relax for a few more moments first?"

The door to the study tore open, and Zombie Icarus shouted, "Gods dammit! Not another mess!"

Sage chuckled. It was one hell of a mess to clean up. The main thing was that they were still alive and they could continue to do all they could to make sure that Maine stayed alive in prison too.

CHAPTER TWENTY-TWO

"So you're really a troll?" Hank asked, back in Maine's cell. "And...a girl?"

Maine rested one of her hands on Hank's wrist. After a short time, her guise faded, and the troll could see her true identity.

"Why go through all this danger?"

"Because I have to get some information from Noolie. I found a living painting and my dad—or some troll who looks like my dad—is inside it. But we don't know anything about the painting. I'd risk anything to get to know more about my dad or to save him if it really is him."

After a time, Hank turned away from her and dropped his gaze to the dark cell floor. "Damn. Just...damn. I've seen and heard a lot, but this is..."

"A lot to take in," Maine finished. "I know. I'm risking everything by sharing my real identity with you. But you knew my dad. And I think I can trust you."

Hank stiffened for a fraction of a second at the mention of her father. "Your secret is safe with me. But why? I mean, geez, you joined one of the gods damned Five Gangs of the Veil. That's not a bond to be taken lightly."

"I've got a deal with the Guardian. If I help him avert a mythical gang war, he'll get me out of the Five Gangs so I won't have to worry about gang assassins for the rest of my life."

Hank whistled. "You weren't kidding that you had history with the Guardian. Not if you could make that kind of deal with him."

Maine shrugged. "We have a love-hate relationship. I love to mess with him, and he hates my guts. As long as I don't mess this thing up, he and I will be all right."

Hank scoffed, then half-smirked. "The Guardian's a real bastard, ain't he?"

"He's not that bad," Maine admitted. "He helped me fight the Corruptor last year."

Hank's eyes widened in the darkness. "Wait. You—you're the one who defeated the Corruptor? You're the Maine Troll?"

"Guilty. I also run the Mantle and Key Detective Agency along with my dire wolf partner Noff."

At the mention of his name, Noff blasted onto the bed, raised on his hind legs, and bowed to Hank. "At your service," he squeaked in his Mickey Mouse voice.

Hank laughed. "Dire wolf? That looks more like a mouse."

"It's called a guise spell, asshole!"

Maine chuckled. "He's using a guise spell too."

Hank leaned back on his bed. He held out his palm and Noff blasted onto it. When Hank could see Noff's true and shrunken identity, he rubbed a callused palm over one eye. "You guys really thought this prison thing through."

"Not really. It was kind of spur of the moment. But my

fiancé is an expert planner, and I've even got contact with the outside world."

"That's…great. So you won't be staying in here for long, I take it?" The troll's words carried a hint of sadness.

"Afraid not. Once I get what I need from Noolie and figure out what's going on with the gang war, I'm out."

"Damn. This is why I don't make friends."

"Why?"

"Because they always leave in the end." Hank smacked himself in the face. "How many times do I have to learn this lesson? I can only trust myself in this life."

Maine's face tightened.

Hank noticed. "Shit. I didn't mean it like that. You're good people. But even you will leave my side in a few days."

"I can come and visit you. Once you get out, you can come and live in Rainwater. It's a great place to live, and it has the best restaurant in the world, the Sacred Sourdough. You'd fit right in."

He gave her a sideways glance. "You really think a misfit like me could fit in there?"

"Yeah. Rainwater is filled with misfits. I'm kind of a misfit myself. So is Noff—he's smaller than the rest of his pack."

"Hey, watch it, woman!"

"And my fiancé is a wizard school dropout."

Hank scratched at his nose. "You really are a weirdo. Hah."

"Yep. So now that you know a little about me, how about you share a little about yourself?"

The troll grumbled for a bit, then wiped his mouth with the back of his hand. "Oh, what the hell. Look, I wasn't always like this. I used to be respectable. That was back before the war, though. Troll War II. I had a steady job at a grocery store.

Even managed to work my way up into management. Things were good. Then the war happened."

He paused, and his hand started to shake. After a few breaths, he got it under control. "The fighting was hard. There was no shortage of demons to ash. You know how trolls like to fight and do battle.

"It was a grand time. Most of the time. Trolls are hardy creatures, but we suffered fatalities. I made a lot of good friends. Friends I'll never see again until I die. Maybe. Your father...he was a good troll. The best. I would have followed that crazy bastard anywhere, even into hell itself."

"What was my dad like back then?" Maine asked.

"Utterly fearless. And honorable. He never left a man behind, no matter how bad things got. He suffered plenty of wounds and scars for his efforts, but he earned the trust of his men. If anyone could lead a successful charge to defeat the Corruptor and his forces, it would be him. And gods damn, he managed to pull it off."

"You didn't take part in the final charge. Because you were injured saving my dad?"

"That's right," he said sadly. "I didn't get to see Victory Day, but I did save your father's life. That meant more to me." He gave a low croak as if he were having a heart attack, then gritted his teeth and continued.

"Well, after Troll War II, things kinda went back to normal again, a new normal I guess. I kept having flashbacks of all the fighting. All those demons. I got my old job back, but I didn't keep it long. I couldn't concentrate. I kept losing myself. To be completely honest with you, I was scared."

"So you turned to petty thievery?" Maine asked carefully.

Hank chuckled. "Oh no. I did what I thought would help me. I went and visited your dad."

"What did he say?"

Hank chuckled again and closed his eyes with the fond recollection. "He was so serious. He told me to get it together. We survived and saved the Veil and the world. Then we had a couple of beers at the Sacred Sourdough.

"As harsh as his words were, he somehow helped to tame the demons in my mind. For the first time since the war, I was able to get a full night's sleep. I felt refreshed again. I even managed to secure my old job. Again.

"Your father and I continued to get drinks off and on for a while. Life was good."

"Then what happened?" Maine asked.

"The Chosen happened, that's what."

Maine frowned. "The Chosen?"

"One night when your father and I were having drinks at the Dough, I could see that he was all torn up inside about something. He hardly ever showed his emotions after the war. So I knew something bad was up that night.

"It took effort and a lot of beer to get him to open up. See, he had a big problem. During a seemingly normal case, he'd stumbled upon something huge in his sleuthing. He found out that Chaos was planning to breach into our world and break reality."

Maine sat tight-lipped on the bed beside Hank, waiting for more.

"I told him that taking on the Corruptor with an army was one thing, but facing off with friggin' Chaos? That was different ballpark. But he was determined and couldn't be dissuaded. So I told him he needed allies to fight with him. He told me he already had some, and they were going to make their move the next day."

"Really?" Maine asked.

"Yeah. I asked, 'You've got some allies?' He said, 'Yeah, the Chosen.'" Hank stopped to turn and stare into Maine's eyes. "You've got to understand he would never have told me this stuff had we not been two kegs into our talk."

Two kegs! Maine thought. She knew trolls could drink, but that was insane. Also, how large was a full troll's bladder anyway?

"Valkious explained that the Chosen were mythical creatures personally selected by him. They had to be strong because they had to give up a part of themselves to perform some sort of 'splitting' ritual. Basically, your father had used a Wish Card to create a Second Nexus to hold off Chaos' army. Don't ask me how he got his hands on a Wish Card. Damn if your father didn't get around in his day."

She was finally learning about her father and his Wish Card. If her father had been wearing the Mantle at the same time, why hadn't the Mantle told her any of this?

The Mantle hissed. *There are some things your father didn't want me to bear witness to, such as his obtaining or using the Wish Card. He had some way of turning me off and erasing knowledge he wanted me to forget.*

I wish I knew how to turn you off, Maine mentally projected to the Mantle.

She turned her attention back to Hank and leaned forward. "What do you mean my father got around?"

"He didn't only take detective jobs in Rainwater. Sometimes your father worked jobs in other countries for wealthy clients. How else do you think he could have afforded to build the Trollcave?"

"You know about that?"

Hank nodded. "Anyway, your father was making copies of himself and the rest of the Chosen to defend the Second

RAMY VANCE & MICHAEL ANDERLE

Nexus against Chaos. To do so, he had to fragment off a sliver of their essence, or soul, to create the copy—a very dangerous and tricky process, and not everyone who underwent the splitting ritual survived.

"When I asked him why he didn't ask me to be one of the Chosen, he gave me a look. That look, well, it said I was broken. Hell, after I was wounded in Troll War II, I could never move the same.

"That demonic spear to the chest had been tipped with poison. It slowed me down some, both physically and mentally. It shaved some years off my life. That look he gave me that night said I was unworthy. That I was weak."

"How do you know that's why my dad didn't choose you? Maybe he thought you were happy with your life and wanted to keep you from more fighting like in the Second Troll War."

Hank passed a hand over his scalp. "Surely you understand that trolls are made to fight. Tell me, have you ever fought a horde of demons?"

She nodded.

"Did you ever feel like you could take on the whole horde all on your own?"

"Yeah. You know what? I think I know what you mean."

"Good. So you understand what a huge blow to the psyche that was. When Valkious didn't choose me to fight by his side... I sort of lost my grip on life again. My PTSD set in again, worse this time around.

"I don't know what exactly your father and the Chosen did, but they must have been successful. We didn't go out for drinks anymore after that, but when I ran into him again one time in town and asked him how it had gone, he said he'd taken care of it for the moment."

The puzzle pieces of the living painting were starting to

come together in Maine's mind. What if the picture showed live footage of the Second Nexus, whatever and wherever that was, and the troll in it was her father's copy—one of the Chosen! So basically, it *was* her father or at least a part of him.

She couldn't wait to fill in the team back in Rainwater on this new development. She wanted to jump up and down in victory, but Hank was having a difficult time recounting these memories.

Hank formed a fist and ground it into his other palm. "I would have been strong enough to survive the Chosen process. I know I would have been. On the off chance that I had died, it would have been an honorable death."

Tell him he IS weak. Go get a job, you loser! Provoke him. Do it. Do it now.

Maine rested a hand on Hank's shoulder. "I don't think you're weak."

"Thanks, but kind words don't mean much to a washed-out vet like me. I wasn't weak then, but I sure as hell am now. I guess I made it a reality." His fist started to shake, and he steadied it with his other hand.

Maine didn't know why her father wouldn't have chosen Hank. It certainly seemed like a slight to not include a troll war buddy. Even if Hank had died in the process, he would have wanted to take the chance.

More than wanting to understand her father's decision, she wanted to help this troll find his way in life again, as her father had done.

"I know he's dead, but do you still want to honor my father?"

Hank nodded. "I've got to prove myself."

She held out her hand to him. "Then I might need your help in carrying out my mission. Do you have my back?"

He looked at her long and hard, then shook her hand. "Hell yeah. Trolls don't let trolls go it alone." He swallowed. "But, if you don't mind, I don't want to talk about this stuff any longer tonight. Give me some quiet time?"

"Of course. I'm sorry if I made you dredge up painful memories."

"Nah, don't worry about it. It felt good to get some of that stuff off my chest. Hell, maybe I'll even be able to get some decent sleep tonight. Night."

"Night." She climbed to her bunk.

Although she was buzzing with the excitement of the new information on her father, his copy, and the Nexus, she laid down to get some sleep. She considered calling Sage and Maki-Mae, but they probably weren't still awake at this hour. They were probably sleeping peacefully in their beds. Rainwater was probably quite boring without her around.

CHAPTER TWENTY-THREE

The next morning at breakfast, Maine separated from Hank and sat at the Seeing Eye gang's table. None of the gang members congratulated or celebrated her as the other gangs had after seeing the Guardian's fake rap sheet. It was kind of bizarre.

While she ate her breakfast, she caught glances from gang members at the other tables. Some looked confused, others disappointed. She accidentally locked eyes with the spider shifter at the oddball table for a moment. He licked his lips and patted the empty seat next to him. Maine shook her head and turned back to her food.

None of the Seeing Eye gang would talk to her. Even weirder, they didn't seem to talk to each other except for occasional knowing looks and head bobs. Were they communicating via nonverbal methods? That was kind of cool but creepy because she wasn't in on it. The Seeing Eye gang was secretive, but maybe all would be explained at the "initiation" tonight.

She waited for the Seeing Eye gang's leader to show up,

but he never did. Maybe he meditated instead of eating breakfast. Just what kind of weirdos did she get involved with? Also, the Guardian had better keep his word and protect her once she got out of prison.

She couldn't wait to finish her breakfast. While she was dumping her tray, a gang member brushed up against her and slipped a piece of paper into her pocket.

Had it been a Parchment gang member?

She wanted to look at the paper but decided to wait until she got back to her cell.

Back in the cell, she tore the paper from her pocket and read the simple message.

Initiation Ceremony – six p.m. Leader's room.

This meant it was from the Seeing Eye gang. Whew. It was time to call Sage and Maki-Mae and fill them in on everything that had happened so far.

Maine didn't go to the rec area after lunch. She didn't want to cause any more trouble before her initiation, where she would hopefully have a better chance to talk to Noolie now that she was a full-blown gang member. At least, she hoped she was. What if she had to perform some kind of hazing ritual or something?

She shuddered. She hoped not.

When she told Hank about the initiation ceremony, he wished her good luck.

The hours passed slowly. Maine spent some of it calling Sage and Maki-Mae and relaying what Hank had told her about her father, the Chosen, and the Second Nexus. They had been equally excited and nervous about this new development.

If there was a Second Nexus, how did anyone reach it? Its existence raised so many questions, but Sage and Maki-Mae said to let them worry about that. They wished Maine good luck with the gang initiation.

When it was time for the initiation, Maine left a little early, testing her new Seeing Eye extra senses as she walked. Her vision was a little crisper, and it enhanced her hearing and sense of smell too. She wished she could have turned the smell enhancer down a few notches.

When she reached the Seeing Eye leader's room, she found it packed with Seeing Eye gang members, which was odd. The guards were okay with formal gang meetings like this? What kind of prison was this?

Then Maine recalled the two corrupt guards who hadn't intervened during the rec yard fight. How many corrupt guards were at the prison?

As with breakfast, most of the Seeing Eye inmates didn't speak. The only people talking were the new inductees standing off to one side.

Maine recognized a couple of the inductees from her bus ride here. The green leshy, one of Maine's biggest enemies since she arrived, was among them. When he caught her eye, he grinned in victory as if he was about to receive his dream come true. She had kicked the leshy's ass in the rec yard fight. Now because they were about to be in the same gang, every-thing was cool? He still had a black eye and a bruised chin.

Inmates were weird.

As she waited, she tried to find Noolie among the inmates. There were a lot of gang members in the room, but he wasn't one of them.

Finally, the gang leader stepped into the room with a glass

of tea in one hand. The power crystal hanging from his neck glowed brighter than usual in the presence of all the inmates, and she felt a magical energy stirring in the tattoo on her shoulder. She inspected it, but it wasn't glowing or anything. It looked like a normal tattoo.

The lean, meditative gang leader stepped to the front of the room, set his iced tea down, and raised his arms. "My brothers. Welcome."

All the inmates clasped their hands together and bowed to him, uttering, "Thank you, daywalker!"

They seemed like such a grateful bunch.

"I trust that all early inductees are enjoying their Seeing Eye abilities?"

Maine saw a couple of other inmates nodding so she nodded too.

"Good. As new members, that is a taste of the powers you shall be granted as you ascend the ranks of our organization. Your powers will grow as you prove your loyalty."

General cheers and assertations that they were the strongest and best of the Five Gangs ensued from those gathered.

"Now on to the formalities of the general initiation," the gang leader called, turning to the new inductees of the gang. "Do you wish to join the Seeing Eye gang?"

"Yes!" they all shouted, the leshy loudest among them.

"Very well." The gang leader snapped his fingers. "Noolie!"

Noolie shuffled into the room with his archaic-looking magic tattoo needle clenched in his hand.

"This may hurt," the daywalker said as if in an afterthought and some of the gang members laughed raunchily.

Noolie stepped up to the first of the new gang members and began to administer the tattoo. The inmate instantly broke into a sweat as he clenched his teeth together. About halfway through the inking, the inmate collapsed to the floor.

"Is he still alive?" the daywalker asked casually.

Noolie crouched and checked the inmate's pulse. "Yes, leader."

"Then finish the tattoo. And be quick about it. This isn't the only new inductee."

Noolie gritted his teeth and finished the first inductee's tattoo while in a crouch. Then he proceeded to ink the next inmate.

Isn't this so much fun? the Mantle hissed. *I wonder if any of them will perish during the process.*

Maine found it disturbing to watch the rest of the new inductees receive their tattoos. All of them screamed from the pain, but luckily none of them died during the agonizing process. The leshy sobbed while receiving his tattoo, his eyes leaking more water than Maine had ever cried in her life.

As difficult as it was to watch, Noolie finished all the tattoos surprisingly fast.

She wondered how long the rest of the meeting might last so she could grab Noolie afterward to ask him about the painting.

The leader spoke up again. "Now, are all new initiates ready for their first task?"

First task? Maine thought grimly.

The daywalker continued. "To prove yourselves to the gang, you must each bring me the heart of another inmate." He gave them all a terrifying grin.

What? Maine thought.

The Mantle hissed in delight. *Do not worry—I shall guide you through the process, my dark apprentice.*

The daywalker suddenly clapped once. "I am kidding.

There shall be no murder inside this prison for that would draw too much attention to ourselves. You should have seen your faces."

Uneasy laughter filtered through the new inmates still recovering from receiving their tattoos while the older inmates smirked.

"There is no initiation rite," the gang leader announced. "The tattoo process weeds out the weak so you have my congratulations."

The daywalker sipped his ginger tea and licked his lips. "Now for the next part of tonight's meeting. Is everyone ready to go to the plane of the Seeing Eye?"

There were nods and verbal acknowledgments.

Maine was wondering what the plane of the Seeing Eye was and how to reach it when her eyes snapped wide open and whited over.

The next thing she knew, she was standing on a flat dirt plain accompanied by the rest of the inmates who had gathered in the prison along with thousands of other rough-looking characters. These people weren't wearing orange jumpsuits but rather street clothes. They all had a seeing eye tattoo somewhere on their bodies.

The Mantle hissed in her mind. *The tattoos act as a conduit to this astral plane. Every Seeing Eye gang member with the symbol tattoo can be brought here to receive instruction from their leader, the bearer of the power crystal and the source of their special powers.*

Wow. That was crazy.

If the gang leader was going to speak to all of his gang members, something big was probably about to go down. Hopefully, this would be the information the Guardian needed to shut down the global gang war before it happened.

Maine glanced around for Noff, but his consciousness

wasn't here. He didn't have a tattoo so that made sense. She wished he was here, though.

"Brothers and sisters." The gang leader spoke, and Maine realized there were plenty of women among the outside-of-prison gang members. The Seeing Eye gang wasn't sexist.

He spoke as though he were a savior. "We have all long awaited the fulfillment of the prophecy that speaks of unifying the Five Gangs of the Veil."

"Hear, hear!" many of the gang members chanted.

"That day is fast approaching. It could be tomorrow. Or the day after. Or a week or a month later, but know this, all of you. It will come soon and it will come swiftly."

"Yes!" everyone shouted.

Don't stand there like a sad sack. Pump your fist and cheer! the Mantle hissed.

Maine did her best to imitate the rest of the gang members for the duration of the gang leader's speech.

"The Seeing Eye gang will be victorious. We will strike the other gangs, assert dominance and forge a new alliance, one where the Seeing Eye gang is the top gang. They will serve us. We will gather and convert everyone to our cause—we will be unstoppable!"

More wild cheering.

"Now, I will need everyone's help. We are all part of this. Those outside will have to keep the rest of the gangs in check during the transition period. I would advise you to keep from violence unless necessary.

"Remember, once the gangs have consolidated, we will all be brothers and sisters. Then we will be able to do whatever we want. Whenever we want.

"World governments will bow to us. We will start a new global superpower, the Seeing Eye nation. We will control everything. The people will own nothing and be grateful for it because we will be their protectors and givers. The world is a harsh place, but we will make it safer."

More cheers and wild cries.

This was starting to get too unbelievable for Maine to believe. The power crystals and the evil symbols were powerful, but enslaving the world? That seemed a bit farfetched. However, if this gang was as dangerous as they made themselves sound, the Guardian was right to send someone in to infiltrate and investigate. If mythical gangs with crazy-powerful magic took over the world, that would be bad news.

Maine would have to act very carefully. She didn't want to get caught and end up on the Seeing Eye gang's bad side.

CHAPTER TWENTY-FOUR

The gang leader continued.

"To help achieve our goals, we will work with one of our own—Noolie NasNas. Although he has fallen from power, he was once a big-time player with his finger in all the pies. He also has connections in the Beneath. He understands what it means to control large groups and will be a big help to our cause."

Maine observed as gang members gave Noolie confused, impressed, and surprised looks. Many looked almost embarrassed to be working with him or how they had treated him in the past. Some gang members stifled chuckles.

Noolie's face reddened in the crowd at the extra attention. Maine recalled from working her first case in Rainwater when Noolie was a dangerous and formidable NasNas, one of the most disgusting creatures she had ever dealt with. But Noolie wasn't magical anymore, and during her short time in prison, it seemed he was everyone's bitch and hated every moment of it.

Why was he taking it? Did he hope to regain his former power and glory? If so, the Mantle would be able to help her manipulate his weaknesses.

"Noolie," the gang leader called. "Would you like to come forward and detail some of your helpful suggestions?"

Noolie reddened further. He looked like he would rather be anywhere than here. Instead, he nodded and shuffled forward until he stood next to the gang leader.

"These are but a handful of suggestions," Noolie called rather meekly, not meeting anyone's eyes in the crowd of gang members. "When dealing with underlings or rivals, it is often favorable to offer promises you can't keep, as long as you can string them along long enough for them to think you can until they are ensnared in your web. Where empty promises don't work, use leverage over your enemies."

Cheers and whoops came from the crowd.

"Also, the following are what I refer to as the golden rules of controlling a group. One, start nice, then gradually become the asshole using fear to keep them in check. Remember, fear is more effective than love when governing others. Alienate those who fail to go along with your narrative.

"Two, locate any alphas in a group. The alpha is the guy who would be the leader if you weren't. You will want to make sure that that guy is one hundred percent loyal to you. Remember, true loyalty should not be based upon fear but blind obedience. Make them need you. This may mean killing alpha number one if alpha number two is more loyal to you."

Maine was more than a little concerned by what she was hearing. Noolie had spent a lot of time researching how to be a controlling monster—he sure put the dick in dictator. Although he spoke rather meekly like a dog with his bark removed, his voice picked up momentum as he continued.

As she listened, she wished Noff was here. He didn't have the symbol tattoo and hadn't come into the "plane of the Seeing Eye." When she got back to her cell, she would fill Noff in on everything she had learned about the gang's "take over the world" plan so he could take to the prison's mouse tunnels and relay the information to the Guardian. Surely this would be enough info for the Guardian to call her part done.

She found it hard to believe that people could be this evil or manipulative of others. She reckoned that the right leader could lead a mass of people to believe anything. One thing was clear. The world would not be better served with a power-hungry mythical gang running it.

Noolie went on for a few more minutes. The Mantle loved every minute of it, agreeing with the evil methods described.

When Noolie finished, the gang leader spoke again in generalities about being the best and how to deal with other alphas. It was a bunch of New Age flourish. Maine was only concerned about Noolie now. With his part done, Noolie walked back through the crowd.

As he moved past her, she prepared to step in line with him or call him to her, but the gang leader delivered a chilling warning.

"For all the new initiates: I hope it goes without saying that you shall not tell our plan to anyone outside the gang. I have no tolerance for traitors, and I have my ways of knowing."

After a few more words, the gang leader dismissed them from the plane of the Seeing Eye and bid them good night.

Suddenly, Maine was back in the cramped prison room full of sweaty, stinky male inmates. Ugh, had someone farted while they'd been in la la land? Her magically enhanced sense of smell didn't exactly help.

"Yo!" Noff squeaked from atop her shoulder. "What'd I miss? Huh? Tell me!"

Suddenly lights out was called over the prison's PA system. Inmates grumbled as they left and headed toward their cells.

"I'll tell you when we get back to the cell," she whispered to Noff as she spotted Noolie amid the mass of moving bodies. She picked a way through the crowd. She was stronger than the other inmates and could have easily shoved them aside, but she didn't want to draw attention to herself.

She slowly drew closer to Noolie, who was heading to a wing of the prison she had never been to before.

Another warning about lights out sounded over the speakers, and Maine almost turned away and headed back toward her cell. Still, she needed to talk to Noolie, and he was about to take a turn that would take him out of sight.

"Noolie," she called, not too loud but enough to be heard over the chattering of Seeing Eye members.

Noolie turned to look at her. She seized the opportunity to catch up with him. He gave her an odd look.

"Hey, uh, I wanted to say I liked your talk," she said.

"Thanks." Noolie was about to turn away from her, but a glint of recognition hit his eyes. "You're a persistent one, aren't you?"

She thrust her shoulders back. "Yeah, that's me."

Noolie scowled as he scrutinized her. "You got a crush on me? 'Cause I don't swing that way." His eyes narrowed. "Or are you stalking me?"

"What? No. You said you'd talk to me if I became a gang member. I wanted to chat with you."

"You messing with me? Trying to act like we're cool, then punch me in the gut like all the rest?"

"Whoa." Maine threw up her hands and took a step back. "Didn't mean it like that. Just trying to be nice."

"Nice? We're in prison. People aren't 'nice' in prison."

"Not even if they're in the same gang?"

Noolie's scowl intensified. "Especially when you're in the same gang."

"Dude's paranoid!" Noff squeaked.

Yes, the Mantle hissed. *Paranoid people are the most fun to mess with. Tell him you're a demon in disguise... Wait, no, reveal your true identity!*

"What can I say?" Maine said. "Prison hasn't broken me yet."

Noolie looked like he wasn't buying it, but he finally dropped his glare when the final call for lights out sounded. "It will," he said softly, his fist quivering at his side. "It will."

Maine licked her lips, preparing to find the words to keep him here but she was out of time.

"Anyway, thanks for the sentiment." Noolie disappeared down the hall and around a corner.

Noff squeaked. "Dude's got a stick up his butt a mile long."

"I don't know. I think maybe he's lonely in here."

"Or maybe he's got too many sticks up his butt..."

Loud footsteps sounded behind them, and a commanding voice shouted, "Inmate! You deaf?"

Maine turned to face an imposing guard standing directly behind her, patting a telescoping baton in his palm. Its tip started to spark with electrical energy.

"No, guard, my hearing is fine."

"Oh really? Then why aren't you in your cell?"

"I'm new here," Maine said with an Oni demon growl.

The guard growled back. "I don't care if you were born

here. If you don't get to your cell within the next minute, I'm throwing you in the hole!"

The halls were basically empty now. Maine sprinted toward her cell.

Hank was already in bed when she reached her cell. She made it just before her cell door locked.

"Where were you?" Hank grumbled without lifting his head from his pillow.

"That secret Seeing Eye gang meeting."

"Oh, right."

"You interested in what I learned?"

"Nope. You can tell your mouse partner about it, but I'm tired. Okay?"

"Got it." Maine grinned. Hank must still be in a good mood if he could sleep now.

She climbed onto the top bunk and explained to Noff everything she had heard on the plane of the Seeing Eye.

"Holy shit, that's crazy!" Noff squeaked. "That's a real badass power play they're makin'. Assertin' dominance over the other four gangs and rulin' the world with their combined power? They got balls, is all I got to say."

"Yeah. Now I need you to relay all this to the Guardian. Tell him my part is over, and he has to let us escape when I give him the signal. After I talk to Noolie."

Noff sat back on his hind legs and twitched his mouse whiskers. "Will do, partner." He turned and prepared to blast off the bunk bed when Maine caught him by the scruff of his neck.

"Be careful," she warned. "You know how the Seeing Eye gang has heightened senses."

"Partner, ya worry too much. I'll be quiet as a mouse."

Maine groaned at the pun.

Noff blasted down to the floor and slipped between the prison cell bars.

It was time to fill in Sage and Maki-Mae on what she had learned. She tapped her magic earmic to make the call.

CHAPTER TWENTY-FIVE

Back in the mansion's study, Sage drew a deep breath and applied a mini electrical rod to the living painting. He tensed as an equally powerful jolt of electricity shot out of the painting and used his body as a grounding rod.

"Okay, that's it. I'm taking a break," he said, turning and setting his tool on a table. His face bore numerous scorch and frost marks. Most of his wounds from the bat creatures had mended after taking a couple of health potions. If he kept experimenting with the painting, he would need to brew more health potions.

Maki-Mae glanced up from the email correspondence she was reading on her tablet. "It is good that we are gaining more data points on the painting."

With a groan, Sage fell back onto a sofa. "Yep, fire, electricity, and frost do not harm the painting—it takes what you give it and fires it right back at you." He sighed dramatically. "Too bad I had to be the guinea pig. Maine and Noff love this kind of stuff."

Maki-Mae nodded, reading further down the email correspondence.

Sage ran a hand through his hair. "Based on what Maine said, this painting depicts the Second Nexus. If it is also the portal to get to the Second Nexus, it has some crazy-powerful magical protection."

Maki-Mae glanced over her tablet at Sage. "You think the painting is the portal to the Second Nexus?"

"I don't know. Those bat creatures came through the painting."

"We don't know for sure that they came from the painting," Maki-Mae said. "Only that they came *through* the painting."

"Yeah, maybe. I wish we could figure out how to get to that quaint countryside in the Second Nexus. For Maine—because you know she will have to go there when she gets out of prison."

Maki-Mae's breath caught as she finished reading the email. "I think I got some answers."

"Huh?" Sage sat bolt upright.

"I've been corresponding with a contact who deals with magic technology. I think I know what this painting is."

"Well, don't leave me hanging."

Maki-Mae laughed. "Sage, you're usually so patient. Have you fallen off the path of enlightenment?"

"No, my fiancée is trapped in a supermax prison filled with hardened criminals. All because of this stupid painting. I want to be done with it."

"As do I. My contact says the painting is probably acting like magical satellite imagery."

"We already know that," Sage pointed out.

"What I mean is that this painting is magically embedded with the coordinates of the location it portrays."

Sage nodded. "The Second Nexus."

"Yes. We can use these magical coordinates to get there, but to do so, we must first have the key."

"What's the key?" Sage asked.

Maki-Mae admitted that she didn't know, but Noolie might.

The door to the study opened, and Blue Dots strolled in. After a big yawn, she looked at the pair. "Anything new on your end?"

Sage filled the tech dragonfly in on their latest development, then prepared to call Maine to tell her about their discovery.

"Wow," Blue Dots said before he could make the call. "Hopefully Noolie can tell Maine where the key is, but in the meantime, maybe we can brainstorm where the Second Nexus is. What do we know about the Second Nexus?"

Sage threw a glance back at the painting. As it always did, it depicted a bright, cheerful countryside. "Well. It's always sunny in the Second Nexus."

Blue Dots popped her finger knuckles. "Yeah, that's so weird. I mean, it's always sunny in that painting. How is that possible?"

"Always sunny," Sage repeated. "Always…sunny." He blinked. "Hold on. I've got an idea. A place where the time of day never changes—where have we seen that before?"

Maki-Mae was the first to understand. "The Beneath?"

"Exactly," Sage said. "In the Beneath, it's always eternal dusk."

"So the Second Nexus is in the Beneath?" Blue Dots asked.

Sage canted his head. "I don't know. Can you have a Nexus within a Nexus?"

They were still considering this when Maine called.

"Maine, are you okay?" Sage asked.

"Yeah, but after what I learned at the Seeing Eye meeting, I feel like I need to take a shower. Not that I'm going to in this prison."

She filled in her friends on the Seeing Eye gang's plans, adding that Noff was on his way to tell the Guardian right now.

When Maine had finished, Maki-Mae observed, "It is a good thing the Guardian requested your help. With your intel, you will help him neutralize a big threat to the balance of the world."

"Just be careful," Sage advised. "That gang sounds like it's full of psychotics."

Maine's chuckle sounded uneasy. "Yep. Have you guys figured out anything new about the painting?"

They relayed their thoughts on the painting requiring a key to reach the Second Nexus.

"I'll be sure to ask Noolie all about it when I talk to him," Maine said. "It's so hard to have a conversation with him, but now that I'm a gang member, I should be able to corner him sometime tomorrow. If I can find him first."

Blue Dots cheered. "That's great!"

"What's our next move?" Sage asked.

"I think it's all up to me now," Maine admitted. "Keep providing support until I can make contact with Noolie. I know the waiting will be hard for you."

Sage grinned. "I think I'll survive."

"Why's that?"

"Because. Tomorrow is our conjugal visit. I'll finally get to have you in my arms again."

"I can't wait for that either," Maine agreed. "The reminder has lifted my spirits. Thanks again for arranging that, Maki-Mae."

"Of course, dear. Be safe until then. We are almost at the end. That is the time when we must be most vigilant. Things usually go wrong near the finish line when guards are dropped."

"Well, if Noff were here, he'd probably say, 'Let's finish strong, team!'"

Back at the mansion, everyone smiled.

Sage didn't know what they would find when they found the key to the Second Nexus, but at least Maine's dangerous prison stint was almost finished. Without her getting shivved.

CHAPTER TWENTY-SIX

The time had finally come—it was conjugal visit day!

Maine wasn't the only excited inmate. When she reached the part of the prison where they and their guests had to check in, Maine found long lines.

"I should have gotten here earlier," she muttered.

"Yeah, you should have."

Maine turned to see Hank. "Oh, you're meeting someone special too?"

"Nah. That stuff doesn't excite me like it used to. I'm a loner, always going to be."

"That's sad, but then, why are you here?"

Hank sighed. "Don't feel too important. I was stretching my legs. While I'm here, I ought to tell you some things because you're new here. You don't know how everything works."

She glanced around at all the inmates focused only on the front of their line, getting up there so they could spend quality time with their special other. Most of them looked very masculine and tough.

"Oh," Maine said at last. "I think I know what you mean."

"Really?" Hank asked flatly.

"Yeah. I look like a badass male Oni demon. And I've got a conjugal visit with a dude."

Hank screwed up his eyes. "What?" He shook his head and crossed his arms. "No, that's not what I'm talking about at all. No one gives a shit who you're hooking up with."

"Really?"

"Nah. The fact that you got someone willing to visit you in prison makes everyone who doesn't have someone a bit jealous. This is the happiest day of most of these guys' years. It means a lot to them, even more than cake day."

"Then what's the issue?"

"I know you've made a couple of enemies since you stepped foot in the joint. They might be looking to pick a fight with you and the worst they could do would be to pick that fight on conjugal visit day."

"Why?"

"Have you not learned anything while in here? Because then you'll lose visitation rights. Hell, I know you've only been in here a few days, but I can see how important this 'dude' is to you. All I'm saying is keep your wits about you. Always watch your back. And do not let yourself get tangled up in a fight. 'Cause you won't be able to talk to Noolie in the hole."

Maine nodded. "Thanks. I appreciate the concern."

"Eh, what the hell. I ain't doing it for you. I'm doing it for your old man. Gods know I owe him. Even if I can't understand him."

Hank meandered off, leaving Maine alone with her thoughts while the Mantle watched her back. She wondered what the Valkious double was doing now in the Second

Nexus. Was he fishing? Was he rallying the troops? Was the war with Chaos still going on?

Maybe it had ended years ago. Perhaps the Second Nexus was this peaceful realm now where you could relax. That would be nice, considering she was in prison. Once they found a way to reach the Second Nexus, maybe they would take a vacation there.

Warning, the Mantle hissed. *Over your left shoulder.*

Maine casually twisted her head to look as indicated by the Mantle. A brutish werewolf shifter saw that she had spotted him and abruptly turned off course to avoid her. As he did so, he whispered, "Should have chosen the Brick gang." Then he disappeared into the throng of inmates and left the room.

Did he mean to harm me? Maine mentally projected to the Mantle.

He had a shiv hidden in his right paw. What do you think?

Yikes. That had been close. All because she hadn't accepted Owen's invite to join the Brick gang? Inmates could be so sensitive. She would have to keep a better lookout for threats.

"I'm bored," Noff squeaked from Maine's pants pocket. "I'm ready for sexy time."

"I should have left you back in the cell," Maine muttered.

"Then how would I be able to watch your back, partner?"

It was good to have another set of eyes, but she would have to send Noff away when she and Sage got to do their thing.

The line moved slowly, and Maine began to feel bored. It seemed no one else wanted to do her bodily harm after she'd dissuaded the Brick gang werewolf shifter.

She turned her eyes to the doors leading to the few rooms for the conjugal visits. She watched as inmates entered the visitation rooms with their significant others, excited and some almost teary-eyed.

It was such a spectacle to see. It seemed even the most hard-ened criminals here had soft spots. She kept looking for Sage, but the guests were kept in another room until it was time for their visit. She knew she had to wait longer, but she wished he was here right now so she could talk to him or touch his arm.

Warning, warning!

Maine glanced up to see a centaur inmate galloping at her at full speed with his hand clenched menacingly around an unseen object. It was the same centaur she had fought on her first day.

The centaur was not backing down, and if she didn't want to get shivved, she would have to fight.

Which meant she wouldn't be able to visit with Sage.

"Uh-oh, incoming," Noff squeaked from her pants pocket.

"Mantle, suggestions?" she muttered as she set her stance.

Duck, dodge, and evade. As much as it hurts me to say this, do not strike back. Do not draw blood or you're going in the hole.

That was easier said than done. The centaur was upon her now, lunging at her. The rest of the inmates in the large room backed off, giving them ample room to fight without being entangled.

Maine jumped to the side as a glint of metal sliced through the air, missing her.

"What's your deal?" Maine challenged.

"No one disrespects me." He rounded on her, slicing the air again.

She backstepped just in time to avoid getting her throat slit. Where the hell were the guards? Not that she wanted them to intervene and take away her visiting rights.

"You're gonna pay big time, Oni!" The centaur renewed his attack and Maine continued to backstep and evade, utilizing every ounce of her enhanced agility. She realized then that her Seeing Eye powers were finetuning her senses, which helped improve her movement.

The centaur wiped his forehead with his forearm, struggling to keep up with his weakened leg from the previous fight. "You're too damn fast for an Oni demon."

Maine pulled up her shirt sleeve to indicate her Seeing Eye tattoo. "Cut it out, or my gang will deal with you."

"Hah! The Seeing Eye members are such pushovers." He grunted as he slashed a thin razor blade at her. "They turn on their members so easily."

"Really?" Maine said flatly, dancing out of the way of his blade.

"Yeah, they're such paranoid bastards. Didn't you do your research before joining them?"

Maine closed her eyes and could still easily evade the centaur's attacks. Even with her eyes closed, she could "hear" the blade's path and step out of it in time. When she reopened her eyes, she could see each move the centaur was about to make, telegraphed as if obvious to her.

Wow, this was the first time she'd fully tapped into the powers of the Seeing Eye. What had the gang leader said? Something about she only had low-level powers. She wondered how powerful the daywalker was in a fight. She was glad she'd never have to find out.

She dodged a mean swipe of the razorblade.

Hopefully the Guardian would get her out without the Seeing Eye gang finding out about her true identity.

Damn, where were the guards? She quickly scanned the

room, but the guards there earlier were nowhere in sight. They must have been paid off again.

Maybe I'll chop this guy in the neck, knock him out, and end the fight.

No! the Mantle hissed. *The guards will show up and throw you in the hole. If you strike, you will not see Sage.*

Damn. How much longer did she have to keep this up? Already she felt the power from the Seeing Eye start to wane. When the centaur managed to nick her in the leg, Maine grunted and shoved him back a few steps.

Instantly, a whistle sounded, and multiple guards pushed through the crowd of inmates.

You just had to do it, didn't you? the Mantle hissed.

It was only a little shove. And he started it!

"You two!" a guard shouted, appearing through a doorway and thrusting a finger at her and the centaur. "You're going in the hole."

"I didn't do anything," Maine protested.

"That's what they all say," another guard said.

"It was self-defense. He attacked me with a razor."

The centaur grinned and held up both palms. There was no sign of a razor anywhere on him. He must have tossed it to the side when the guards yelled.

Maine growled as two guards stepped forth and grabbed her by each arm.

"Looks like you're not going to get to see lover boy," the centaur said as guards grabbed him by the arms too. He continued to grin as they swiveled him toward the door leading out of the room.

"I didn't do anything," Maine repeated.

Do not even think of fighting the guards, the Mantle said. *Even if they are crooked, you will receive a worse punishment.*

What was worse than going in the hole for twenty-four hours and missing her conjugal visit with Sage?

She dropped her head and allowed them to walk her to the exit.

Before they reached the door, a voice called from behind her. "Hey, wait, you've got the wrong guy."

The guards holding Maine glanced back to see Hank standing there with his trademark half-smirk and the centaur's razor in one hand.

The guards looked at each other as if unsure of what to do.

"Guards," Hank said. "Take me instead. I started the fight with the centaur, and I realize it was wrong of me to do so." He held the razor out to them like a peace offering. "The Oni demon didn't do anything. You going to take me to the hole now? Or am I going to have to attack some more inmates?"

The two guards growled, glanced at Maine, then glanced back at Hank. Finally, they released Maine and apprehended Hank, who did nothing to fight their rough handling. The troll met Maine's eyes as they pushed Hank toward the door and nodded.

Maine mouthed her thanks to him. Then Hank and the guards were out of the room.

That is one hell of a loyal friend, the Mantle hissed.

Yeah, Hank was. Maine agreed. He might be a criminal, but he was an all-right guy, and she owed him.

CHAPTER TWENTY-SEVEN

When it was finally time for Sage's visit, Maine's boredom jolted to high-adrenaline excitement.

"I'll be damned," Noff squeaked. "You made it without bein' shivved. It was close, though."

"Shut up," she murmured as a door opened and Sage stepped into the room. Maine had to restrain her excitement and not jump up and down or sprint up to him. Instead, she calmly walked up to the guard escorting Sage and smiled. Sage grinned and patted her hand so he didn't disrupt her guise.

The guard led them to the next available visitation room. He opened the door and motioned them inside in a bored way. "I'll lock the door behind you. You have one hour."

"That's all?" Noff squeaked.

The guard squinted, trying to find the source of the high-pitched squeaking but then Maine said, "Do you guys, you know, spray down the room after each couple?"

The guard gave a noncommittal shrug. "The sheets are changed after each visit. Usually. This ain't a hotel."

"You're right," Maine agreed as she and Sage stepped through. The guard wasted no time in locking the door behind them.

Perched atop Maine's shoulder, Noff vigorously sniffed the air. "Is it just me or does it smell like prison sex in here?"

Maine made a face when she took in the room's interior. It consisted of a second-hand sofa and a motel bed. At least the sheets looked like they had been changed.

Maine glanced down at her Oni demon arms and up at Sage. "You probably can't wait to get it on with a male Oni demon, right?"

Sage chuckled and took her hand. "You know me so well." After her guise had faded, he lost himself in her eyes.

"Ya two just gonna stand there makin' googly eyes at each other? Or ya gonna—"

Whoosh!

Maine nearly toppled over to the floor. When she saw the Guardian standing beside them, she cursed. Sage, who used to look up to the Guardian as his hero, now eyed the angel leader carefully.

"Watch your language, half-troll." The Guardian's words were clear and booming.

"What are you doing here? And can you talk any more quietly? The whole prison can probably hear you in here with us."

"They cannot hear us. The visitation rooms are sound-proof. There are no surveillance cameras either."

"Well gee, that's good to know," Maine said. "Why are you here? We only have one hour."

"Fifty-six minutes, now," the Guardian corrected. "I think you know why I'm here. To speak to you about our arrangement."

Maine exchanged a look with Sage. "Okay, go ahead. But make it quick."

He nodded professionally. "Noff filled me in on what you learned about the Seeing Eye gang. Gang subservience and world domination. It is as I suspected. My plan is going according to how I thought it would."

"Your plan?" Sage asked.

The Guardian stood proudly. "Who do you think arranged for the leaders of all Five Gangs of the Veil to be in the same prison at the same time?"

Maine groaned. "You set this all up? You set *me* up?"

"Please." The Guardian shook his head. "The world does not revolve around you. It revolves around the sun."

"I can't believe you," Maine said.

The Guardian crossed his arms as he regarded her. "Why do you complain? You wanted to come here to speak to Noolie, and I wanted you to come here to infiltrate the Seeing Eye gang. This is what humans call a win-win."

"Yeah, but don't you trust me? You could have at least told me this when we talked last time instead of keeping secrets from me."

The Guardian gave her a smug look.

"You also didn't have to throw me in the gods damned hole."

"No, I didn't have to do that," the Guardian agreed. "But I wanted to sell it. You can't fake being in the hole. Perhaps we are about even now."

"Even?" Maine asked incredulously. "You owe me like a gazillion. That was before the hole. I don't think you under-stand how humans really think."

"I know they can be quite talkative," the Guardian said. "Fifty-two minutes left."

"Ugh. You came here to tell me you were satisfied with Noff's report, and you will get me out of prison as soon as I speak to Noolie?"

"Yes. And to request something further of you."

"Is it dangerous?" Sage asked.

"Not particularly." The Guardian shrugged. "If Maine is careful."

"What do you want me to do?" Maine asked.

The Guardian extended his hand. On it was a small tablet.

"What's in the pill?" Noff squeaked.

"It's an alchemical substance that will dampen the powers of any gang leader who ingests it."

"And?" Maine took the tablet and rolled it between her thumb and forefinger. "What do you want me to do with it?"

The angel leader looked at her. "Isn't it obvious? The Seeing Eye gang leader is the strongest mythical creature in the prison. I cannot make my move until the daywalker's powers are dampened. It would be too risky."

Sage gaped at the Guardian. "But not too risky for Maine?"

"She is in the Seeing Eye gang now. It should be easy."

"How is she supposed to give it to the daywalker?" Sage asked in a hysterical voice.

There was a glint in the Guardian's eyes. "She's quite crafty. I'm sure she will think of a way."

Sage gestured with both hands across his chest. "No way—"

"Will the tablet dissolve in liquid?" Maine asked.

The Guardian nodded in approval. "Yes. It will dissolve instantly without a trace."

Maine thought this through. "You understand the motto of the gang I'm in, right?"

"Oh? I am unaware that the Five Gangs have official mottos."

"It's not official, but it might as well be. *Kill the snitches.* That's the creed they live by. The gang members have super hearing and sight and stuff. How am I supposed to spike the daywalker's tea without being caught?"

"I'm sure you'll find a way," the Guardian said.

"Maine, you can't seriously be considering this," Sage protested.

"He'll notice that his drink tastes different after I spike it."

"He will not," the Guardian promised. "This is a special formula. It's physically and magically undetectable."

Maine thought it might be doable if the reward matched the risk. "What's up with an angel leader using magical roofies? That's kind of evil."

The Guardian grunted, and for the briefest of moments, his eyes glowed with smiting energy. "I am not trying to roofie the gang leader. I am only dampening the special abilities granted him by the Seeing Eye symbol."

"So you can arrest him?" Maine prodded. "He's already in prison."

"You don't need to know the rest of my plan. The gang leader only needs to drink a sip of the spiked tea to receive the tablet's full effects. As long as I am in the prison, I will be able to sense when he ingests it. Then I will commence with the final phase of my plan to end this global mythical gang war before it begins."

"My guise spell will only last another day," Maine warned.

"Then you better hurry. Now, will you do it?"

Sage flashed her a look that said, Hell no! while Noff panted excitedly.

"I need to gain Noolie's trust," Maine said. "I don't think he likes it here. If I can promise to extract him from the prison, he might be willing to help me." She met the Guardian's eyes. "Can you get Noolie out when you get Noff and me out?"

"Consider it done." The Guardian answered so quickly that Maine regretted having not asked for more.

"There's also a troll in here by the name of Hank. He's helped me a lot, and he's a good guy. Can you get him out too?"

"Absolutely not. He must serve his time like the rest of the inmates. As for Noolie, I can only promise to transfer him to another prison. No one escapes judgment in my prison."

Maine bit her lip. At least she tried.

She drew a deep breath to clear her mind. "All I have to do is spike the gang leader's tea with this magic tablet?"

"Correct."

"What if he doesn't drink it? What if you're wrong and he detects it and doesn't drink the tea?"

"Make sure he does. I don't care how you manage it. Cause a distraction when you spike it. Its effects are not immediate, but I will know when it affects him."

"Then you'll get me, Noff, and Noolie out of prison?"

"Yes."

"Promise?" Maine asked.

"I swear it."

"Ain't no goin' back on a magical oath," Noff squeaked. "Nice job in gettin' him to agree."

Maine shifted on her feet. "Are you sure you can't get Hank out too?"

"Absolutely not," the Guardian said. "Any other questions?"

"What if we need to reach you?" Sage asked. "If there's an emergency, do you have a phone number we can call?"

Scowling, the Guardian conjured a pen and paper and

wrote down a contact number. He handed it to Sage. "In case of emergency only."

Maine crossed her heart. "I promise not to prank call you."

"Very well." The Guardian grunted. "I am glad that is settled. You can sleep well knowing you are helping to ensure a safer tomorrow for the Veil. Now is there anything else you wish to discuss?"

Maine and Sage exchanged a glance. She considered telling the Guardian what they had discovered about her father, the Chosen, and the Second Nexus. What if the Guardian tried to intervene and shut down their operation? It was true they were dealing with powerful Chaos magic, but they could handle it on their own.

Probably.

"No," Maine said. "Now, if you'll excuse us?"

The Guardian passed a disgusted glance over the room. "Have...fun, I guess."

"Oh," Maine added. "Can you please take Noff with you?"

"Aw, man!" Noff squeaked. "Ya two are the worst!"

Maine and Sage chuckled.

CHAPTER TWENTY-EIGHT

"Whew, I'm glad he's gone," Maine said.

Sage made a slight face. "Why didn't you tell the Guardian about your father, the painting, and the Second Nexus?"

"I don't think much good would have come out of it. You know how he is. He would have wanted to become a big part of it, and maybe he'd shut our operation down. I can't risk losing our shot at meeting my father's double."

Sage scratched his smooth chin. "You're the most persistent girl I've ever known."

"Thanks." She grinned and wrapped her hands around his back. "I have an idea. How about we get married as soon as we figure out this Nexus thing?"

Sage swallowed. "Sure, Maine. I mean, we do have a few things to settle on first regarding the wedding preparations."

"Do we need a big celebration?" Maine pulled herself closer to him.

"We don't have to. Don't you want all our friends to celebrate with us?"

"Yeah, but I'm tired of waiting."

"If you mean that, why did you decide to do this under-cover prison scheme then?"

Maine frowned. "It's one last big case before I settle down a bit."

"Last big case, huh? It's probably going to turn out to be your most dangerous case."

"How so?"

"Because Chaos is involved. After Troll War II, Chaos did something so bad that your father used a Wish Card to create a Second Nexus to... Well, we don't exactly know what the Second Nexus was for. Maybe the war with Chaos is still going on."

She wrapped her arms behind his neck and kissed him lightly. "Or maybe the Chaos war is already over. Maybe we get to the Second Nexus and have a nice happy chat with my dad's double. It could be like a happy homecoming."

Sage looked at her. "Trolls don't have happy homecomings. They fight and wage wars, and sometimes they fall in battle in said wars." He gripped her arms. "All my life I've been searching for a girl like you, and it feels like I've just found you. I don't want to lose you."

"I get that. I don't want to lose you either. We'll take precautions when going to the Second Nexus."

"What if it's still more than a match for us?"

"It won't be. We've got your planning and magic, Maki-Mae's rituals and contacts, Blue Dots and her magic tech. And we've got Noff."

"What can Noff do?"

"Well, you know. He's Noff. He's descended from *the* Noff, the dire wolf of legends."

"He probably isn't, you know."

Maine giggled and put her nose against his chest. "We'll be

fine. I've got a good feeling about it, and if all else fails, my in-flux destiny will keep us all safe."

"That's what I'm afraid of. Your in-flux destiny."

"Oh, so you're not afraid of my prison cooties?"

"You're ridiculous." Sage kissed her. "I can't believe we're about to do it in a disgusting prison room."

"We did it before. When *you* were the one behind bars."

Sage rolled his eyes. "Don't remind me. Prison life did not suit me like it seems to suit you."

"The Oni demon guise probably helps."

"Probably."

She gripped him tighter. "That was our first time. And even though it was in a prison, it was magical to me."

Sage blushed. "Well, uh." He glanced around the small room containing the sloppy sofa and the bed. "You're saying it will be hard to beat?"

"I'm not complaining. Any time I get to spend with you is magical."

"Okay, now you're flattering me."

She looked up at him with puppy dog eyes. "It's working then?"

They came together and kissed again. They meandered over to the bed, and Sage broke for a breath as he touched the comforter on top. His fingers came away wet, and he retched.

"Crap. Well, that killed the mood." Maine laughed. She passed her gaze across the room, landing on the sofa. Then she winced. "Maybe the floor would be better?"

The next thing she knew, Sage was down on one knee.

"Um, Sage, what are you doing?"

Sage cleared his throat.

"Are you about to propose to me again?"

He shook his head and fumbled something out from under his jacket. "I was going to save this for our honeymoon, but…"

"What is it?" Maine's curiosity was stoked.

"I saved up for a few months to afford it, but it should be worth every bit."

"Seriously, what is it?"

Grinning, Sage held up what appeared to be a round, fully expanded whoopie cushion.

Maine's smile faded. "This place is gross enough, and you brought a fart bag?"

Blinking, Sage chuckled. "Oh, this is no fart bag. Remember Maki-Mae's Bag of Wind that she used to dispel the Chaos Mists?"

"Yeah."

"Well, this is a miniature version of that. It releases its wind much slower." He set the mini Bag of Wind on the floor and positioned the opening upward. "When you set it up like this…"

He uttered an incantation, and warm, pleasant air blasted up in a continual gust. Sage took off his jacket and tossed it over the Bag of Wind. Maine stared in amazement as the jacket hovered in the air.

"That's so cool! But why is this so expensive and special? What are we—" Then she understood. "Oh, so we're going to get it on in the air?"

"Exactly. Are you impressed?"

She grabbed him by the belt and tugged him closer to her. When he reached her, she tilted backward over the Bag of Wind. Her eyes widened in amazement as their bodies gently hovered off the floor. "A little bit," she admitted with a wild grin. "Now, how about we not waste any more of our time."

Sage beamed. "That is an excellent plan."

CHAPTER TWENTY-NINE

The Bag of Wind was worth every dollar, Maine decided while sitting on the edge of her bunk bed in her cell. That experience with Sage had been mesmerizing.

"C'mon," Noff squeaked from beside her. "Can't ya just tell me a little bit 'bout what happened? You're glowin' like ya just got back from Cloud Nine."

"In a way, I kind of did."

"That makes no sense, partner. This ain't fair."

"Then maybe you should quit snooping."

Noff squeaked. "That's rich comin' from a detective."

Maine kept waiting for Hank to comment on her "glow-ing-ness." Then she remembered he was currently in the hole. Without his sacrifice, she wouldn't have been able to spend time with Sage.

That damn centaur. He was one enemy she would be glad to be rid of once she got out of prison.

She couldn't wait to be free again and back in Rainwater. To do that, she needed to A, talk to Noolie and B, spike the Seeing Eye leader's tea. She figured she had a better chance at achieving goal A first so that was her immediate next move. She didn't know Noolie's exact cell location, but she knew the general area and the block of cells he had been walking toward the last she'd spoken with him. Was she being too forward going to see him at his cell? What if it scared him into not talking?

The dinner bell sounded, but Maine didn't get up.

"Ya ain't hungry?" Noff squeaked.

Her stomach growled. "With my troll blood, I can always eat. But I need to talk to Noolie."

"Well, I'm famished. Maybe we'll run into him at the cafeteria. Ya two are in the same gang after all."

Maine thought about that. "Yeah, we are in the same gang. But when have I ever seen Noolie eating in the cafeteria? With the amount of teasing he receives, he probably stays in his cell during meals."

"Not a bad observation, partner. What if he ain't in his cell now? What if he's somewhere else?"

Maine tried to recall everything she had learned about Noolie since being in prison. He was the best tattoo artist in the prison, a high-ranking member of the Seeing Eye gang, and was kind of a pushover. There was something else, she was sure of it, but she couldn't think of it at the moment. It probably wasn't important anyway.

She hopped down from her bed. "I've got to try to find Noolie. The daywalker could start the gang war at any time, and my guise expires tomorrow. That means I'm running out of time—I don't want to get stuck in prison."

Noff stood on his hind legs and twitched his whiskers. "Yeah, me neither. It was cool for a while, but the novelty is startin' to wear off."

She smirked at him. "Oh, you mean you miss watching TV?"

He lowered his mouse head with a squeak. "Guilty. Ain't no nature documentaries to watch in prison."

"Ew."

"Besides," Noff squeaked. "You're startin' to stink, partner."

"Like you couldn't use a shower, too." She laughed and patted her shoulder for him to sit on. "Come on, we've got to hurry, and I might need your nose."

Noff blasted off the bunk bed and landed on her shoulder with barely a sound. "Let's do it!"

The prison halls were mostly empty as Maine went to find Noolie's cell. Most of the inmates would be in the cafeteria now. After eating, most would retire to the rec area. Maine hoped today wasn't the day Noolie decided to break his pattern.

On the way, she passed the leshy that had been inducted into the Seeing Eye gang. His black eye was a lot better now.

"Hey, Oni, buddy." The leshy grinned and pointed at Maine.

Maine forced an awkward smile. "Hey."

"Am I gonna see you at the lunch table today?"

"In a bit. I need to talk to someone first."

The leshy gave her a quizzical look. "Who?"

She didn't like his eager smile. It didn't feel genuine considering how mad he must be at her for kicking his ass. Now that they were in the same gang, he wanted to be best buds?

"None of your business."

At first the leshy frowned at her, then he licked his lips with glee. "You really do belong in the Seeing Eye gang. So secretive. Just as long as you're not betraying the gang…"

Maine gave a throaty Oni demon grunt. "I would never do that."

The leshy's face tightened, and he took half a step back. "Whoa, big guy. I didn't mean to insinuate anything. I think you're an upstanding guy. And tough too. You'd never deceive the Seeing Eye gang."

Maine peeled down her lower lip to expose more of her tusks. "I'll see you later."

After gulping down some air, the leshy turned and trotted toward the cafeteria.

Nicely done, the Mantle hissed.

"Look at ya," Noff squeaked. "Shot-caller!"

"Damn straight," Maine muttered as she trudged toward Noolie's cell block, channeling every bit of Oni demon bravado she could muster.

She passed a few more inmates, but none tried to initiate a conversation with her.

As she reached the cell block, she started peeking into cells. Most were empty. Now and then there was an inmate inside sleeping on his bed.

"Ya sure this is the right area?" Noff squeaked.

"Do you smell Noolie?"

Niff sniffed. "I do smell him. He's not far off."

Maine knew she was close when she heard voices around a bend in the corridor. One of the voices was Noolie's, but she didn't recognize the others. She couldn't distinguish the words, but their tone suggested a disagreement. Eventually, she came upon a cell with two Parchment gang members and Noolie inside.

Noolie was finishing up tattooing the second Parchment gang member. "I'll be with you in a minute," Noolie called without looking in Maine's direction. There was a weariness to his voice, but Maine was more interested in how he knew she had been standing there in the first place. She had been moving about as quietly as an assassin.

Because of his Seeing Eye abilities, the Mantle hissed. *He is at a higher level than you. Hence he has stronger senses than you.*

That made sense. It was also a bit creepy that he could detect her like that.

"These guys giving you trouble?" Maine indicated the two Parchment gang members.

"Ugh. It's you, Oni," he said without looking at her. "No, we're good."

"Then why are you tatting up a rival gang?" Maine asked.

The two Parchment gang members gave her the evil eye.

"Are you that dumb?" Noolie finally looked up at her. "Because I am the best tattoo artist in the whole joint and I gotta tat up every single gods damned initiate sent to me."

Maine raised a hand in peace. "Damn, man. Chill. I forgot." That was what she had forgotten. He tattooed other gangs too. It explained why Noolie was never at lunch. He was too busy doing tattoo work.

"How's that look?" Noolie asked when he had finished.

The two inmates looked impressed. Noolie patted his hands together, careful not to drop the archaic-looking ink quill. "Two more satisfied customers."

The two Parchment gang members took their leave, giving Maine a clear berth as they did so.

"I didn't mean to embarrass you," Maine said.

"Shut it. You only embarrassed yourself." Noolie turned and opened a small wooden box on a desk in his cell. He gingerly set the magic tattoo needle inside. "Now why'd you come all the way out to my cell? Did the daywalker request me or something?"

Before Maine could answer, footsteps sounded outside the cell. She turned as two Seeing Eye gang members stepped inside.

"Hey, Noolie," one of them said. "Can you touch up my tattoos?"

"No, I'm going to lunch now."

The other inmate shook his head and whistled. "Wrong answer, Noolie. You're gonna touch up our tattoos first."

"Really?" Maine popped her knuckles, much to Noolie's chagrin. "Because I think maybe you should come back tomorrow."

"Who the hell do you think you are?" the first inmate asked. "Wait, aren't you that Oni demon that couldn't get the barbell up?"

The other inmate grinned stupidly. "He couldn't get it up. Ha ha. Get it?"

"Yeah, I got it, you dolt," the other one said. He grinned at Noolie. "So pal, what's it gonna be? You gonna touch up our tattoos or are we gonna have to have a little fun in the showers later tonight?"

Noolie's face tightened, and a vein stood out on his neck with such contrast that Maine thought it might burst right then and there. Which wouldn't be good because if he died, she wouldn't be able to get the information she needed from him.

Maine inserted herself between Noolie and the two other Seeing Eye gang members. "Boys, I'm going to have to object."

The two inmates laughed, then one of them said, "Is that right?"

The other inmate peeked out into the hallway. "It's clear. No guards."

"Good." The other inmate punched his fist into his palm. "Looks like we get to settle this the old way. Time to show Fresh Meat to mind his own damn business."

CHAPTER THIRTY

"Well, tell us, how is she holding up?" Maki-Mae asked.

Back at the mansion, Sage folded his hands behind his neck and leaned back on a sofa in the study. "She's doing well. Prison life and food haven't hurt her yet. It sounds like she's over picking fights with the rest of the inmates."

Maki-Mae smiled. "That's great to hear."

"I see you two enjoyed yourself," Blue Dots remarked as she tinkered with a miniature magic drone at a coffee table. Her computer setup had also been returned to the study.

"Our alone time was well-spent," Sage said. "After we finished speaking to the Guardian."

Both of Maki-Mae's eyebrows raised involuntarily. "The Guardian?"

"He wants Maine to roofie the Seeing Eye gang leader so he can wrap up his 'prevent global mythical gang war' plan."

"What did Maine say?" Maki-Mae asked with concern.

"She agreed in exchange that he transfer Noolie to another prison." Sage let out an exasperated breath. "You know what they say about 'never meet your heroes?' Yeah, they're right. The Guardian is a straight-up jerk."

"The 'good' ones usually are." Blue Dots sighed.

Maki-Mae sat up and straightened her kimono. "This is quite concerning. Gathering intel on the gang's activities is one thing but targeting a gang leader like that? And the most powerful one in the prison... You know what the Seeing Eye gang will do to her if she gets caught, right?"

"Nothing good," Sage agreed. "That's not going to happen. Especially since we'll be helping her too."

"What do you mean?" Maki-Mae asked.

"I'm not leaving Maine's escape up to Fate. If by some chance Maine fails or gets caught, we've got to have a backup plan." He jerked a thumb at Blue Dots. "While you were performing your protection ritual for Maine, Blue Dots has been busy."

"Mini support drone," Blue Dots explained. "To smuggle in some small items to her. With all the gear we're going to pack inside here, she'll be able to survive even a prison riot."

Sage added, "Knock on wood there will be no prison riots."

"Impressive," Maki-Mae observed. "I'm glad you two have been productive in my absence."

"How was your ritual?" Sage asked.

"Not as fruitful as I had hoped. I reached out to a guardian spirit to provide magical protection for Maine. But my plea was rejected."

Sage scratched his chin. "Why?"

"I did not have enough magical energy to offer in exchange. Although I probably don't show it, Maine's decision to go undercover at the prison has caused me much stress. I guess this is what it feels like to be the mother of a headstrong young girl."

Sage offered his future stepmom a weak smile, and she patted his hand gratefully for the kind gesture.

Blue Dots set down her drone next to several other slightly larger drones and turned to Maki-Mae and Sage. "Guys, I'm keeping my eyes on the prison's surveillance cameras, and we can reach Maine through her earmic at any time. We've got this."

"Thanks," Sage said. "Keep it up."

Al appeared then in the study with a tray of scones and tea. "You all are working up an appetite, I am sure."

"Al, you're the best." Blue Dots gobbled up a scone.

"I am hungry," Sage admitted.

Al blinked. "You all have been working so hard to keep Master Maine safe, and I thank you for it." He paused, standing professional and upright. "Also, I wanted to inform you that the appointment with the DJ for the wedding is in twenty minutes. Shall I reschedule?"

Sage groaned. "I forgot all about that. Yes, please."

Maki-Mae looked frustrated as well. "I forgot about my dress-resizing appointment."

"No need to fret," Al said. "I'll reschedule that as well."

"And the flowers appointment," Sage said. "That's tomorrow. Crap."

"On it," Al said.

Sage grinned at the ghost butler. "Al, you're a lifesaver."

Al straightened his ghostly tie. "Just doing my job. You all focus on what you're best at, and I will take care of my specialty. Together, we shall ensure Maine gets home safely *and* that the wedding goes off without a hitch."

As Sage grabbed a scone and some tea, he thought they all felt like a family here. They were just missing the most important person: Maine.

CHAPTER THIRTY-ONE

"This ought to be fun," one of the two Seeing Eye gang members said as he popped his neck from side to side in Noolie's cell.

"Yeah," the other agreed, rolling his shoulders.

Strike now! the Mantle hissed. *Exactly as I instructed!*

Both of these inmates looked like high-ranking Seeing Eye members with corresponding abilities. Maine thought it probably would have been wiser to come back to Noolie's cell later to talk to him, but it was too late to back out of this fight.

She closed the distance between her two fellow gang members and slugged one across the jaw before either could react. As the first one slumped backward, she followed up on the other by chopping his neck, kneeing him in the gut, and finally shoving his head back against the cell wall. Just like that, the fight was over.

They let their guards down, and it cost them, the Mantle hissed.

"Holy shit, you kill them?" Noolie gasped.

"No." Maine crouched by each one to make sure. "They should sleep for quite a while."

Noolie's eyes bulged. "I can't believe you! Attacking two Seeing Eye members? In my cell?"

"Are you grateful or what?" Maine said. "They were treating you like garbage."

"Um, he is garbage," Noff squeaked. Maine flashed him a look that told him to stay in her pocket and stay quiet.

"I, uh…" Noolie's eyes wobbled in their sockets. "You can't come to my cell and do *that*. You're as bad as them."

"No, I'm not. For the record, I want to help you—not that I should." Noolie had murdered her father. Still, it was pathetic to see how prison was treating Noolie.

"Yes, that's become apparent since you got off the prison bus. Why help me? It makes no sense. What's your angle?"

"You're right. I do have an angle. I need information you have."

Noolie glanced from the unconscious bodies of his fellow gang members slumped on the floor back to her. "You joined one of the friggin' Five Gangs of the Veil for information?"

"Yeah. You said you wouldn't talk to me unless I was in your gang."

"That's suicide."

"We'll see." Maine crossed her arms.

"Why the hell is an Oni demon so interested in me?"

Maine considered how to proceed. It was probably better to stick as close to the truth as possible. "I was passing through Rainwater before I wound up here. I was in your mansion."

Noolie's eyes bulged again. "My mansion? I mean…it's not mine anymore, but why were you—"

"I found something of value to me in your mansion."

Noolie frowned. "So? I had plenty of valuable relics and artifacts in my mansion."

"It was no ordinary artifact," Maine growled.

Noolie cringed. "What item are you interested in?"

"A painting of a quaint countryside in your study. Know anything about it?"

Noolie gulped. "Not a clue. I got it at an art auction in the Beneath, I think."

Liar! the Mantle hissed.

Maine continued. "Funny thing is that when I scratched off the top layer of paint, there was an identical painting underneath. A *living* painting."

"A living painting?" Noolie was sweating profusely. He clutched his prison uniform collar and fanned his chest. "Don't know anything about that."

"I can hear your heart rate picking up," Maine said. "I can smell the sweat leaking through your pores. Aren't Seeing Eye abilities great?" She took a step closer to him, and Noolie threw his hands up in defeat.

"Shit, okay you win! Don't eat me! I'll tell you what you need to know."

Your intimidation tactics make this demonic weapon proud.

Maine took another step closer to Noolie. "I want to know how to get to the location in the painting. I know it's a real place. It's just not on Earth. I need the key."

Noolie's back came up against the wall. "You're right. It's not in this world. It's in… Shit, you're not going to believe me."

"The Second Nexus, I know." Maine held up a claw to the light and inspected it.

With a shaky hand, Noolie knocked some sweat out of his face. "How? Only a handful of people know about that."

"Tell me everything you know about it."

Noolie swallowed. "After Troll War II, reality was a bit wonky due to all the fighting and all the hell dimensions opening. Chaos saw his chance and prepared to break reality. To combat Chaos, a troll by the name of Val—uh, his name isn't important—stole a Wish Card from me."

"A Wish Card?" Maine feigned ignorance. "Aren't those pretty rare?"

"Extremely rare. I just had to have one in my collection. I never dreamed of using it—not at first, at least. It's a direct line to Chaos. Anyway, this troll stole it from me back when he was working a case—"

"Is that why you eventually murdered Valkious?" Maine asked coldly and abruptly.

"What? Y-yes. It took many years before I finally worked up the courage to do that. He was always such a pain in my ass with his investigations in Rainwater. He was always trying to catch me in the act, but he could never get anything that could stick. Finally, I had to do him in myself."

He swallowed violently and pierced her with trembling eyes. "How did you know about that?"

Maine flared her lower lip to reveal more of her protruding tusks. "I know a lot about you. What I really want to know is what the painting has to do with this troll, Valkious."

It wasn't easy for Maine to listen to Noolie talk about her dad. She wanted to hit him for what he had done to him. At least it was helping to provide closure.

"Okay, back off, will you? Only a few souls living today know what Valkious did with the Wish Card. He used it to create a Second Nexus—an island of sorts amid the Seas of Chaos."

"The Seas of Chaos? What the hell is that? How do you know all this?"

Noolie tugged his shirt collar. "The Seas of Chaos are Chaos' domain. They are what threaten to rush into the world if reality ever breaks. I know all this because I was surveilling Valkious' activities. As I said, he was a thorn in my side."

Noolie caught his breath. "Valkious used a very intricate ritual to split himself and his 'Chosen' so they could go to the Second Nexus and defend the Veil from Chaos there. You could think of it as the first line of defense to stop Chaos from ever getting to our world."

Wow, that was a lot to take in. She couldn't wait to tell Sage and Maki-Mae about this.

She flexed her Oni demon claws. "All this while, you were secretly worshipping and working for Chaos?"

"Well, sort of," Noolie said glumly. "My endgame was to ultimately betray Chaos and the Corruptor. I was out of my league. The Corruptor had his weaknesses, but Chaos is not one to be messed with. In the end, Chaos wasn't the one who did me in."

"Who was?" Maine was curious about how Noolie would respond.

All the energy went out of Noolie's body and voice. "Valkious' daughter, can you believe it? And she was just starting her career as a detective. Do you know how embarrassing that was for me? It's part of why I'm the butt of everyone's jokes here."

Reveal your true identity to him. Grip him by the throat and show him who you are beneath your guise. You will break him so completely he'll have to be committed to an insane asylum. Do it— do it quickly!

Maine didn't. As much as she would like to pay back

Noolie a bit more for what he had done to her and her father, she wasn't like Noolie. She still needed his help. Besides, he was in a pretty pathetic condition as it was, locked in a supermax prison and made everyone's prison bitch.

However, she wasn't done.

"I've heard of this troll," Maine said. "I believe they call her the Great Troll Detective. Or the Maine Troll. Would you seek revenge against her if given a chance?"

As Noolie stared into her eyes, his words grew hard. "That half-troll took everything away from me. Everything. But I think… Maybe I had it coming. No. I wouldn't seek vengeance."

Maine felt her eye twitch. Had he expressed remorse?

She shook her head to clear it. "The living painting or Second Nexus or whatever. Do you know where the key is?"

Noolie's eyes widened in amusement. "Ah, you wish to speak to Valkious' double?"

"Would that be possible?"

"Of course. If you had the key. The painting provides you with the living coordinates of the Second Nexus deep within the Seas of Chaos. But to open a portal to the Second Nexus, safely bypassing the Seas of Chaos, you must possess the key and use it at the designated location on Earth."

"That sounds complicated."

"It's really not."

"Can you get me the key?"

Noolie looked deep in thought.

This conversation was taking a long time. If someone came to Noolie's cell for a tattoo and found the two knocked-out inmates, that would not be good. "Come on, answer me!"

Noolie winced. "Y-yes. But why should I tell you where it is?"

"Because I have powerful connections on the outside. I can help you."

Noolie gave a weak laugh and shook his head. "Yes, I do have the Key. It's even in this prison. But you can't have it. It's all I have left to hold onto."

"Is that your final answer?" Maine asked.

"Yes. You can't have it, and you can't help me. There is nothing you can offer me that will make me change my mind."

"Nothing?" Maine prodded.

"Nothing," Noolie confirmed sadly.

He is clearly beyond help, the Mantle hissed. *Tell him you'll kill him quickly rather than slowly.*

Maine eased off from her tough guy routine and crossed her arms. "It's clear that this prison has become your personal hell. Would you give me the key if I got you transferred to a minimum security prison?"

Noolie's eyes brightened "With windows?"

"No, even better, I'll get you transferred to a Martha Stewart prison. You know, the kind with pretty gardens and shit where you can walk around wherever you want. And there won't be any other prisoners—"

Noolie threw himself upon his hands and knees in front of her. "I'll do anything. Anything!"

"You'll, uh, give me the key then?"

Noolie kneeled before her. "Oni, I will praise your name for the rest of my days if you carry through with your word. Yes, of course, you can have the key. It's in the prison, but it's not on me."

"Great. I've got some other business to take care of first, but we'll have to move quickly." She glanced at the two unconscious Seeing Eye members in Noolie's cell. "Because those two goons weren't in the plan, and I don't know how much longer we have until our cover is blown."

Noolie scampered to his feet. "Yes, of course, we must move quickly."

First you should hide the bodies, the Mantle hissed.

That would buy them some time if someone came looking for the two Seeing Eye members. Maine grabbed the two unconscious men by the feet and dragged them beneath Noolie's bed.

Now drape some bedsheets over the edge.

Maine did as the Mantle suggested, concealing the gap between the bottom of the bed and the floor so the two unconscious gang members were out of sight. Surveying her handiwork, she couldn't help but feel like a criminal.

While Maine hid the bodies, Noolie gathered some small items from his cell. When they finished, they stepped out into the hallway after using their Seeing Eye senses to ensure no one was outside. Then Noolie closed his cell door behind him. It locked.

"Isn't that going to be suspicious to the guards?" Maine asked.

"No. Sometimes I shut my door when I want to be alone. The guards can always open it at any time. It should buy us some time."

"Good. Now the key?"

"I'll have to retrieve it. How about I get it, and you meet me at the laundry area in an hour?"

Maine wondered if Noolie was somehow trying to deceive or betray her, but the Mantle confirmed that Noolie had no ill intent.

"All right, I'll see you in an hour."

Before they set off in different directions, Noolie asked in a whispered hiss, "What are you going to do now?"

She leaned her mouth next to Noolie's ear. "I've got some business to finish with the Seeing Eye leader."

Noolie's eyes shot wide. "The daywalker? What kind of business?"

"I've got to spike his tea for the Guardian."

Noolie slapped his hand to his forehead. "Our plan is doomed."

She smacked him on the shoulder with as much force as she thought an Oni demon might. "Toughen up. I'll get it done."

"He'll *sense* you."

"Not if I cause a distraction while I do it."

Noolie gulped. "I'm a dead man."

Maine gripped him tightly by the shoulder. "You are not. You're going to make it through this. You've got to trust me."

Social distance!

Maine released Noolie and set off for her cell to get the Guardian's tablet.

When she reached her cell, she was surprised it wasn't empty.

"Hank, what are you doing in here?" she asked.

Hank was lying in bed with a pillow over his head. "The guards let me out early from the hole. Two times in one week. Sucks like a hangover from hell."

This is rather suspicious, the Mantle hissed.

Is he lying?

I don't detect a lie.

That was good enough for her.

She retrieved the magic tablet and sent Noff to inform the Guardian that they would need to be rescued from the prison ASAP because she was on the way to spike the daywalker's tea. Noff promised to join her and Noolie in the laundry room and scampered into the corridor.

Hank watched all this with a curious eye. After Noff left, Maine quickly filled the troll in on her impromptu plan.

"Hank, I know you feel like crap, but you said you would help me. I'm not expecting trouble, but it sure likes to find me. You in?"

The troll threw back his head and chuckled. "Hell yes. Thanks for asking."

CHAPTER THIRTY-TWO

Maine called her friends over her earmic and briefly explained the situation about how she talked to Noolie and was carrying out the Guardian's mission right now. They were equally nervous and excited that Maine would soon finish her time in prison.

Maine walked down the corridor. "Guys, I'm going to have to turn off the earmic while I spike the daywalker's tea."

"I don't like it," Sage fretted. "But I understand."

Blue Dots chimed in. "The mini drones aren't quite ready to deploy yet. I'll try to work faster."

"Thanks." Maine slowly passed the empty cells on both sides. Everyone was either still at lunch or in the rec area. "Hopefully I won't need them."

"Better safe than sorry." Sage sounded perturbed. "Does the Guardian know about your impromptu plan?"

"Noff's on his way to tell him right now. The Guardian will get us out. He swore it."

"I don't have a good feeling about this," Sage divulged.

"Be safe, dear," Maki-Mae added. "May you traverse your path with a clear heart and mind."

"Thanks. Now I have to go. I'm running out of time."

"Where are you going after you see the, uh, daywalker?" Sage asked.

"The laundry room. It's where I'm meeting Noolie."

"You honestly trust him to bring you the key?" Sage didn't sound confident.

"The Mantle trusts Noolie. So do I."

"The Mantle is a demonic weapon," Sage reminded her.

"I'll be prepared in case anything goes wrong," Maine said. "Besides, Hank will help watch my back to ensure I make it to the laundry room. In case it's a setup, which it isn't."

"Sounds like you've thought things through," Maki-Mae observed.

"A few things. I'll admit, it's a pretty fluid plan, but I'll be all right. I mean, the Guardian is on my side if things go really sideways."

"I checked the laundry room surveillance camera," Blue Dots informed her. "It looks empty."

"That's good." At least Noolie had picked a good meeting place. Maine finished her goodbyes with her team.

"I love you," Sage said.

"Love you too. See you soon." Maine shut off her earmic.

Then she breathed calmly until her heart rate and other bodily functions were back to normal. "Mantle, I trust you to help keep my vitals even."

I'll do what I can, but the magic dampeners are hampering me. You will be mostly on your own in there.

"Well, keep an eye and ear out for me, okay?"

Always.

When Maine reached the Seeing Eye leader's cell, she found two brutish inmates standing outside with their arms crossed.

"What do you want, Fresh Meat?" one asked.

Maine kept her voice gruff, low, and calm. "I need to speak to our leader on a most urgent matter."

"He's not here at the moment," the other said.

Maine peeked between the two sentries. While she couldn't see the gang leader, she could see the corner of his yoga mat off to one side. On it sat the gang leader's glass of tea.

"It's urgent." She kept her voice level.

One of the gang members tried to shove her back a step, but she held her ground. "What part of 'he's not available' don't you understand? Geez, you fresh meats can be so intolerable."

"Hush," a soothing voice called inside the cell. "For you were once 'fresh meat' yourself. Or have you forgotten?"

Both of the sentries suddenly looked uncomfortable.

"I'm sorry, leader, I did forget for a moment. With your guidance, I have remembered." To Maine, the inmate said, "I am sorry, new initiate. I did not mean to degrade you." His tone suggested that he did indeed mean to degrade her.

"Okay?" Maine said. "So…"

"Let the Oni demon come to me," the daywalker commanded in a strong but soothing voice.

"Yes, sir!" Both sentries stepped aside, allowing entrance to the gang leader's room.

Use utmost caution. The daywalker sees and hears everything. Speak no more than necessary.

Maine stepped inside. "Sorry to disturb your meditation, leader." She took in the room's interior. It looked the same as the prior two times she had been here—huge and filled with tapestries.

"Why are you sorry? If it truly is urgent, I would be glad to hear it. We don't like keeping secrets in the Seeing Eye gang."

"Okay. Well, it's the Guardian. I just heard that he's trying to infiltrate the gangs, that he might already have a mole in this one."

"That is quite important." This whole time, the gang leader had kept his eyes closed. Maine meandered up to the glass of tea on the corner of the meditation mat and crouched beside it. "Can you explain it a bit more in-depth?"

"You mean where did I get my source of information?" Maine asked hesitantly, edging closer to the tea glass.

"Of course not. We of the Seeing Eye are founded on trust. We do not need to divulge sources. If you say it is so, I take it as so. Now the Guardian. What exactly is he planning?"

It was best to keep as close to the truth as possible.

"It is my understanding that he wants to take down all the Five Gangs of the Veil but through the use of spies and moles."

The leader chuckled dryly, which was creepy considering his eyes were still closed, and he was a redneck-looking, meditating daywalker. "Good luck getting one into my gang. I will be on the lookout and sniff him—or her—out before they cause any damage."

Crap. Was he onto her?

Play it cool, the Mantle hissed.

Still crouching, Maine shifted her position slightly. "What if the Guardian inserts a spy into our gang outside the prison? I know you are our leader, but you can't possibly hear and see that far away."

His lips curled up into an eerie smile. "I have my ways, new initiate. That damned angel leader may be able to infiltrate the other gangs, but he's in for a nasty surprise if he thinks he can infiltrate mine."

Maine's fingers closed over the Guardian's tablet in her pocket. She was ready to drop it into the tea glass at any time.

"Now, is that all?" the gang leader prompted.

Hurry, say something else! the Mantle hissed.

"Y-yes. I've been, uh, having strange dreams."

For the first time in their conversation, the gang leader cracked one eyelid open to look at her. "What kind of dreams?"

"Um, that's what I hoped you could help me with." She glanced around the room as she tried to figure out what to say next.

Now the gang leader opened both eyes wide. "How fortunate for you. I am a master interpreter of dreams. Extend your hand to me, and I will read them via the blood in your veins."

Crap! Not only were the gang leader's eyes wide open now, but he wanted to maintain an extended physical connection to her that would make her guise fade.

"I'm sorry, leader." Maine drew back in her seated position. "My skin condition. I really shouldn't have bothered you with such a trivial matter."

The daywalker flashed a hungry smile. "I must insist you extend your arm to me. You do trust me, correct?"

"I trust you, but I don't feel comfortable letting you into my blood, er, mind."

The daywalker ran his tongue around his lips. "You fear the daywalker? And an Oni demon? You humor me. I do not have to touch you to read your dreams."

She stiffened. "You mean you can read my mind without touching me?" Uh-oh, maybe the gang leader had a heightened sixth sense she didn't know about.

He smiled at her for a time longer than seemed necessary. Then he thankfully closed his eyes again. "Would that I could read minds. That is not what I meant.

"I can understand your...hesitation in opening up to another. It's quite common among inmates. Something we shall cure you of. I meant that if you could describe your dream, I could connect to it and interpret it for you. Dreams are insights into the soul, you know."

Maine forced a chuckle, starting to relax a bit now that the gang leader had closed his eyes again. She glanced around the room again. Her gaze landed upon a tapestry with a wolf head on it. "There's a big wolf in my dream. It's pursuing me."

"I see. What is the environment like?"

"Huh?"

"The landscape of your dream. Are you on a back country road, in a busy city, at the beach?"

"Uh..."

Now's your chance. Spike the tea—spike it quickly!

She raised her voice quite suddenly. "It's an overgrown field." When the gang leader's eyes didn't open, she continued, keeping her voice uneven and loud as she slowly extended her hand over the glass. She dropped the tablet into the glass. "Lots of wildflowers and thorns. A miniature dire wolf is chasing me from behind, but the big dire wolf is in front of me. They come upon me so suddenly. I wake up in a sweat every time."

"I see," the daywalker said evenly. "A big dire wolf and a small dire wolf..."

Was he buying it?

"What time of day is it?"

"Time of day? It's a dream."

"Is it night or day or morning in the dream?"

"I don't know. Daytime, I think. There's a heavy mist all around. It's difficult to see through it."

The gang leader lifted a long finger to his chin and scratched. "A very interesting dream, but quite easy to interpret."

"It is?"

"But of course. The big dire wolf in front of you is a big life event, and you are rushing toward it. The small dire wolf behind you is egging you ever closer to your big life event. It could be a fear, like running out of time.

"The wildflowers and thornbushes are the obstacles in your path. The mist is your hesitation. You want to know: Am I making the correct choice?"

The gang leader's eyes snapped wide open and locked onto her face. "Does that provide any clarity to you? Any big life events for you before you came to the joint?"

"I have a wedding coming up," Maine said softly. "Had a wedding. I got caught and thrown in here before I could tie the knot."

"I'm sure he is a lovely fellow," the gang leader said.

"How did you know he's a he?" Maine asked sharply.

"Just a feeling. Don't worry. It's nothing to be ashamed of. We don't care about stuff like that. That's your business and yours alone."

"Well, um, thanks. You're probably right. I guess my dreams are about that." She rose. "Thank you for your time, leader. I'd like to spend a few minutes in the rec area before it's over for the day."

"Don't mention it. Thank *you* for the information."

She held her breath.

"Your information on the Guardian's plans."

"Just doing my duty." Maine turned toward the room's entrance.

"Oh, one more thing," the gang leader said calmly.

She slowly turned back to face him. "Yes?"

"A small favor. Can you hand me my glass of tea?"

Maine swallowed a gulp of air and did as requested. She stood before the cross-legged gang leader while he took a few swallows of spiked tea.

"Such a unique taste this tea has. Oolong with a hint of ginger. You should try it one day. It's eye-opening."

Okay, now he was messing with her, right? He knew the game she was playing.

Quit being paranoid! the Mantle hissed. *You'll give yourself away.*

She nodded, and he wiped his mouth with the back of his hand. As he did so, he momentarily displayed his imposing daywalker canines.

He handed her the glass back, and Maine was relieved that the Guardian had said only a sip was required for the tablet to work. "You have my appreciation, new initiate. I can see great things in store for you. Now, best hurry if you hope to have any time in the rec area today."

"Yes, leader." She set the glass down and headed for the door. She didn't breathe again until she was outside the cell.

That was so creepy! she mentally projected to the Mantle.

Look on the bright side. You accomplished your mission without him tearing open your jugular and sucking down your life's blood.

Maine gulped. She had survived the encounter, and the gang leader had drunk some of the spiked tea. She had seen it so that meant the Guardian would be able to tell shortly when the gang leader's powers were dampened or whatever. Whew. She did *not* want the daywalker as an enemy.

Now there was only one thing left to do.

She headed to the laundry room to meet up with Noolie.

CHAPTER THIRTY-THREE

Hank joined her as she headed toward the laundry room, breaking away from his waiting place against the wall.

Maine was glad for him to be there. She couldn't help but worry if he was okay because of the stupid grin plastered across his face. "You okay?" she asked. "For just getting out of the hole, you look like you're having the time of your life."

He flexed his fingers. "I'm psyching myself up for the coming fight."

"We're not going to fight unless it's necessary."

"Of course, just want to be ready is all."

Maine thought Hank was acting kind of suspicious. "Stick to the plan. We're going to meet Noolie. He's going to give me the key. Then the Guardian will whisk him and me out of prison."

"I've got it," Hank confirmed as they continued walking toward the laundry room on the other side of the prison. He no longer walked slouched over. He was moving confidently for the first time since she had met him. Like he had a purpose.

"I wish I could get you a free ride out of prison too, but the Guardian denied my request."

The troll shrugged. "It's all good. I deserve to be in this place. I can't speak for Noolie, but you don't belong here. If it comes down to me having to fight and getting thrown in the hole again...well, that's just me repaying my debt to your father."

"Okay. Just stay alert. We're not to the laundry room yet."

It seemed that every other corridor had a clock hanging on it. The clocks notified her that she was running out of time to meet Noolie, but they couldn't run. They had to be careful traversing the hallways.

They rounded a corner. As they did so, Maine made out a person at the other end walking toward them. When they got closer, she saw that it was a guard.

"Crap," Maine muttered.

"Ah hell, let me deal with him." Hank ground a fist into his palm.

She nudged him in the side. "No. Let me."

As the guard neared them, the guard called, "What are you two doing in this block?"

They stopped walking, and Maine kept her eyes on the floor as she spoke. "Going to work some overtime in the laundry room, sir."

The guard studied both of them. "The laundry room? You two ought to be finishing up lunch."

"Not hungry," Maine said.

"It's cake day," the guard said. "You missed cake day? No inmate misses cake day." Suspicion filled his eyes as the guard drew his baton from his side. "You two not feeling well or something?"

Maine focused on the weapon in the guard's hand. If he

tried to come at them with it, she would take him out nonlethally. She hoped she could avoid that. She glanced up at a clock on the wall. If they didn't keep moving, they would be late, and she couldn't afford for Noolie to get cold feet.

"I feel fine." Maine turned to Hank, who was eyeing the guard tersely. She elbowed him in the side.

"Me too," Hank said good-naturedly. "We're on the keto diet, can't have cake anyway."

The guard wrinkled both brows. "Even if that's true, your being in this hall is very suspicious."

Weakness: hates to be told he's paranoid.

"I think you're being paranoid," Maine said calmly.

"What? I am not," the guard objected.

He's frustrated, calm him down—but confuse him.

"Then why do you look like you want to take out your frustration on a couple of reformed inmates looking to put in some overtime doing laundry for our fellow inmates?"

The guard looked down at the baton in his hands. "That's not true."

"Your knuckles are bone white," Maine said calmly. "Are you sure there isn't something else on your mind right now?" A glance at the clock said they were about to be late to meet Noolie.

"Well, maybe," the guard said uneasily. "But I ain't gonna talk about it to you two. Now turn around and get a move on before I write you up and throw the both of you in the hole."

It's his wife.

Maine fisted her hands at her hips. "Your wife about to leave you?"

All tightness seemed to leave the guard's face as gravity pulled his features—and the baton—downward. "Hey, how'd you know?"

"You've got that look," Hank said before Maine could speak. "I ought to know. Happened to me once. It got better."

The guard looked a bit consoled for a few moments. Then he straightened. "It got better for you? You're in prison."

"Because I stole a car," Hank clarified. "I wouldn't recommend doing that part."

The guard chuckled as if he felt morally better than the criminally inclined troll.

"Want to talk about it?" Maine was still eyeing the ticking clock in her peripheral vision.

After a long pause, the guard sighed. "Nah. I'm good now." He closed the telescoping baton and holstered it at his side. "You two really going to do laundry now?"

"Scout's honor." Hank winked.

"Well, all right. I'll be back around to check on you two later. No funny business, you hear?"

Maine solemnly nodded while Hank grinned.

When the guard had walked out of sight, Hank chuckled. "Hah. The poor schlep just needed someone to talk to."

"You should know. You were holding things in too the other night."

Hank's face soured. "Yeah, yeah. You're not my psychiatrist."

"Come on. We're late."

When they reached the laundry room, it was empty. There was a clock on the laundry room wall, and Maine checked it to ensure it was the time she thought it was. It was.

"Crap. He's not here."

"Take it easy," Hank soothed. "I'm sure he's just running a little behind. Maybe he ran into a guard like we did."

"What if he got caught?"

"Noolie's a squirrely one, but he's capable. He's got high-ranking gang member special abilities, remember?"

"Yeah, but still." Maine searched for Noolie as she explored the expansive laundry room. She tried to move as inconspicuously as possible since there were surveillance cameras.

She had never been on laundry duty because she was still new. She hadn't been in here before. The place was creepy with the lights off and the only illumination in the room coming through some high, dirty windows. The numerous shadows in the room seemed unnaturally dark, and for a place of cleaning, she found the grimy windows ironic.

"Hey, I think I hear someone," Hank said.

They both stood still and Maine used her Seeing Eye abilities to listen for a few seconds. "I don't hear anything," she said at last.

"Damn. Must be hearing things," Hank said. "Could have sworn I heard someone moving in here."

Maine scoured the darkened laundry room with her gaze. Rows upon stacked rows of electric washers and driers filled it. They were all front-loading and had clear windows so you could see inside them at all times. As Maine walked through the big laundry room, she glanced inside each washer and drier she passed. The front-loading doors were all open, presumably so they could air out.

She didn't expect to find Noolie in one of them, but maybe he was hiding. Or what if this was a trap and someone had stuffed Noolie's corpse in one of the machines? Was it just her or did she feel like she was being watched?

Who's the paranoid one now? the Mantle hissed with delight.

"Shut up, rag," she muttered and finished inspecting all the washers and driers on her side of the room. "See anything?" she called to Hank on the other side of the laundry room.

"Nothing. Like I said, he's probably running behind. Or maybe he stopped by the cafeteria for some cake."

"Can everyone please shut up about the cake?"

"What? It only comes once a month. You know the quality of our regular food..."

Maine wrapped up her search, her instincts telling her to stay clear of all the patches of thick shadows in the room, and returned to Hank. She considered flipping on the lights but decided against it.

Again, paranoid. I detect no one else in the room.

"You know," Hank said when she rejoined him. "You remind me of your old man. Even when he was scared, he never showed it. Never backed down from a fight, either. He always had to help people, even his enemies if they needed it. He was a different breed, Valkious. It's good to see he passed on his best qualities."

"Um, thanks." Maine kept searching the darkened interior, waiting for Noolie to burst into the laundry room, explaining that he'd been held up and that's why he was late.

Noolie didn't show.

It didn't make sense. Noolie was so insistent on getting out of this place. He'd practically been sobbing when she'd mentioned she could get him into a Martha Stewart prison. He'd been praising her as if she were a god. The Mantle hadn't detected him lying so she was now almost convinced that something bad had happened to him.

The two continued to wait in silence in the middle of the room. That's when Maine realized something else was bothering her.

At the same time, Hank scratched his cheek. "Hey, where's your annoying Mickey Mouse dire wolf partner?"

That was a very good—and disturbing—question. Noff should have been here already too. All he had to do was take the mouse holes straight to the Guardian like the Guardian had instructed Noff to do in case he needed to get urgent info to him fast.

Dammit! What the hell was going on?

"I don't like this one bit." She bit her nail.

This time, Hank didn't try to make an excuse for Noolie. The troll let out a long sigh instead of replying directly.

Maine's enhanced hearing picked up footsteps from the other side of one of the laundry room doors. Four doors led into the laundry room, and the footsteps were coming from a different one than Maine and Hank had entered.

"Get ready to fight," Maine whispered over her shoulder to Hank.

Hank popped his neck from side to side. "Oh, I'm ready."

They backed up a few steps to stand in partial shadows from the stacked washers and dryers.

After what seemed like too long, the door finally opened, and in stepped Noolie, his face ashen.

"What's wrong?" Maine asked in a soft voice.

Noolie didn't say anything.

Maine realized then that she had forgotten to turn her earmic back on after spiking the tea. She reached up and turned it on.

"Maine, get out—" Sage warned, but then the comm link became static.

Suddenly all the lights in the laundry room blared to life, blinding her and Hank. She raised her arms to block out the light. Despite the direct lighting, many thick pools of shadows remained on the floor. The shadows throughout the room began to quiver, and a few moments later, they began to ooze upward and take on the shape of humanoid figures.

When Maine's eyes had fully adjusted to the bright lights, she recognized some of her fellow Seeing Eye gang members standing where the inky shadows had been.

What kind of magic could turn shadows into inmates?

This wasn't good.

It's a trap! the Mantle hissed.

"A bit late, you think?" she muttered.

CHAPTER THIRTY-FOUR

All of the gang members materializing in the laundry room belonged to the Seeing Eye gang. They were the inmates she'd been eating with in the cafeteria, the ones who would silently eat their food beside her, always observing, always looking for secrets...

Among them, Maine saw the green leshy, his previously go-lucky, chummy demeanor replaced with one of disappointment and anger.

"Well... Shit," Hank said. "I love a good fight, but I think we might be outmatched."

There were now at least fifty gang members in the laundry room. Where the hell had they come from? How did they know she was going to be here?

Maine shared a quick look with Hank. "Outmatched, huh? Since when has that ever stopped you before?"

The troll flashed her his half-smirk. "I didn't say I was going to surrender. Whether it's the hole or death that faces me afterward, I'm ready to fight by your side."

"Very touching." An annoyingly calm and powerful voice drifted into the room from the doorway Noolie had stepped through.

A figure entered after Noolie and shoved Noolie toward Maine and Hank. The overhead lights revealed the daywalker. His mouth twitched when he looked in Maine's direction.

"We've got all the doors covered," the gang leader said. "You're not getting out of here unless we allow you to. I don't think that looks likely."

Maine tried to focus on the daywalker, but in the blink of an eye he had shifted to the side, then he seemed to skate forward a few yards before braking and appearing a couple of feet to the side again. He moved like the cross between a snake and a ghost.

Daywalker, the Mantle hissed. *Possesses extreme speed, strength, and agility. A true equal to the toughest of troll war chieftains. Good luck.*

"Good luck?" Maine muttered. "What's his damn weakness?"

Daywalkers are weak against lightning magic. A lightning bolt might hobble him.

"The only elemental spell I know is fireball."

The daywalker looked at Maine as if she were a specimen in a jar that couldn't escape. "Who are you talking to, Dead Meat? Your friends in your ear?"

She wondered if the daywalker was somehow disrupting her earmic's comm link. How had he known she'd been communicating with the outside world?

The daywalker tapped his ear with a long slender finger. "You know the answer to that. I have *very* good hearing."

"Can you read my mind?" Maine's palms were sweating.

"I might as well be able to. Alas, there's no need. Not when your every muscle twitch betrays your next move. My enhanced senses vastly outperform yours. I can hear a bee buzzing a mile away. I can practically hear your neurons firing."

As I said, the Mantle hissed. *Good luck.*

Noolie picked himself off the floor and backed up to join Maine and Hank.

"How long have you known?" Maine asked the gang leader.

The daywalker chuckled. "From the moment I spotted you stepping off that prison bus, I knew you weren't what you appeared to be."

"You were watching me from the shadows?" Maine asked.

"No. I was meditating in my cell. I *heard* you step off the bus. I *felt* your intentions. You signed your death warrant the second you set foot on this prison's grounds."

Try to maintain your confidence, the Mantle hissed. *Do not betray weakness or the daywalker will impale you with his fist quicker than you can blink.*

"Then why go through all the charades?" Maine asked.

"What do you mean?"

"Why didn't you kill me on the spot? Or sneak into my cell at night? That was you at night, watching me, wasn't it?" A wave of goosebumps shimmied across her skin at the recollection.

"Perhaps you forget that this is the Seeing Eye gang. Our specialty is secrets and deception."

"So why induct me into your little gang?"

"Isn't it obvious? To draw out the Guardian's pawn. To uncover his plan. Those visitation rooms aren't soundproof against me. I heard every word he spoke to you and your fiancé."

He doesn't appear to be lying.

Crap. So the gang leader had known that she was a mole this whole time.

"You drank the spiked tea," Maine said.

His smile was wicked. "Why would I drink the tea if I knew you had spiked it?"

"I watched you drink it. You took a sip, and that's all the Guardian said you needed to drink."

The daywalker rolled his eyes. "You saw what I wanted you to see. I dry-swallowed air is all. It was a good 'guise,' don't you think?"

Guise. Was he referring to her guise spell?

"While I may not be able to see through your guise spell, I can detect its presence with my master-level sensing abilities. It won't be long until your guise fades for all here to see who you are."

At this, Noolie gave Maine a confused and terrified look.

Maine didn't understand what the daywalker's cryptic message was all about. Her guise spell had another day left, not that it would help her now.

She didn't know how she would get out of this situation yet so she felt it best to keep stalling for time. Stalling until Noff and the Guardian could reach her.

She gestured at her sides at all the gang members glaring her way. "What's up with the magic shadow trick? I thought the magic dampeners would prevent all magic inside the prison."

The daywalker picked his teeth with a slender clawlike fingernail. "Who says the magic dampeners are still on at this moment?"

"What are you talking about?" Maine asked. "Of course they're…"

She conjured a fireball above both palms and realized his words were true.

"Wait," she said, "if the magic dampeners are down, that means you…"

"Have full power," the gang leader finished. "The funny thing about the magic dampeners is they're like Wi-Fi signals. You can't 'feel' when they are off and on. You have to check your device—or magic in this case—to see if it's active or not."

"What about the guards?" Maine recalled her fireballs into her palms. "They'll be here any moment."

The daywalker looked somewhat perturbed. "No, they won't. Some of the guards are Seeing Eye members. They're in the know and will ensure no one intervenes with what we are about to do."

When Maine glanced up at the surveillance cameras in the room, the daywalker sneered. "In addition to disabling the magic dampeners, the surveillance cameras in this room are all on a loop. No one is going to come to save you."

Maine blinked, trying to think straight. "The Guardian will be here at any moment. Even if you can all use your magic now, he will kick all your asses."

"Ha. Don't make me laugh," the daywalker scoffed. "The Guardian is off in LA at this exact moment, trying to prevent the start of the mythical gang war."

"No, he's here in the prison," Maine insisted. He had to be here. Why would he leave now?

"To answer the question most likely swimming through your head right now, he's tracking down a red herring I planted. See, as soon as I knew you were making your move today, I had to get the Guardian as far away from here as possible. True, he is powerful, but I dare say I would give him a run for his money, especially with my gang at full power and some of the guards on my payroll. If he were here right now, we'd be able to make that cocky, stuck-up angel beg for us not to kill him."

The daywalker paused long enough to flash his fangs at her. "He's no idiot, I'll give him that, but by the time he realizes what's going on, you'll be drained of blood and stiff as a board. And you, Noolie. I always knew you were a snake. A real shame because you're a damn good tattoo artist."

Noolie gave Maine the most sorrowful look she'd ever seen on a person. "There's no other way to say it—we are dead," Noolie croaked.

"Not without a fight, we aren't." Hank's muscles tensed. Moving with more speed than he looked like he should possess, he threw himself at the nearest inmate, who raised his dukes. The troll instead swept the inmate's legs out beneath him, then bashed his head against the floor.

A second gang member jumped at Hank, but he ducked and threw the inmate over his back with a judo move. The inmate landed on his back with a *thud* and Hank stomped on his chest. The inmate groaned and rolled over onto his side.

"Well, you going to join me or what?" Hank called to Maine.

Three inmates were already darting Maine's way. Instead of trying to evade, she took a note from Hank's playbook and tackled the lead inmate in the legs. He toppled to the floor over her like a struck bowling pin. She uppercut one of the inmates under the chin and brought the third inmate's nose down onto her rising knee. She was about to deliver a power kick to the inmate on the floor when the daywalker called in a loud, clear voice.

"Stop right now. Or I'll squish your little friend to a pulp."

Maine stopped mid-fight and twisted her head back to look at the gang leader. Noff hung suspended by his neck fat between two slender fingers.

CHAPTER THIRTY-FIVE

Noff looked about as helpless as a mouse-sized dire wolf could look under the circumstances. He gave Maine an embarrassed look as he dangled from the daywalker's fingers.

"Sorry, partner," he squeaked. "They caught me."

She could have told him she said to be careful, but both of them had underestimated the daywalker's abilities and his reach inside the prison.

"I knew I smelled a rat," the daywalker said. "I didn't know it was a real rat. Now don't do anything you'll regret. Wouldn't want your 'partner' to die."

Maine knew the gang leader had no intention of letting them live. Still, she couldn't live with herself for however short that time would be if her actions caused Noff to die right now. She eased her offensive posture and stepped away from the groaning inmates she had incapacitated.

"Very good," the daywalker said. "I knew you would listen to reason."

Maine wasn't going to let the daywalker talk them to death before he killed them. But what could she do?

Attack the daywalker now—he won't expect it!

But that would get Noff killed, Maine mentally projected back to the Mantle.

So? You must think about yourself. If the daywalker strikes you first, you will not last long.

Now that the magic dampeners are off, you've got your full powers back, right? Maine asked. That meant so did she.

True. Perhaps you do stand a chance.

Maine wasn't going to risk Noff's life. Until she thought of a plan, there would be no provoking the daywalker.

The gang leader stretched his jaw open and closed a few times. He had a surprisingly elastic jaw. "Aside from my extra senses, I know every mouse hole and comm line into this prison. It was easy to intercept your mouse spy. Even easier to send word to my boys in LA to cause a big scene to draw the Guardian away."

Unless the Guardian teleported back here ASAP, Maine's and Noolie's way out was gone, and Maine didn't see another way appearing anytime soon. She was on her own against one of the most powerful mythical creatures on the planet.

There had to be a way out of this.

The daywalker lifted Noff to eye level and licked his lips.

"You know, as a Seeing Eye, I hate rats. It's a good thing they're so tasty."

Noff twitched and squirmed in the gang leader's grip. "I'm a dire wolf, asshole!" He managed to twist his head around and bite the gang leader's finger.

"You'll pay for that—"

The key-shaped marking on Noff's rump began to glow, and in the next moment, a blinding white ball of light exploded from Noff's tiny body, illuminating the room.

The daywalker shuffled back a step, dropping Noff in the

process. The dire wolf blasted off in midair and landed on Maine's shoulder with a squeak. Then he stood on his hind legs so he was closer to Maine's ear and squeaked, "I think it's time to fight now."

"All right!" Hank roared and commenced shoving his fist into an inmate's face.

"Stop them!" the daywalker hissed, still recovering from Noff's intense sunburst attack directly in front of his eyes.

At least ten inmates rushed Maine, but instead of meeting them, she bear-hugged a washing machine, lifted it, and chucked it at them. They all scrambled to the side as it struck the floor with a loud *crunch* of metal.

Way to use your strength, the Mantle hissed.

"You are damn strong, my friend," Hank called as she kicked an inmate in the chest, sending the goon flying backward into an open washing machine.

A few more inmates leapt at Maine, but she swiftly evaded, then delivered a sweeping blow against the back of their heads in one fluid motion that sent them tumbling to the floor.

"The Oni demon is too strong!" an inmate cried.

The daywalker cursed. "Weakling," he mumbled, then struck down his gang member with a clawed hand. The inmate didn't get back up. Then the daywalker raised his hand and snapped his fingers. It sounded extremely loud amid all the fighting, which was odd, Maine thought.

The inmate nearest her gasped. "The Oni demon is a...girl?"

"What the hell?" another inmate gasped.

Glancing down at her arms, Maine saw that her intimidating Oni demon skin had reverted to hers. She looked like a twenty-something girl in a laundry room filled with hardened mythical criminals.

"Shit!" Noff squeaked from her shoulder. His guise too had faded, revealing a dire wolf the size of a mouse perched upon Maine's shoulder.

Maki-Mae had said that the only way for someone to break the guise spell was if they figured out the exact guise spell and performed the necessary counter-ritual. The daywalker did meditate quite a lot—he must have spent a lot of time figuring out how to undo her guise and performed the ritual.

Pissed-off gang members charged Maine's way with renewed vigor now that her appearance wasn't so intimidating. She looked past them at the daywalker who had nearly recovered from Noff's sunburst. Dealing with him took priority since he was the most powerful entity here.

She looked at Hank. "Can you take care of these guys?"

Hank grunted as he applied pressure to the headlock he was giving his current opponent. He tilted his head up at the fifteen or so gang members closing in on Maine. "Oh, hell yeah. What are you—"

Maine was already picking through the oncoming inmates, shoving one to the side and kicking another out of the way.

The daywalker saw her approach and sneered. "Girl, you are severely outmatched."

Maine raised her palms as she neared him. "You going to fight me or talk me to death?" She conjured twin fireballs and sent them flying.

The daywalker, who she knew was incredibly fast—faster than her—didn't even try to evade them. He stood there as the two fireballs slammed into his chest with a raging fury. When the smoke and fire dissipated, the gang leader was unscathed. His prison uniform shirt had burned away, revealing a lean hard torso of chiseled muscle.

He popped his neck from side to side, then glared at her with a look of mad glee. "Been a while since I had this much fun."

Maine scoffed, trying to fight off the creeping alarm attempting to seize her. "Is that all you prison guys know how to do is to pop your knuckles and try not to look weak?"

The gang leader pivoted away from Maine and prepared to leap at Noolie who was cowering backward against a wall of washers and driers. "Traitor…"

Maine tried to reach the gang leader in time, but he leapt clear of her grasp and landed in front of Noolie without a sound. Noolie emitted a terrified squeak.

"Like I said," the daywalker repeated. "I don't like rats."

"I'd never—"

The gang leader punched Noolie, but Noolie slipped and fell to the floor. The daywalker's fist punched a hole through a washing machine instead. As Noolie scrambled away, he tore his fist out of the appliance and prepared to pounce.

Maine tackled him, throwing him up against the washers and driers. The appliances were crushed and smashed with the impact and silence fell over the inmates as they watched their leader disappear inside a washer.

Seizing the unexpected moment, Hank started punching again. Inmate after inmate crumpled to the floor, but the blows he was taking were adding up. An inmate jumped on his back and threatened to take him to the floor. Instead, Hank backed up into a washer. When the inmate cried out, he threw the inmate off his back. But now five angry inmates who were fresher than him had cornered him.

Maine saw this as she crawled out from under the crumpled machines. She launched a couple of fireballs at the inmates, throwing several of them clear of the area when the fireballs exploded. When the rest of Hank's attackers turned her way, Hank took care of them.

"Nicely done," he said, flashing Maine a half-smirk. "You know, we make quite a good team—Gahh!"

An inky shadow had formed behind Hank. Now a hand shot out of it and raked a claw down the troll's back. Hank collapsed forward to his knees. The clawed hand belonged to the daywalker.

"No!" Maine shouted as Hank wavered on his knees for a few moments.

"We did good." Hank crashed forward onto his chest.

Maine fired a fireball at the inky shadows. The shadow quivered. Then the daywalker stood there, shaking himself off. Maine didn't know if Hank was alive or not, but she had to deal with the daywalker right now before he took her down too.

She shouted, "If you can walk in the day, how come you can make magic shadows?"

"Precisely because I can walk in the day." The daywalker moved slowly and confidently toward her like a steamroller preparing to flatten what was in front of it. "With the sunlight comes shadows. Daywalkers can use their magic to make people look like shadows, much like your guise spell can change one's appearance."

"Mantle, it would have been nice to know that ahead of time," Maine seethed.

I'll, uh, add that to my database on daywalkers, the Mantle hissed. *I'm not omniscient!*

234

"Now, where did Noolie go?" the gang leader hissed, searching the laundry room as he moved.

Maine didn't see Noolie either. What had happened to him? Where had he gone?

One of the high windows atop the laundry room wall shattered as a tiny buzzing object flew into the room.

Maine's eyes widened. The mini drone! It would have supplies and potions for her—

Quicker than her mind could process, the daywalker sprang up, drew back his arm, and sent a clawed swipe across Blue Dots' mini drone.

It exploded in the air, raining down bits and pieces of plastic, metal, and glass.

"Damn," Noff squeaked. "That was prob'ly our last chance at makin' it out of this alive!"

CHAPTER THIRTY-SIX

"Welp, there goes our only support drone," Noff squeaked. "What we gonna do now?"

Ten yards away from her, the daywalker touched down on the floor, eyeing her hungrily. On the other side of him, Hank lay toppled over onto his chest. He looked dead, but her Seeing Eye senses detected a faint heartbeat and shallow breathing. He was still alive.

The door off to the side is clear, the Mantle hissed. *If you sprint, you might make it.*

Judging by how the daywalker looked at her like dinner, the gang leader wouldn't let her escape.

"I like playing with my food," the daywalker said. "I get so hungry in this prison. They don't serve my kind of food if you understand my meaning."

Maine thought back to the disgusting slop the cafeteria tried to pass off as food. "We can't have everything. What do you expect—you're in prison."

There was no way she was leaving without checking on Hank. He was still alive. Maybe it wasn't too late to get him help.

It probably is, the Mantle hissed. *Sometimes you must make hard decisions in life.*

What were Maine's options? Even with all the Seeing Eye gang members she and Hank had taken out, more were filtering in through the doors leading into the laundry room. What she needed was more fighters on her side. How was she going to get them? She was fighting her damned gang. The other gangs wouldn't come to her aid.

Not unless they saw it as an opportunity to cripple a rival gang, the Mantle added.

That wasn't a bad point. How could she reach the other gangs in the rec area on the other side of the prison? Too bad the guards weren't here either.

"Any last words?" the gang leader called.

"Yeah. I'm not dying until after my damn wedding."

A confused look crossed the daywalker's face as a new sound filled the air above them.

Bzzzzzz...

All the inmates except the daywalker looked up at a second mini drone that had flown in through the open window high in the wall.

"Your friends, I take it?" The daywalker was unconcerned.

"Yeah. Must be a *backup* backup plan. If I know my fiancé, you're about to have your hands full."

The daywalker blinked. "I shall take it out of the sky, the same as the first—Zhhhhrr!"

A lightning bolt zapped the daywalker, shot from the mini drone's bottom-mounted cannon.

The rest of the inmates who were still standing gasped and pointed up at the mini drone. It zapped the daywalker with a second magic lightning bolt. This time the electricity arced outward and zapped the nearest inmates too.

Smoke and shouts of pain filled the air.

Thank troll for magic attack drones.

The way out is now unguarded. Go—go quickly!

Maine ran toward the daywalker.

What are you doing?

"I'm not leaving Hank."

Foolish troll woman! Save yourself! The exit won't stay unguarded for long.

Maine wove around the smoldering daywalker and fell to the ground beside Hank. She lifted his head and cradled it in her hands. "Hank. Hank, are you still there?"

Hank didn't move. At last the troll's eyelids twitched, then his fingers. "Yeah, I'm still kicking. Did we win?" He tried to half-smirk but winced.

"Don't move. Your back is bleeding pretty bad."

Hank groaned as he flexed both knees and elbows. "Could've been worse, I guess."

Maine gripped one of his shoulders and gently set his head back on the floor. "I said don't move. You're going to make it worse."

The drone was taking fire from some magic projectiles an inmate wizard was casting. It was doing its best to avoid the magic attacks while intermittently zapping the daywalker with its lightning cannon. As long as the drone kept that up, Maine and her crew might stand a chance to make it out of this. With all the loud noises coming from the laundry room, the non-crooked guards would have to investigate sooner rather than later.

Hank shut his eyes. "Did you get the key?"

"No. Noolie disappeared when the fighting got heavy. I

don't know where he is."

Noff wriggled his tiny butt atop her shoulder. "I'll find the squirrely bastard." He blasted off Maine's shoulder and scampered amid the carnage, pausing now and then to rear up on his hind legs and sniff the air.

"He's a good partner," Hank said. "A bit odd, though." When he started chuckling, a fit of coughing took him. It didn't sound good.

"I'm going to get you some help," Maine said.

Hank blinked his eyes open. "Don't throw your life away for me. I'm a deadbeat."

"My friends can help you. They're the ones sending the drones…"

The attack drone started smoking high in the laundry room. It flashed red, then descended in a beeline toward the daywalker, who was recovering. The drone's aim was true. It crashed into the daywalker, exploding and showering him with further electrocution.

Hank chuckled, then started coughing again.

Bzzzzzz…

Maine glanced behind her at another drone that had made it inside the laundry room, although this one didn't have a lightning cannon. Instead, it contained supplies strapped to its sides and undercarriage. Maine reached for the drone, but it buzzed away from her and rounded a stack of washers and dryers away from the fighting.

Maine scooped up Hank under the knees and back.

"Hey, what the hell are you doing?" Hank blubbered. "I said don't risk your life for me. Get out of here!"

"I'm not leaving you behind." Maine trotted toward where the drone had disappeared. Hank was heavy, and she almost fell but righted herself. As she moved, the daywalker glared at her with utter hate. Half his face was scorched and blackened, and his body smoldered from all the electricity that had pelted him.

"You're not getting away—Zzzzzt!"

Another magic attack drone had buzzed inside the laundry room and attacked the gang leader and the others with lightning bolts.

Smirking, Maine ran toward the supply drone.

An inmate jumped out at her and yelled, "I'm going to get you!"

Then there was a streaking blur, and Noff had blasted in front of his face. "I am the Noff, and I'm hot like the sun!"

Maine closed her eyes as Noff sunburst, blinding the inmate. Maine ran up and kicked him in the gut. The inmate fell and rolled onto his side, moaning.

"Thanks," Maine said as yet another attack drone buzzed inside the laundry room and started dropping smoke canisters all around. Soon the laundry room was full of a smokescreen so thick she barely made it to the drone before she lost sight of it. It buzzed forward a bit, leading her toward a back section of the laundry room and under a desk that was out of general sight.

Maine set Hank down as easily as she could.

"Dammit, I said leave me," he sputtered. "I'll only slow you down."

Maine reached for the supply drone and plucked a health potion from its reserves. "Sorry, that's not my style." She uncorked the vial with her teeth and poured the potion down Hank's throat. He swallowed it and cursed.

"You're a stubborn one, aren't you? Hah. Just like your father."

Maine went through the rest of the drone's supplies while the health potion started to seep into Hank's body.

"Why are you doing this?" Hank demanded, sitting up when his body had enough strength.

Maine found a couple of tactical vests, another health potion, an unlabeled green potion, and some other supplies. "What do you mean?"

"Aw hell, you know what I mean. You saw me out there fighting. I'm practically an old man compared to you. I'm weak."

"Weak?" She stopped searching through the supply drone's contents. "What battle were you watching? I saw you take out like twenty inmates rushing you all at once."

"I took my share of licks too. Getting older is a bitch. I can still hit just as hard but can't move as fast. And my heart's never been the same since the war..." He clutched his chest where his scar was, where he had stepped in front of her father during the war and saved his life. He was breathing pretty hard, harder than he should be after taking a break from fighting.

In short, Hank was falling apart when she needed him most.

"I'm telling you, you're better off on your own," he said. "Leave me. I'll buy you some time here."

Yes, do as the stupid oaf of a troll insists, and leave while you still can!

Maine studied the troll sitting on the floor beside her. The health potion should have revived him more than it seemed to have. His injuries from the daywalker must have been more severe than she had first thought.

Noff barked—er, squeaked—as he rode atop Noolie's

shoulder through the smokescreen. "Keep goin' straight!" Noff squeaked.

"I can't see anything!" Noolie whimpered.

"Me neither, but I can smell my partner... Whoa, boy, stop!"

Noolie stopped in front of Maine, still crouched over the drone. "Gods, Maine Half-Troll?" Noolie's face was pale and sweaty. "It was you the whole time? Don't kill me, please!"

"I'm not going to kill you." Now that the guise spell was no longer working, Maine didn't have to worry about him finding out it was her, his worst enemy. "Does this change anything?" she asked.

"No." He gulped. "Why would you help me?"

"Because I need the key to that painting. You have it?"

"Y-yes."

"Give it to me."

"I'd feel better if I held onto it until we're safe." He gulped again and jerked a thumb at the nearest door leading out of the laundry room. "Now come on, this is our chance to escape."

Maine knew that Noolie was trying to keep himself useful to her so she would get him out of here.

"Now!" Noolie said. "Those drones aren't going to keep the daywalker pinned down for much longer."

Maine switched her gaze from Noolie to Hank still sitting weakly on the floor. Hank was right. He would only slow them down. Plus, he was still in no condition to fight.

"Leave me, dammit," Hank insisted.

Yes, leave him, the Mantle hissed.

"Come on!" Noolie shouted, waving for her to join him.

Noff met her eyes. "Well, partner, what's it gonna be?"

CHAPTER THIRTY-SEVEN

Maine reached for her second and final health potion. She'd sustained some small cuts and bruises from the fighting, but she bit off the cork and poured the health potion down Hank's throat before he could object. He sputtered and fought her, but by then he'd already swallowed the potion. It wouldn't be long before it started to rejuvenate him further.

"Why'd you do that?" Hank asked. "Valkious was right— I'm weak. I'm worthless. I'm no hero. I deserve to be left here—"

Maine smacked the troll hard across the cheek.

"Shut up, Hank. You're not worthless. You survived a friggin' daywalker claw to the back. You're one of the bravest trolls I know."

Noff squeaked. "Considerin' your Uncle Joffrey is the only other troll you know, that ain't really sayin' much…"

Maine lightly swatted Noff, careful not to break him in his current mouse-sized form. Then she took Hank by the shoulders. "Get it together, man. You're a fucking troll. Act like it!"

Hank recoiled, then sat up straight. After a tight swallow,

he raised a hand to his forehead in the salute her father used to give her when she was a child.

"Yes, ma'am." He glanced down at his hands and flexed his fingers. "All right, looks like that second potion is kicking in now." As he shifted into a crouch, his joints popped. "Damn arthritis, you got a potion for that too?"

Maine smiled. "Glad to have you back. Okay, now we need a plan." She tried to think over the sounds of the latest magic attack drone zapping the daywalker and the other inmates. Noolie had decided against running off on his own and hunkered down beside them.

Suddenly, her earmic crackled.

"Maine? Maine, can you hear me?" Sage asked.

Her hand moved to her ear to block out the external sounds. "Yes! I'm all right. Thanks to the badass drone support."

"Woohoo!" Blue Dots cheered. "Glad to be of help. I think the daywalker is jamming my signal with his magic somehow. Our connection might go out again at any time."

"How many more drones do you have?" Maine asked.

There was a terse pause. "We're down to the last drone," Blue Dots said. "As soon as it blows up, you're on your own."

"Except you're not on your own," Sage picked up. "Unless you didn't reach the supply drone."

"I've got it in front of me," Maine said. "What's the green potion for?"

She heard the pride in Sage's voice. "That's a magic detox potion. It'll soothe malignant magic in your system if you get overpowered by an attack. It was all I could scrape together at the last moment."

Maine eyed the potion. "I don't know what good a magic detox will do in the middle of a battle, but you never know."

Maki-Mae's voice came over the earmic. "Dear, what's the situation? Have you gotten the key?"

Maine pierced Noolie with her eyes. "Noolie has the key. I don't currently have eyes on it."

"What happened?" Sage asked. "Why are you still in the prison? Where's the Guardian? He said he would get you out as soon as you spiked the tea."

Maine shook her head. "This was all a setup. The Seeing Eye leader has been one step ahead of me the whole time. He figured out I was under a guise spell and managed to break it."

On the other end of the line, her friends gasped.

"The Guardian isn't there?" Maki-Mae asked. "Where is he?"

"He's in LA dealing with some mythical gang violence. But it's all a setup to lure him away from the prison."

"Not good!" Blue Dots said.

"I'll call him," Sage said. "I knew that emergency contact number might come in handy."

Blue Dots made an *eek* sound. "Uh-oh, the last drone is about to—"

Boom!

Fire and electricity spouted out from the center of the laundry room. It would only be a matter of seconds before the gang found them now. The gang leader would not be in any mood to spare them.

"Hold on," Blue Dots said. "We still have the supply drone. I'll take control of it."

A moment later, the supply drone lifted into the air. Without all the supplies weighing it down, it moved much faster than the attack drones.

"I'll pilot the drone around the room to draw their attention. You'll have to hurry!"

The gang members cursed as the supply drone buzzed through the smokescreen-filled laundry room. Some of them shot magic spells at it. By the sound of it, it was evading all the projectiles so far. However, the smokescreen was starting to lift, and they'd be exposed.

The nearest door to the laundry room had only two inmates guarding it. Maine looked from Hank to Noolie to Noff perched on her shoulder. "Whatever happens, I trust you guys completely."

Hank and Noff nodded while Noolie whimpered that they would all die.

"Ready?" Maine asked. "Okay, stay low!"

She led the way to the door in a half-crouch. When one of the inmates at the entrance spotted her, she quick-launched a fireball at him that exploded against his chest. He fell backward with arms splayed out in the air. The other inmate assumed a tackling stance, preparing to lunge at Maine.

Hank tackled him first. The troll stood from the groaning inmate and clapped the dust from his hands. "Hah. Still got it."

Maine led the way into a corridor outside the laundry room. She didn't know where she was.

"Hang in there, Maine," Sage encouraged. "I'm trying to reach the Guardian, but he's not picking up. Damn it."

"Keep trying," Maine instructed. "Daywalkers are no joke. I don't think I can handle him on my own."

Hank nudged her shoulder. "You're not alone, remember? You got us."

Noff looked ready to fight, but Noolie looked like he'd rather huddle under some blankets.

"Where the hell are we, Noolie?" Maine asked.

Noolie looked around as they ran down the hallway. "I

know where we are. I know a safe place where we can wait for the Guardian to come. But we'll never make it."

"Then find us a place to hide for a bit," Maine said.

Noolie bit his lip. "There's a supply closet up ahead."

They reached the closet as the supply drone exploded in the laundry room. The closet door was locked, but Maine forced it open, and they clambered inside before inmates ran down the hall.

"Where'd they go?" one of the inmates shouted.

"Hey, stop!" a prison guard called.

"About time," Maine muttered. They were all scrunched together near the back of the closet, and she had both hands up to cast fireballs if the door opened. Noff's key marking on his rump lit up faintly, and a moment later his body emitted a low nightlight glow inside the supply closet.

"Turn back. It's the guards!" one of the inmates shouted.

"I say we fight 'em!" another inmate shouted.

Maine heard a fireball or spell being cast. Then a prison guard cried, "What the hell? I think the magic dampeners are down! Sound the alar—" His voice sputtered, and a body struck the floor.

This was getting ugly fast.

"There are more inmates than guards," Maine said in a hushed voice. "We know some of the guards are loyal to the Seeing Eye. This isn't good. We need a plan!"

The Mantle hissed. *Perhaps you should ask Noolie.*

That made sense. Noolie used to be a criminal mastermind. She spun and found Noolie in the dark closet and grabbed him by the prison uniform in both hands. "Look, the Guardian isn't coming. At least not for a while. I know you used to be a badass. I need you to channel that badassery and come up with a plan to get us out of here."

"I don't have any power anymore," Noolie whimpered. "I'm like a neutered dog."

Maine snapped on him. "Neutered dogs can still bite. So bite."

Noolie's eyes glistened in the low light of the supply closet, then grew cold.

"You're right. I'm underselling myself. I have an idea…"

CHAPTER THIRTY-EIGHT

Footsteps ran past the supply closet in both directions as guards and Seeing Eye members clashed physically and magically. It sounded like an all-out war.

Luckily it masked the sounds of their escape plan.

"The halls are too congested right now," Noolie stated. "If we can lure all the gangs to a big space…"

"What do you have in mind?" Maine asked. The four of them were cramped up against the far back wall of the storage closet, ready to attack and bug out in case the door opened at any moment, while Noff continued providing a low nightlight with his glowing body.

Noolie spoke in hurried confident breaths. "We've got to take out the five gang leaders."

"Easier said than done, wee man," Hank said. "They've got the power crystals around their necks."

"That's what I mean by take them out," Noolie continued. "We take out the leaders by snatching their crystals."

"How do we get close enough to them without getting

killed?" Maine asked. A body *thumped* against the other side of the closet door, but thankfully the door remained closed.

Noolie grinned. "Currently, the leaders of the Five Gangs of the Veil are honoring an uneasy truce among themselves. Now that they're all in one place, it's very tempting for one of them to make a power play against the others."

"Why haven't they yet?" Maine asked.

"Each gang's power crystal has a special attribute. For example, the Brick gang has the most physical strength, but the Light Burst gang has the strongest magic attacks. For each gang's unique strength, they are no match against the combined might of the other four gangs."

"Why don't two or three gangs agree to team up temporarily and take out or weaken the other gangs?"

Noolie looked at Maine like she was crazy. "Because the gangs don't trust each other. They all want all the power for themselves. The one gang that might be capable of pulling it off in terms of strategy and planning is the Seeing Eye gang. You've seen how paranoid that bunch is. Their members don't trust each other."

Maine relented. "Good point. It seems so simple, though. Just set aside your differences and work together for once."

Noolie sighed. "Such naïveté. And you're the one who defeated me... Truly embarrassing."

"Watch it, or I'll give you a troll punch to the gut."

"Easy now, folks," Noff squeaked. "We're on the same side. For the moment."

Noolie raised both hands in a sign of peace. "Please don't hit me. I would hate to throw up the disgusting slop that was breakfast."

Maine's nose wrinkled. Yeah, they were in a tight closet, and no one needed puke on them.

"Okay," Maine said. "To sum up, we get the gang leaders to attack each other because gang leaders are the only ones strong enough to take each other out. When they're reeling on the floor, we grab their power crystals to de-power the rest of the inmates."

"Yes," Noolie said. "Then we head to a safe place until the Guardian arrives."

"Not a bad plan," Hank admitted. "We'll need a place big enough to fit all the gangs."

Maine thought about it. The fighting had died away from the hallway outside the supply closet for the moment. "The laundry room is out—it's a wreck and probably not big enough. How about the rec yard?"

Noolie shook his head. "It's too open. We need somewhere with a ceiling and some walls to add a sense of confinement and immediacy. You know, to get everyone at each other's throats."

"Wow. Are you an evil psychiatrist on the side?"

Hank *harrumphed* and crossed his arms. "See, that's why I don't see shrinks. They know how to mess with your head."

"What about the cafeteria?" Maine suggested.

"Yes!" Noolie exclaimed. "That could work."

Noff squeaked and blasted off the closet's floor. "Food fight! Woohoo!"

"How are we going to lure them all there?" Hank asked.

Maine considered. "Hey, Blue Dots, are you there?"

"Yes!"

"Think you can patch into the prison's PA speakers? We need to get all the inmates back into the cafeteria."

Blue Dots giggled. "That's easy. What should I say?"

Maine turned to Hank and Noolie. "How do we lure them?"

"Announce that there is leftover cake," Noolie said.

"Will that work?" Maine asked.

The un-Mythed NasNas flashed her a conspiratorial grin. "Oh, for cake, they will come."

After filling Blue Dots in on the new plan, they filtered out of the supply closet. With Noolie in the lead, they snuck through the prison corridors, listening for the sounds of fighting and doing their best to avoid those areas.

So far they had come across no conscious bodies although they passed a few inmates knocked out by the guards' electrified batons.

When they came to a corner, Maine proceeded up to it, whispering, "Mantle, any threats up ahead?"

I detect none in this general area. You may proceed.

"Thanks for the permission," Maine said sarcastically.

Noolie looked sideways at Hank. "Is she talking to herself?"

"You get used to it," Hank said gruffly. The two followed Maine.

"The cafeteria is close," Noolie advised. "Only a few more corridors."

They were making their way down a cell-lined hallway when a figure darted out of one of the cells with his hands in his pockets. It was the spider shifter from the cafeteria. "A lady inmate? Hm... You'll do. Won't you step into my parlor?"

"Not this weirdo," Maine muttered. "We don't want any trouble," she called to him.

The spider shifter licked his lips. "Oh, I don't want trouble —I want some real food." He opened his mouth and spat a glob of super-fast webbing at Maine. She sidestepped it, and the projectile struck Noolie. A web instantly ensnared him, and he tipped over and fell to the floor with a *splat*.

"I warned you." Maine launched a fireball at the spider inmate, who ducked back inside his cell.

"Got to be quicker than that!" the spider man cackled.

"Hank, check Noolie. See if you can get him out of that web."

"What are you going to do?" Hank asked.

"I'm going to go squash a bug."

Noff squeaked from atop her shoulder. "Spiders ain't bugs. Someone needs to watch some nature documentaries."

Maine picked Noff off her shoulder and set him on the floor. "Remember how you hunted that rabbit the one time in LA?"

"Yeah." He panted energetically.

"You're small. I need you to squeeze between that spider guy's cell bars and flush him out for me."

"Heh. And here I thought Spider-Man was one of the good guys." He set his ears back and prepared to blast off toward the prison cell. "On it!"

Maine watched as Noff launched himself.

"Come on out!" she called.

"Nah, how about you step into my parlor!"

Maine readied two fireballs, preparing to launch them at the open cell door.

A moment later, "I am the Noff!" was followed by a sunburst.

"Gah!" the spider shifter shouted and stumbled out of his cell, right into both of Maine's loosed fireballs. They exploded like gunshots, throwing the inmate back into his cell.

"I'm good, I'm good," Noolie was saying behind her, no

longer enmeshed in the webbing. Maine turned in time to see Hank sliding a shiv into a shoe. Hank nodded at her, and the three of them continued down the corridor. Maine shut the spider guy's cell door in case he was still mobile, locking him inside.

"Well, that guy was rude," Noff squeaked once he had blasted atop Maine's shoulder. "Definitely not friend material. And don't tell me ya told me so."

They rounded the next corner. The cafeteria was directly ahead on the right. However, so were two guards standing fifteen yards away from them.

"Get them!" one of them shouted.

The other one gawked. "It's a girl. What the hell? Why is there a girl in here?"

In the guards' confusion, Maine noticed they each toted what she could only think of as a magic rifle in their arms. The barrels of the guns glowed an eerie blue.

"Shit," Hank said, seeing the guns too. He and Noolie immediately raised their arms above their heads and Maine followed suit.

"Don't let them shoot you." Noolie quick-stepped behind Maine so she served as a shield.

Maine was about to ask why when a rhinoceros shifter trundled into the hallway from the other direction. One of the guards swiveled and trained his gun on him. When the shifter did not raise his hands in surrender, the guard pulled the trigger, and the rifle fired a bluish orb. It struck the rhino shifter, and he instantly slumped unconscious to the floor.

"Great, magic tranquilizers," Maine muttered.

Beside her, Hank licked his dry lips. "What are we going to do now?"

The Mantle hissed. *Send out the troll as a diversion, using him as a shield. Then troll-force your way through them and into the cafeteria.*

Maine wasn't going to sacrifice her ally in such a stupid move. Instead, she said, "Sage, can you still hear me?"

"Yes!"

"Tell Blue Dots to make that announcement."

"Hey you, girl!" one of the guards said. "Whoever you are talking to, stop. I don't want to have to shoot you."

"Roger," Blue Dots called over the earmic. "I can do you one better. Cover your ears!"

A moment later, the PA system in the prison squealed so loudly that both guards dropped their guns and clapped their hands over their ears.

"Let's go!" Maine shouted over the screeching as she took off down the hallway. As she reached the floundering guards, she stooped and picked up both magic rifles. As she tossed one to Hank, the two guards cursed and ran away. Hank handed his tranquilizer rifle to Noolie and punched his open palm.

"Trolls don't need guns." His familiar half-smirk appeared.

When Maine reached the double doors leading into the cafeteria, she raised her leg and kicked with such force that both doors blasted off their hinges and skidded along the cafeteria floor.

Maine, Hank, Noff, and Noolie rushed inside and turned to face the open doorway. They ran to the far corner where they could see the entire room.

Blue Dots' sexy voice came over the PA system then. "Hello, boys. The cafeteria is now serving leftover cake. I repeat: the cafeteria is now serving leftover cake."

A few moments later, a low thunder of feet stampeded through the prison halls.

Maine brought the magic tranquilizer rifle to her shoulder. "Get ready, guys."

CHAPTER THIRTY-NINE

It wasn't long until the first inmates ran into the cafeteria, shoving each other to the side like kids trying to reach the cafeteria first.

"All this for cake?" Maine asked.

The inmates were in such a rush to get to the cafeteria line for the cake that wasn't there that they didn't notice Maine and Noolie standing in the far corner with the magic guns.

"Ya know they're gonna be pissed when they find there ain't no cake left, right?" Noff squeaked from her shoulder.

More inmates filtered into the cafeteria. They belonged to all five gangs, which meant their plan was working. The gangs were all coming. However, there was no sign of any of the gang leaders yet.

Still, no one paid attention to Maine and Noolie with the guns.

Sighting down his magic rifle, Noolie wiped sweat off his bald head with his sleeve. "I can't take much more waiting," he muttered nervously.

"Take it easy," Maine soothed. "Don't start tranquilizing

until the gang leaders show up. Our goal is to provide chaos and distraction."

"If anything can cause chaos and distraction, it'd be cake day," Noolie said.

The cafeteria was filling up. The inmates were starting to get antsy with no cake in sight. Some were getting rowdy, pushing and shoving, but there was no hard-core fighting. There was still no sign of the gang leaders, but if they didn't carry on with the plan soon, it would all fall apart.

Maine spoke into her earmic. "Time to enact Phase Two of Operation Cake."

The PA system squawked, and Blue Dots' sexy voice sounded again. "Oh dear, there has been a mistake. It looks like there is no cake left after all."

Groans and shouts of protest filled the cafeteria.

"This ain't right!" someone shouted.

"I'm hungry!"

"For cake!"

Blue Dots' voice sounded again. "Apologies. It looks like the Brick gang ate the last piece."

Shouts and growls rumbled through the cafeteria.

"Why, you pigs!"

"I'm gonna kill ya!"

"Stupid Bricks!"

Fists and elbows started flying, then bolts of magic crackled and blasted. Wizard inmates cast spells, and shifters attacked with claws. It was a nightmare.

Behind her magic rifle, Maine observed that the Brick gang members appeared to be getting mobbed by the other four gangs.

Noff squeaked sorrowfully. "Poor bastards don't stand a chance outnumbered like that."

Part of the cafeteria wall exploded inward, and the Brick gang leader burst inside like the Incredible Hulk, sweeping terrified inmates aside with his arms.

"What is going on?" he roared over the din of the fighting.

For a moment, silence fell upon the cafeteria. Then Maine whispered, "Now!" She and Noolie started picking off inmates with their magic tranquilizer rifles.

"What's going on?" inmates started shouting as the cafeteria chaos bloomed.

Maine climbed atop a cafeteria table and started taking potshots at the massive Brick gang leader. Maybe there was an easy way to take down the gang leaders...

The blue tranquilizer orbs staggered the gang leader, but he soon regained his footing.

"It's his power crystal!" Noolie shouted. "He's too powerful."

Maine gritted her teeth. Damn. They weren't going to knock out the gang leaders that easily.

The Brick gang leader locked eyes with her then. He had opened his mouth to presumably order his gang to tear Maine to shreds when Blue Dots spoke over the intercom again. "It looks like the Seeing Eye leader ate all the cake himself."

"Whaaat?" someone cried.

"Death to the Seeing Eye!"

Maine winced as gang members started tearing into each other. Sitting atop her shoulder, Noff panted with excitement. "Prison rehabilitation at its finest."

"Where is the gang leader?" someone shouted.

Meanwhile, the Brick gang leader had not broken his stare at Maine. He pushed inmates aside as if they weighed nothing as he trudged toward her and Noolie's corner.

Noolie squeaked. "Quick, do something! He's going to turn us into sloppy Joe!"

Maine rapid-fired the magic rifle at the Brick gang leader, but the tranquilizer orbs had no effect on him. She tossed the weapon to the side when her magic rifle overheated and started smoking.

Noolie squeezed her arm. "You've got to do something!"

Maine hopped down from the table and ran along the cafeteria's back wall. As she did so, she caught sight of the Parchment gang leader and the Light Burst gang leader entering the cafeteria. In her peripheral vision, the Brick gang leader was closing on her.

Blue Dots' voice came over the speaker. "Would the leaders of the Parchment gang and the Light Burst gang please report to the warden's office?"

"What?" the Parchment gang leader shouted at the nearest PA speaker.

"The Guardian is tired of your gangs graffitiing in the bathrooms," Blue Dots answered.

Maine saw an incredible elemental blast of magic as the Light Burst gang leader blew the Parchment gang leader out into the hallway.

"Can't run from me!" the Brick gang leader roared, swiping at Maine from behind.

Maine put on a burst of speed as she reached the empty food line. She vaulted over the empty food tables while the gang leader stomped through them.

The counter leading to the kitchen was directly ahead. Maine hopped over it.

Duck!

She landed in the kitchen, barely avoiding running head-first into a hanging cast iron pan.

The gang leader crashed right through the countertop. Maine grabbed the heavy pan and swung it at him. It ricocheted off his skull with no effect.

The Brick gang leader grinned like a madman. "You're making me angry."

There was a pot of cold, congealing lunch slop behind Maine. She grabbed it and upended the contents at the gang leader. "I have that effect on some people." She sprinted to the side, nearly colliding with the green leshy.

His breath was as foul as garbage. "Traitor! I'm going to enjoy pulverizing—"

A swift kick to the crotch shut the leshy up. Maine moved around him and shoved him at the Brick gang leader. The brute grabbed the leshy by the ankles and swung him like a baseball bat through the kitchen.

"Let go of my new initiate," a voice rumbled through the cafeteria. It belonged to the daywalker.

"Make me," the Brick gang leader snarled.

The Mantle hissed. *You probably already know this, but you need to get out of here now!*

Maine dove over what remained of the cafeteria counter as inky shadows engulfed the food prep area.

Maine picked herself up and surveyed the craziness of the kitchen.

"This is insane!" Noff squeaked.

Maine ducked as a refrigerator was thrown clear of the kitchen. The Brick gang leader was putting up quite a fight against the Seeing Eye leader.

"They're like friggin' gods," Maine said. "I'm not sure we'll be able to get the power crystals off their necks."

"I'm not sure there's gonna be a prison left after this," Noff squeaked.

Maine pushed through the crowd of clashing inmates, punching them out whenever one of them got too close to her. "I need to find Hank."

She located Hank, but before she could reach him, a pair of Oni demon hands gripped her and held her in place.

"Who the hell are you?" Owen demanded.

"Oh, Owen, it's me. The uh, other Oni demon who could lift as much as you."

The Oni demon gave her a hard look. "What kind of trick is this supposed to be?" His claws began to dig into her arms.

"Look, I don't have time to explain everything, but I got arrested on purpose. I had a guise spell cast on me to make me look like a dude Oni demon so I could infiltrate the Seeing Eye gang and get some info."

The Oni demon's eyebrows wrinkled. "Hmm. Really? You're Mantle?"

"Yes."

Owen released his claws from her. "Sorry about that."

"Not that I'm not grateful, but why do you believe me and why aren't you trying to kill me?"

"One, I like your style. Two, you're pretty hot. You really started this prison fight?"

"Yeah—" She and Owen jumped out of the way as another refrigerator landed near her. When the door opened, she was granted a quick peek inside. She saw a couple of items she might be able to use.

She dashed over to the fridge and pulled out a commercial-sized pouch of ketchup and a carton of eggs. She stuffed both of them under her tactical vest.

"Raidin' the fridge at a time like this?" Noff squeaked. "I know you get hangry but—"

"I might be able to use these during the fight."

"Ketchup and eggs? Did you see any leftover cake?"

"What do you need from me?" Owen asked eagerly, picking himself up.

He has a crush on you, the Mantle hissed. *Let him think he has a chance and after this is all over, tell him you're engaged.*

"Can you clear a path to Noolie in the corner?" Maine asked. "I've got to find Hank."

Owen didn't move for a moment. "You trust me?"

"What's the worst that can happen?" Maine asked. "I'm in the middle of a magical gang fight in a prison cafeteria, and refrigerators are flying over my head."

Owen grinned. "Never a dull moment in the joint, that's for sure. After this, though… I think we're *all* going in the hole."

Maine broke away from Owen and came upon Hank throttling an inmate. When the inmate passed out, Hank tossed the guy aside.

"Hank!" she yelled a few feet away.

At first, he didn't hear her, but he snapped out of his rage and nodded at her. "Isn't this the best day of your life?" he shouted.

"We've got to find a way to get the power crystals from the leaders. Can you help me?"

Two more inmates rushed Hank. He backstepped and slammed their skulls together. They dropped to the floor.

"Sounds crazy. I'm in."

"All five of them are in here." Maine winced as a powerful heatwave of magic surged through the cafeteria courtesy of the Light Burst leader. "Maybe we can take out the Light Burst leader before he incinerates everyone?"

"Good idea." Hank located the Light Burst leader. "What's the plan?"

Use the dumb troll as a distraction. Have him run out in front of the gang leader while you sneak up from behind.

"I'll run out in front of him and grab his attention. Meanwhile, you sneak up behind him and steal his power crystal."

Hank gave her a tight salute. "Hell yeah. Let's go."

CHAPTER FORTY

By this point, broken glass and ceiling tiles littered the cafeteria floor. Maine shoved an inmate out of the way and jumped up and down, waving both arms at the Light Burst leader as he prepared to unleash another wave of intense magic at his next target. When he didn't look her way, she pulled the egg carton out from under her vest.

She selected an egg and threw it at the gang leader. It *splatted* right above his forehead. As runny yolk slid between his eyes and dripped down his nose, the gang leader finally turned his attention to her.

"Who the hell are you?"

"Your worst nightmare," Maine quipped in a half-joking tone to keep the gang leader's eyes off Hank quickly approaching his backside. She launched a few more eggs at the leader in rapid succession.

The gang leader raised a hand, and a fireball the size of an oven flared to life.

"Uh-oh," Maine muttered. If Hank didn't act fast, she

would be burned crispy. She conjured a fireball, which looked like a puny ember in comparison.

The gang leader laughed, providing the extra time Maine needed for Hank to jump on the gang leader's back and tear the power crystal off his neck. The ginormous fireball exploded on the gang leader's hand, blasting him backward into the hall.

"Woohoo!" Noff squeaked. "Power crystal number one!"

A large figure hurtled Maine's way, and she barely stepped aside long enough to avoid the Brick gang leader landing on top of her. The Seeing Eye leader had thrown him out of the kitchen.

As he picked himself up off the floor, the Brick leader looked at her with a disoriented expression. Maine snatched the power crystal from around his neck.

"No!" the Brick leader shouted, but it was lost to the din of the fighting around them. He reached for her leg, but she kicked him swiftly across the jaw, and he passed out.

"Woohoo, two power crystals!" Noff squeaked.

An inky shadow materialized in front of Maine, and the daywalker emerged from it like a tar monster. When his body took form and color a moment later, he saw the power crystal in her hand and roared. "What is going on? We are being deceived—"

Maine threw a straight jab at the daywalker's side, unleashing a fireball as she made contact. The daywalker grunted, and when she tried to grab the power crystal from around his neck, he lashed out with speed much faster than hers and knocked her hand away.

There was no way she would be fast enough to grab the power crystal from him as long as he was conscious. He was so quick and powerful. How could she get the jump on him now that he understood what was going on?

Even with the Mantle, he outclassed her. Not even Hank would be able to help her with the daywalker.

"You made a big mistake coming to my prison," the daywalker said. The two of them danced in a circle.

"Your prison?" Maine sounded amused, hoping he wouldn't murder her before she could blink.

"Yes. It will be once the rest of the gangs are dealt with. Which is what I see you and your troll friend are doing. Hah. Doing all the hard work for me. Don't you love it when what Fate has in store for you works out better than your plan?"

"I don't much care for Fate."

"Because you're not immortal like me?" The gang leader grinned. "Your fate is to die, just like every insignificant puny mortal—"

The daywalker staggered to the side as Hank bulldozed into him from the other side. Hank tossed a power crystal to Maine as the daywalker shook himself out. She barely caught it. On the crystal, she saw the symbol of a triangle. So Hank had managed to get the Triangle gang's power crystal too? That left only the Parchment gang crystal and the Seeing Eye crystal.

As the daywalker grabbed Hank and flung him halfway across the cafeteria, Maine focused on the two power crystals in her hands, Brick and Triangle.

She was outmatched, true. But she had low-level Seeing Eye powers from her tattoo. If she donned both power crystals, that ought to juice her up enough to stand a chance against the daywalker.

The daywalker turned back to face her, and she lifted the crystals over her head.

Don't don them! the Mantle hissed. *You don't know what you're doing!*

She knew that if she didn't try this last gambit, she was dead. What did they say about fortune? That it favored the brave?

As the necklaces dropped over her head and jangled against the back of her neck, the Mantle hissed, *What have you done?*

"I'm taking care of business," she said as immense power flooded her entire body from foot to crown.

Your body won't be able to handle all that power—

"Oh yeah? 'Cause I feel great."

For a time, but then...

"Then what?" Maine asked.

You'll spontaneously combust into an exploding meat bag!

While Maine grimaced at that imagery, the daywalker chuckled harshly. "You really are a foolish one. Your mortal body cannot handle all that raw power."

Maine shrugged. The power still surged through her as if from an infinite energy source. "What can I say? I never went to magic school."

Before the daywalker could quip back, Maine threw a punch so fast it smashed in the daywalker's teeth before she realized her punch had hit.

The daywalker stumbled back a few feet, then spat a couple of broken fangs to the floor. He flashed a bloody grin. "Finally, an equal match."

Noff squeaked. "As badass as ya are, ya ain't gonna be able to control that much power for long."

"I don't have to control it for long. I just have to beat this asshole!"

Maine went for another quick punch, but the daywalker

darted to the side and kneed her in the gut. Then he disappeared into a thick, inky shadow.

"Dammit," Maine cursed, searching the cafeteria for any signs of the gang leader. She noticed that virtually all the fighting had stopped and all eyes were on her.

When she noticed the thick shadows pooling under her feet, it was too late. The daywalker's hand latched onto her ankle and tried to pull her inside the shadow. She fired twin fireballs at the hand, and the shadow disappeared.

"That was a close one!" Noff squeaked from atop her shoulder.

Duck! the Mantle hissed.

Maine managed to swat aside a cafeteria tray thrown with dangerous force. She realized that the leshy had thrown it at her. He was all banged up but still full of hate.

"No one messes with our gang leader!" he wailed.

Maine picked up the tray and with lightning speed, slung it back at the leshy before he knew what was happening. Her aim was true with the Mantle's assistance, and the tray struck a glancing blow off the leshy's temple. The leshy groaned and fell in a zigzag pattern.

Daywalker! the Mantle hissed.

Maine turned as the daywalker appeared from a shadowy puddle on the ceiling. He dropped to the cafeteria floor like a pile of sludge, then formed into his regular shelf.

"You're disgusting. You know that?" Maine said.

"Let's finish this!" the daywalker roared. He raised a fist and charged with impossible speed and force.

Maine did likewise, throwing all she had into her punch. A thunderclap sounded when their fists struck, sending invisible shockwaves throughout the cafeteria. The remaining windows shattered and ventilation tubing fell from the ceiling with sparking electrical wires. Water dripped from all over the ceiling and the floor cracked outward in a spiderweb fashion from where the two stood.

Maine sucked in an exhilarating breath. It felt like she'd been sucked through a tornado and come out unscathed. She felt like... Her body was on fire.

That's because it is, the Mantle hissed. *You're about to explode from the inside out.*

Maine glanced down at her arms. Sure enough, tiny magic flames protruded from the pores of her skin.

"Youch!" Noff squeaked and blasted off her shoulder, his fur fuzzed up from the massive punch attack and his tail smoldering.

"What do I do?" Maine asked, flailing her arms at her sides, which only made the flames worse.

Take off the power crystals! You'll probably still die, but at least you won't explode.

"I can't take them off yet." She breathed raggedly as the daywalker appraised her with hungry eyes. He knew this fight was about to end. He took a few steps backward, knowing he only had to wait it out.

Maine felt like she was about to puke. A cold sensation was sluicing through her body, but it didn't seem to worsen if she remained relatively still.

She needed a plan. She needed a way to defeat the daywalker and take his crystal...

Her body was nearly spent. She was done for.

She fell to one knee.

Then, for some reason, the leshy's last words echoed in Maine's mind. *No one messes with our gang leader!*

That was it... She now had not one but two of the Five Gangs of the Veil loyal to her: the Bricks and the Triangles. If she concentrated on her magic core, she could feel Brick and Triangle energies being diverted outward to all the members.

How had it been explained to her? The gang members were loyal to whoever bore the symbols of power. Maybe she didn't have to fight the daywalker herself. Maybe she could command her gangs to do it for her.

Gritting back the pain, she rose and pointed at the daywalker, who was still slowly backing away from her with a look of triumph.

"Get him!" she yelled as loud and hard as she could.

The cocky look faded from the daywalker's face as the gang members rushed him from the crowd.

Feels good to be Queen, doesn't it? the Mantle hissed. *Few ever get to experience this level of power and command in their lives. Of course, you're about to turn into an exploding meat bag so I guess it all balances out.*

Maine's legs gave out, and she wobbled to the floor. The magic flames coming out of her skin rose higher too.

She needed to take the power crystals off. If she did, she would lose command of the gangs and die either from the daywalker or the aftereffects of the crystals' powers. She felt like all that power and magic were poisoning her body. If only she had a way to negate some of it, she could finish this fight and prevent a global mythical gang war.

She realized that she did.

Sage's green potion!

She fished it out of her pocket, weakly bit out the cork, and drained the contents. It looked like the green drink at the juice bar and tasted like raw sewage. Couldn't Sage have given it a better flavor?

The potion was supposed to soothe an overload of magic or magic poisoning in her system. When a few moments

271

passed, and her stomach cramped, she hoped this potion didn't have the same effects as invisibility potions.

It became harder to breathe for a few seconds. Then her lungs seemed to have better capacity.

She realized she had closed her eyes. When she opened them, the magic flames had receded into her skin.

Yes!

It's only temporary, the Mantle hissed. *If you continue to wear the power crystals, you will die.*

She had an idea. What if she took off one of the power crystals?

That could perhaps prolong your death.

Which one should she keep?

She decided to keep the Brick power crystal, reckoning that she only needed one good power hit to knock out the daywalker. Still, maybe it would be better to boost all of her stats instead…

She kept the Brick crystal, removed the Triangle, and shoved it in her pocket.

Her head felt clearer now, and she still had plenty of energy surging inside her. It was time to end the daywalker once and for all.

CHAPTER FORTY-ONE

The daywalker had knocked out a ring of inmates all around him. He looked a bit fatigued so maybe finishing him wouldn't be so bad. He was picking up a Brick member and throwing him into the crowd when Maine ran up to him.

The daywalker lunged to meet her, but she got out of the way in time. She reached for his power crystal as he passed, but he smacked her hand away with his claw, which drew blood.

"I will drain you shortly. Then I'll rule over the Five Gangs."

Maine feinted and landed a solid blow to the gang leader's shoulder. She poured all the Brick energy into it and saw that the impact had fazed him.

He quickly knocked her to the floor, though. Then he loomed over her like a shadow of death, licking his lips.

Some Bricks rushed him, giving her time to rise. She reached for the necklace at the back of his neck, but he smacked her hand away again with super-fast reflexes.

They locked hands then, interlocking their fingers and trying to push the other back.

"You're rather persistently annoying." The daywalker grunted.

"I think we're almost done here." Maine grunted too.

They were nearly matched in terms of power, and neither was gaining any ground. They were near the back wall of the cafeteria.

Suddenly, inky shadows wrapped around Maine's arms. She struggled to escape the shadow hands and the daywalker's hands. The daywalker sensed a moment of opportunity and tore his hands free, then slammed them palms outward into Maine, blasting her backward with incredible force.

The cafeteria wall gave way at her back. Then she was lying on the hot asphalt of the rec area directly outside the cafeteria. She groaned as dust spewed out from the cafeteria and into the air. The asshole had punched her through a wall, and she did not appreciate it. At least, aided by the power crystal, her body didn't feel broken.

The flames are back, the Mantle warned her.

A glance confirmed the magic flames were burning out from her skin again. That meant she didn't have long until her body burned out from all the raw power coursing through her.

She got up as the daywalker stooped and stepped out through the hole in the wall onto the strewn rubble.

"Ready for recreation time?" He picked up the barbell from the weight bench. There weren't any weights on the ends, but it made a dangerous weapon. The daywalker's grim look said he was putting everything into his next attack. That meant she had to do the same.

He streaked like a blur toward her.

She set her back leg. With timing help from the Mantle, she crouched at the moment before impact. The daywalker was leading with the barbell, like a harpoon strike.

Maine sprang up before impact. Her fist struck solid chest as the barbell slammed downward against her shoulder in a numbing strike.

They stood frozen for a few moments. Then the breath exploded from the daywalker's chest. With the flames rising higher on her skin, Maine wasted no time snatching the power crystal from around the gang leader's throat.

Then she lifted the daywalker's body with her free hand, closed her fingers into a fist around his crystal, and delivered an uppercut he'd never forget. She hit with such force that his body sailed into the air, arced over the rec area, and sprawled him out over one of the basketball hoops.

The daywalker weakly lifted his head and groaned. "You win…" He passed out atop the basketball goal.

"You did it," Hank said softly from the opening in the cafeteria. "You defeated the daywalker."

Maine tore the Brick crystal from her neck and gathered the Seeing Eye and Triangle crystals in her hand. She saw the Light Burst and Parchment crystals hanging from Hank's hand.

"You got the rest of the power crystals. I'm proud of you."

The magic flames had extinguished from her skin, but now that she had no source of infinite power, her body was losing energy fast. She stumbled. Hank moved toward her, but he wasn't going to catch her in time. Before she hit the asphalt, a pair of burly Oni demon arms caught her.

"Thanks, Owen." She fought her exhaustion. The Oni demon had sustained some wounds in the fighting, but he looked like a handsome devil in the sunlight. Not that she was into that—she already had a guy waiting for her.

"You are one crazy half-troll." Owen grinned. "Hella lucky too. I can't believe someone took out the daywalker, and a girl, too." He met her eyes. "I think I'm in love—will you marry me?"

Distract him by telling him, no, you'll break his heart—then break his face.

Maine smiled. "Sorry, I'm taken."

Owen shook his head. "Damn."

Hank stepped up to them. "Maine, you don't look so good."

"The power crystals," she gasped. She blinked, fighting back fiery pain. "Noolie. Where's Noolie?"

"He's here," Owen said. Noolie stepped forth from the cafeteria hole.

"Any sign of the Guardian yet?" Maine said. "My team was trying to call him."

"No," Hank said.

Noolie looked ready to freak out. "We've got to get the hell out of here. The gangs are in disarray, fighting for who will be the next leaders."

Hank chuckled and lifted the five power crystals. "Well, they won't be real leaders unless they're wearing one of these."

"You idiot!" Noolie cried out. "That means they're going to be coming right for us. Unless you all can climb barbed wire fences, we've got to get out of the rec yard."

"You have a safe place in mind?" Maine stood on her own. She wobbled, and Owen steadied her.

"Yes. We have to be quick. Follow me!"

Hank and Owen shared a look. "Okay, we'll clear a way through the cafeteria," Hank said.

"Can you walk?" Owen asked.

"Yeah, I feel better now." Maine stood on her own again. "Let's go."

As they ducked inside the cafeteria, fighting broke out once again among the inmates. Small fires burned in parts of the rubble, and wires hissed and sparked. When the inmates saw Maine and her friends, some broke away from the crowd to fight them.

Owen rushed ahead, plowing a path through the inmates. "Hurry!"

Maine, Hank, and Noolie followed the Oni demon. Noff clung to Maine's shoulder.

They only made it halfway through the cafeteria when all the inmates closed in on them in a circle.

"Damn," Owen remarked.

Noff squeaked. "Damage, destruction, terror...and mayhem!" He blasted into the air and sunburst so bright it blinded all the inmates.

"Nice." Owen finished opening a path through the cafeteria. When they made it to the hallway outside, Owen said, "I'll stay and hold them back as long as I can. Good luck!"

"You're up." Maine patted Noolie on the back and pushed him to the front.

He nodded and ran onward.

"We've got to watch out for any stragglers," Hank said wearily. "And for corrupt prison guards."

Maine hoped they had passed the worst of the obstacles. Her body was tired, and her legs felt like lead. She didn't know how much her body could take let alone if the power crystals were still going to kill her.

I'm trying to negate as much of the magical damage as I can, the Mantle hissed.

Maine grunted her thanks as she did her best to catch up with Noolie.

"It's not too far," Noolie said, "it's just around the corner."

They came around the corner, and a guard standing five yards away raised his rifle. Except this gun looked lethal and not like the magic rifles from before.

"For the daywalker," the guard hissed and pulled the trigger.

He was aiming at Noolie. Noolie had the key and knew how to use it.

Maine threw herself in front of the bullet, wincing as it struck her chest.

CHAPTER FORTY-TWO

Thankfully her tactical vest stopped the bullet, but that didn't lessen any of the pain.

As she groaned on the floor, she was vaguely aware of Hank rushing up and dealing with the corrupt guard.

The world was hazy and spun in slow motion as Noolie stooped over her. "Are you okay? Geez, you took a bullet for me. Why? I killed your father."

Maine didn't trust herself to speak. Her strength was fading. The Mantle was frantically sharing some of its energy with her, but it would only last so long. If the Guardian didn't show up ASAP and whisk her away to healing, there would be no wedding.

"You okay?" Hank asked a short time later.

"Yeah, thank troll for Sage's tactical vest."

"Seriously, why did you save my life?" Noolie was still saying. "Now I owe you a blood debt."

"Just get me to the safe spot," Maine mumbled, blinking and trying to stop the world from spinning.

Hank helped her to her feet, and they entered a door

Maine had never seen before. On the other side was a long corridor with offices on either side leading to a flight of stairs. There was a door atop the stairs.

Maine pointed up at it. "What's up there?"

"The prison helipad," Noolie said.

"You know how to fly a helicopter?" she asked incredulously.

"What? No. There's no helicopter there. But that's the first place the Guardian teleports to when he comes to visit. It's a safe place, and that's where he'll show up when he gets here!"

"Oh." Maine stumbled, and Hank helped her stand.

Meanwhile, Noolie started climbing the stairs two at a time.

From outside the corridor came many footsteps, inmates trying to stop Maine and Noolie from escaping.

When he was sure that Maine could stand alone, Hank headed back for the door leading to the corridor. "I'll try to hold them off!"

Left on her own, Maine winced as she eyed the long corridor. The prison's walls seemed to close in on her like a trap as she hobbled forward. Behind her, the sounds of inmates fighting renewed as guards started intervening. She heard Hank shout as he fought the inmates trying to get to Maine and Noolie.

She made it a few more steps before Noff squeaked from her pants pocket, "Look out, yo!"

Maine evaded to the side of the corridor as a tattooed prisoner lunged at her from behind. He must have slipped past Hank. She elbowed him in the face and kept moving forward. The corridor was long, and when she reached the end of it, she groaned.

"I've got to go up there now?" Maine muttered when she came to the stairwell leading up to the exit.

"There she is!" a voice called from behind her.

She barely had time to turn as three inmates entered the corridor and rushed her, a vampire, a goblin, and a rhino shifter. As they fell upon her position, mouse-sized Noff blasted out of Maine's pocket and sunburst in front of the first prisoner's face. The vampire went cross-eyed. The rhino shifter trampled him.

Noff blasted to the side and sunburst a second time, blinding the other two with a miniature dazzling fireworks display. While they threw up their hands to guard their eyes, Maine dispatched them with quick jabs to the chin and solar plexus. Maine had already turned before their groaning bodies slumped to the floor.

"Mantle," Maine muttered. "Can you give me a little more energy?"

I am nearly depleted. You need healing.

Maine grunted and placed her foot on the first step. Safety lay at the top beyond that door. She had to make it there.

Hurry! the Mantle hissed.

Exhausted, Maine huffed in air and started up the steps.

Before she could get far, two ogre prison guards stepped into the corridor behind her, eyeing her warily and hungrily. Behind them, three mythical gang members with their arms and necks sleeved in arcane tattoos cracked their knuckles.

So close and yet so far, the Mantle hissed. *You're outnumbered and spent. You'll never make it up the rest of these steps.*

Maine turned and descended the few steps she had climbed. "You don't scare me," she shouted in challenge to the five newly arrived opponents. She tried not to wobble, but her body ached all over. She was so tired.

The first guard threw himself forward, leading with his fist. Maine blocked his uppercut and shoved him to the side. Then the second ogre guard grabbed her by the arm and shoulder, holding her in place like a bully.

"Shiv!" Noff squeaked, but it was too late.

While Maine focused on dealing with the second ogre guard, one of the gang members had shot forward, plunging a thin, sharpened piece of metal into her side.

She grunted, slipped out of the guard's hold, and swiveled away from her attackers, heaving in a breath and pausing long enough to clutch at her side. Warm red liquid oozed through her fingers.

As she backstepped and lost her footing, the Mantle hissed disappointedly.

Congratulations. That is a fatal wound. I always knew your blood would stain my cloth.

You're such a drama queen, Maine projected as she reached out for the wall for support. Her hand slipped off it, and she collapsed backward. *It's only ketchup from the cafeteria.*

She blinked and realized she was sitting against the wall with her five attackers looming. As her eyes fluttered shut, she heard Noff's frantic Mickey Mouse squeaks in her ear, telling her not to go to sleep.

Sleep. Ah, yes, that seemed like such a good idea.

Her eyelids fluttered closed.

Whoosh!

Her eyelids fluttered open, and she saw the Guardian standing atop the stairway, glaring daggers down at the two corrupt guards and three gang members gathered around Maine's body.

"S-self-defense!" one of the guards cried.

All five of them backstepped as the Guardian *whooshed* down the steps and crouched beside Maine's body.

The Guardian's face was inches from Maine's. He swiped his finger in the blood, and when he saw it was ketchup, he winked at her. "Play dead," he whispered so only she could hear.

Then the Guardian rose and turned to face the other five mythical creatures in the room. At the snap of his fingers, the door leading into the corridor slammed shut and locked.

"We didn't mean to do it!" the gang member with the shiv blurted.

The Guardian took a step closer to them, and the five cowered. The Guardian solemnly shook his head.

"Aren't you going to revive her?" the other corrupt prison guard asked.

"It's too late. She's beyond this world. Looks like I'll have to add a murder charge to your records."

"No!" the guards and inmates cried, dropping to their knees and begging forgiveness. Soldiers of the Angel Guard filtered through the door atop the stairs armed with batons and handcuffs.

Maine watched through slitted eyelids, unable to conceal the hint of a smile. After the Angel Guard escorted the guards and inmates out of the corridor, they started to quell the riot within the rest of the prison.

When they were alone, Noff hopped out of Maine's pocket and blasted onto Maine's shoulder. "Hell yeah, we did it! We survived prison!"

CHAPTER FORTY-THREE

A Few Days Later

"Home sweet home." Maine relished the soft cushion of the sofa at her back. She stretched out and nestled her head on Sage's shoulder. It felt amazing to be back at the mansion in the study. It also felt good to recover from all the prison fighting.

"What was the worst part of prison?" Sage draped an arm around her.

She looked at him. "You really want me to dredge up such horrible memories?" When he flinched, she laughed. "Just kidding. Those orange jumpsuits were pretty bad, though."

"Not as bad as that food," Noff barked, prancing into the study. He was back to his normal tomcat size and as full of energy as ever.

"Yeah, that was the worst part of it."

Sage teased, "Just remember, it was your idea to go undercover in a mythical supermax prison."

"I know. On the upside, it felt good to reconcile with Noolie. He came through with his promise to give me the key

284

to the painting." She glanced at Noolie's archaic-looking tattoo needle resting on a coffee table.

"Who would have thought that a magical tattoo needle would be the key to unlocking the Second Nexus?" Sage asked.

Maine yawned and settled into a comfortable position on the sofa. "After the Guardian extracted us from the prison, Noolie explained that the tattoo needle also serves as a magical quill. It's what created the living painting in the first place."

At that, Sage eyed the Seeing Eye tattoo on Maine's shoulder. "It can also ink tattoos?"

"I know, magic, right? Now do you understand why it's so confusing to me?"

Sage laughed. "I still cannot believe you decided to keep that Seeing Eye tattoo."

Maine grinned. "The Guardian said there's no way the gangs can ever trace me through the tattoo. Also, the Guardian and Maki-Mae performed some kind of super-charged mind-wipe on all the inmates—except Hank—so no one will remember I was there."

"Then what was the point of faking your death?" Sage asked.

"For dramatic flair."

"Ya really sold it too," Noff barked. "I bet even Ma in LA would be impressed with your actin'. Hey, wonder how she's doin'."

"I don't know. As crazy as LA is, she could probably write a book about her exploits. Probably a whole series."

Noff scratched behind his ear. "Ya think people would really wanna read about an elf in LA?"

"Depends on how it was presented," Sage interjected.

"What's she doing out in LA anyway? Helping mythical creatures who are down on their luck? Solving mythical mysteries?"

"Dunno," Noff barked. "I think I'll wait until they make the movie of it. Hey, too bad Owen don't remember ya."

"Who's Owen?" Sage asked.

Maine shifted on the sofa. "Some guy I met in prison. Whoa, don't worry, he was an Oni demon."

"You were an Oni demon too," Sage reminded her. "Is there something you're not telling me?"

"Nah, they didn't do nothin'," Noff barked. "But he did have the hots for her."

Maine smirked at Sage. "I have the hots for you."

They kissed and settled back into the sofa.

Finally, Sage prompted, "Noolie did tell you how to use the key to get to the Second Nexus, right?"

"Yep, I have to utter an incantation, and the key will guide me like a compass to the spot in Rainwater where my father used his Wish Card. When I reach the spot, I insert the key into the painting, which will open a portal to the Second Nexus."

"We are going to the Second Nexus?" Sage asked. "There's no changing your mind?"

Maine kissed him lightly on the lips. "What do you think?"

Noff wriggled his butt and blasted into the air. "Woohoo! I think we've got one more adventure left in us. Team on three. One, two, three!"

"Team!" the three of them shouted.

The door to the study flew open, and Al glided in. "Master Maine, I heard a commotion. Everything all right?"

Noff barked. "No, Al, we need more cookies!"

Al chuckled. "Oh, Master Maine, I spoke with the

Guardian on the phone. He said he would be stopping by soon—"

Whoosh!

Al cleared his throat. "Master Maine, the Guardian has arrived."

The angel leader stood tall and edged his shoulders back as he surveyed the study.

"Thanks for knocking," Maine quipped. When the Guardian glared at her, she added, "I'm especially grateful to you for getting Noolie and me out of prison. Did Noolie make it to that Martha Stewart prison I promised him?"

The Guardian scoffed. "It can hardly be called a prison where Noolie went. There are no bars on the cells. Or even cells there. It's a disgrace to justice." He gave a low growl.

"Yeah...sorry about throwing in that condition without telling you first."

The Guardian grunted.

Maine added, "I managed to take down all five gang leaders. I basically stopped a mythical global gang war, so cut me some slack."

The Guardian grimaced. "Yes. You have my thanks. You did a very reckless and dangerous thing, obtaining the power crystals yourself."

"Well, I had help. It wouldn't have been so dangerous if you had been there when the daywalker revealed my true identity to the entire prison."

The Guardian stroked his chin. "I admit that I am embarrassed for falling for their ploy to get me away from the prison."

"Is that your way of congratulating me for a job well done?"

The Guardian's eyes quivered. "Congratulate you? You

destroyed half of the prison. Do you know how much repairs are going to cost?"

"Hold up there, that wasn't all me. Why don't you use the demonic Needle to mend the damages? That would be free."

The Guardian glared at her with pursed lips. "I shall take that into consideration. But the demonic weapons aren't to be tinkered with lightly."

Tell the Guardian I said hi, the Mantle hissed.

Maine didn't.

"Did the power crystals find new homes yet?" Maine asked.

"That's partly the reason for me coming over today. I chose Hank to be the bearer of one of the power crystals."

"Really? Which one?" Maine asked.

Disregarding her question, the Guardian continued. "I also assigned him to choose the least-worst inmates to receive the rest of the power crystals to avoid a power vacuum among the Five Gangs. I think he has chosen well. I thank you for recommending him to me."

"You're welcome." Maine remembered a talk she had with the Guardian after her extraction.

The Guardian paused. "I am quite proud of Hank. He is reforming nicely. He has found his purpose, I think, thanks to you. With his newly appointed power, he has gotten most of the inmates to renounce the Corruptor and his ways."

"They've vowed to live on the straight and narrow?" Maine asked.

"No. At least they do not serve the Corruptor anymore."

The Guardian snapped his fingers and conjured an envelope into his hand. "This is the second reason I came here today. To give you this." He handed Maine the envelope. "I must go now. I am very busy."

As Maine wondered who the envelope was from, the Guardian disappeared in a *whoosh.*

Maine opened the envelope and read the letter inside. It was from Hank.

Maine,

So much has changed in my life since I met you in the joint. All of it for the better. You have my utmost thanks and know that I will never be able to repay you.

I now know that I am not weak. True strength comes from within and from trusting yourself. It also means opening yourself up to others at times and asking for help when you need it.

I now bear one of the power crystals. It is quite a responsibility, but I am managing. I am the new leader of the Seeing Eye gang. Can you believe it?

I've made some changes to the way the gang operates. We now emphasize trusting each other instead of keeping secrets from each other. By working together, maybe we can set an example for the other gangs. Hell, when I get out of prison, maybe I can start spreading some good in this world.

Thank you for trusting in me when no one else in the world did or had any right to. Be safe.

—Hank

CHAPTER FORTY-FOUR

The next day, they were packed and ready to venture to the Second Nexus. It was time to activate the key.

Maine, Sage, Maki-Mae, and Noff gathered in a circle in the mansion study. Sage held the painting while Maine held the tattoo needle. They all exchanged excited looks, then Maine spoke the incantation Noolie had provided her.

Suddenly both the living painting and the tattoo needle began to pulse with magical energy.

"It's working!" Maine exclaimed. "We're so close now…"

The pulsing tattoo needle acted like a compass, directing them toward the spot where Maine would insert the needle into the painting to open the portal to the Second Nexus. The tattoo needle guided them outside and deep into the forest behind the mansion where they had faced off against the Mists and Baba Yaga.

Traversing the forest was much easier this time around. They walked in silence, the anticipation building as the tattoo needle and painting pulsed more intensely the farther they walked.

The path was starting to seem familiar, and Maine guessed she shouldn't have been surprised when the tattoo needle led them to a clearing with the cave that had contained the Chaos leak they had sealed.

The cave looked the same as she had remembered it—collapsed. Except there were a bunch of rocks piled outside it that she didn't recall being there the last time. When Maine held the tattoo needle toward the cave, it pulsed even more intensely, signaling that they had to venture inside the cave.

Sage rubbed his jaw. In his free hand, he held the painting. "So the Chaos leak must have been where Valkious used the Wish Card back in his day. It must have left a weakness in the fabric of reality there."

"Too bad the cave collapsed," Noff barked.

As they stepped closer to the cave's mouth, they discovered someone had carved a narrow tunnel out of the collapsed cave. All the rocks and boulders piled outside must have come from inside. Who had cleared the path?

A twig *snapped* from the tree line surrounding the clearing. They spun as one toward the sound. Maine conjured a fireball while Sage and Maki-Mae prepared to cast spells.

Some bushes parted, and a tall, gangly figure appeared. "Rah?"

Maine recalled her fireball and lowered her hands. "Cookie Monster myth?"

The figure stepped into the sunlight and threw his long fuzzy arms into the air. "Rah rah rah!"

"Not this guy," Noff barked.

The Cookie Monster myth burst out of the tree line and ran up to them in ecstatic glee. He swallowed Maine in a giant gangly bear hug when he reached them. "Rah."

After a few moments, Maine pulled back from the fuzzy

myth. "Cookie Monster myth, did you remove all these rocks from the cave?"

He nodded. "Rah."

"But why?"

"Rah rah."

While Maine tried to interpret the creature's sounds, Maki-Mae noted, "Doesn't he look bigger than last time?"

"He does," Sage agreed.

Noff barked as he padded around the Cookie Monster myth to get a better look at him. "Yup, got some bigger muscles on him. Myths sure grow up so fast, don't they?"

Maine switched her gaze from the myth to the piles of rocks and back to the myth. "You moved them because you knew we would be back?"

The creature clapped his hands in excitement. "Rah, rah!"

"This is weird, guys, but I think Cookie Monster myth knew we'd be back."

Maki-Mae smiled warmly. "I do not think it is so odd. All of Baba Yaga's myths are born for a purpose. Perhaps this myth was born to ensure we got to the Second Nexus."

Noff trotted over to a rock pile and lifted his leg. "If so, sure feels nice for somethin' to finally go our way for once."

Even Sage looked a little relieved to hear of the possible positive connection between them and the myth.

Maine turned back to the Cookie Monster myth. "Are you done clearing the path? Or do you have more rocks to move?"

The fuzzy creature grinned. "Rah." He pointed into the cave.

"I think he wants us to go in," Noff barked, rejoining the group.

"Is it safe?" Sage asked.

"Rah."

"Yes?" Sage asked.

The Cookie Monster myth nodded. "Rah."

"Okay, we're going in there." Maine stepped toward the opening.

The Cookie Monster myth clapped and followed her.

"Okay, so you're going in too?" Maine asked.

"Rah."

"Want me to bite him?" Noff barked.

"No."

"Ya sure? 'Cause there's only room for one loveable side-kick in this party."

"I thought I was the loveable sidekick." Sage feigned hurt feelings.

Maine kissed him on the cheek. "You're definitely loveable."

The narrow tunnel running through the collapsed cave soon grew completely dark. Noff squeezed up to the front and sunburst softly so his body became a nightlight for them. He trotted ahead of the group to lead the way as the rest followed single file.

There wasn't much to see along the path besides a bunch of stone. The Cookie Monster myth must have been working overtime to clear the path so fast.

When they had been walking through the tunnel for a couple of minutes, they stepped over some greenish chaos Mist lingering on the ground.

Maine asked, "Mantle, is that Mist going to attack us?"

No. I do not sense Chaos in this realm.

"What's he sayin'?" Noff called over his shoulder.

"The Mantle says it's safe. Chaos isn't here."

"I don't sense an abundance of chaos either," Maki-Mae confirmed.

They continued through the tunnel.

"Is it me or is the tunnel narrowing?" Sage asked. "Also, the painting is vibrating like crazy."

"It is getting a little tight," Maine confirmed. "The tattoo needle is going crazy too. Cookie Monster myth, are we almost there?"

"Rah."

After another minute of navigating through the increasingly narrow tunnel, the passage opened into a wide, high-ceilinged space.

"This is where the Chaos leak was." Maine looked around. "This part of the cave must not have collapsed."

"Rah."

Suddenly, the tattoo needle began to glow with white light. The painting in Sage's hands glowed too. They were standing at the center of the expansive stone room.

"I think it's time," she said softly.

Sage nodded.

Noff blasted into the air in a twirl, trying to bite his tail. "Woohoo!"

Maine stepped up to Sage. "I promise that we will get married after we get back from the Second Nexus. No more wild, dangerous adventures—"

Sage leaned in and kissed her.

"For a while," Maine finished.

Sage grinned. "Okay, sounds good." He held up the painting and Maine raised the tattoo needle. Both objects shone brighter as they neared each other until Maine carefully plunged the tattoo needle into the painting.

A moment later, a glowing portal opened against the far wall near where the Chaos leak had been.

"Sweet," Noff barked. "Our ticket to the Second Nexus."

The Mantle hissed. *Yes, I can confirm that leads to the Second Nexus.*

"You're sure?" Maine asked.

Yes.

Suddenly the ground began to rumble.

"Partner, either you're really hungry, or I think Chaos senses us here."

"It's not me," Maine confirmed.

Sage groaned. "I knew this wouldn't be so easy."

Rocks dropped from the ceiling, cracking when they struck the ground.

"Rah rah rah!" the Cookie Monster exclaimed, flapping his long arms. "Rah!"

Swaths of dust poured down from the ceiling.

"We must hurry!" Maki-Mae urged. They all ran.

"Everyone keep headin' toward the light at the end of the tunnel," Noff barked as he scampered along the rock fall. He skidded to a stop before colliding with a fallen rock and blasted over it. "Course, seein' a light at the end of a tunnel usually means death..."

Maine reached the glowing portal first and stopped to ensure that Maki-Mae and the Cookie Monster myth made it through. Their bodies disappeared as soon as they entered the portal.

Noff blasted through the portal next. "Woohoo!"

Then Sage appeared through the dust. He grabbed Maine's hand, and together they jumped into the portal while Sage yelled, "'Til death do us part!"

When they came to, they were sitting upon a quaint hillside awash in cheery sunlight.

Noff blasted into the air with glee. "We made it! We're in the paintin'!"

Maine picked herself up and surveyed the countryside. It looked even more peaceful than in the painting. The fishing pond wasn't far away. Over the crest of the hill was a sprawling village of thatched-roof houses.

"Wow, this is awesome," Maine said. "I can't wait to go down there and explore…" She let her words trail off as she spotted a small group of troll soldiers marching up the hillside toward her. Some of the soldiers carried spears, others clubs and swords. Leading the small group was the Valkious double.

Maine's heart skipped a beat. She was finally about to meet her father. Sort of.

Sage, Maki-Mae, Noff, and the Cookie Monster myth joined her by her side as the soldiers approached.

"Ya think they're gonna attack us?" Noff barked.

"Let me do the talking," Maine directed.

Finally, the small group of soldiers arrived at the top of the hillside. The Valkious double stepped forth and spoke in a commanding voice. "Send forth your leader."

Blinking, Maine stepped forward. "Hey, Da—"

"What is your name?" the Valkious double demanded.

Maine brushed some bangs out of her eyes. "Don't you recognize me? I'm Maine. Your daughter."

AUTHOR NOTES RAMY VANCE

SEPTEMBER 29, 2022

What's in an elbow?

My sister-in-law recently got married. It was a whirlwind affair set in a tiny cottage in northern Ontario. There were exactly 19 guests (20, if you count Joni, their black Labrador).

It was a bit last minute (no, not a shotgun wedding... that said, they did suddenly decide to pull the matrimonial trigger) and very limited and exclusive guest list.

A guest list that included my 7-year-old.

Prepping a wedding while the guests are there is hell. Prepping a wedding while the guests are there AND have multiple children (my own amongst them) is pure chaos.

Things get forgotten... important things like a wedding photographer.

I know, it's crazy right? But we absolutely forgot to assign someone to take photographs. There was one person who took professional photos BEFORE the ceremony. But that person went home because no one booked her for the ACTUAL ceremony.

The icing on the cake? We didn't notice until the next day, when – at breakfast – my mother asked to see the wedding photos...

What wedding photos? There was a moment of tension. A second where tears were forming in the eyes of the bride, the mother of the bride and the niece of the bride (I know, I know – I could have said, bride's mother and niece ... but the 'of the bride' adds gravitas to the situation, don't you think?).

Until, that is, my 7-year-old piped up and said, "I took photos."

Seems the little guy took my phone – and bored, took a ton of photos (or should I say, a giga of photos). He took so many, that I got a notification from iCloud Storage, that my account was full and no longer backing up to the cloud.

All in all, it was something like 7 gigabytes of photos and videos.

Now, he's 7. So his aim was… off.

But his spirit was dead on.

We got our wedding photos. A lot of knees. But the photos are there.

Tears (mostly) saved and a wedding album to cherish forever.

(Note – the elbow photo is a screenshot from the only video we have of the wedding speeches.)

(meet the photographer)

AUTHOR NOTES MICHAEL ANDERLE

OCTOBER 12, 2022

Thank you for not only reading this book but these author notes as well!

Do you read romance? I don't, but...

I'm not a reader of the romance genre, but I recognize how a romantic subplot (done well) might resonate with me in stories I read.

As many of you know, I run a publishing company named LMBPN which has released over 1,600 books since 2015, over 120 audiobooks ourselves, over 600 books we have licensed for audio, and over 200 books in 5 different languages.

What I haven't done is published much in romance.

Enter Lantia, a publishing company based in Spain. Recently, we contracted to translate five (5) romance books into English, and to say it's been humorous for our Alpha readers is putting it *nicely.*

I'm aware of situations when my English books get translated into foreign languages the occasional odd (to me) questions on what a particular euphemism means—I've just never encountered it coming from a foreign language into English.

Here is an example (a direct translation): "You didn't have to be a lynx to see that he was a very attractive, manly, and edible man. He was like a cheese."

He was like a cheese?

I understand the readers reviewing the book had a righteous time learning about foreign euphemisms. Far be it from me to take away their pleasure, right?

So, I translated three (3) more to keep them entertained.

Everyone remembers I said I am a publisher, right? A publisher doesn't eat unless we publish…

Even if our romance guys taste like cheese.

Talk to you in the next book!

Ad Aeternitatem,

Michael Anderle

I have a couple of short stories you can read that I am sharing from my STORIES with Michael Anderle newsletter here:
https://michael.beehiiv.com/

BOOKS BY RAMY VANCE

Middang3ard
Never Split The Party (01)
Late To the Party (02)
It's My Party (03)
Blue Hell And Alien Fire (04)

Death Of An Author: A Middang3ard Novella

Dark Gate Angels
Dark Gate Angels (01)
Shades of Death (02)
The Allies of Death (03)
The Deadliness of Light (04)

Dragon Approved
The First Human Rider (01)
Ascent to the Nest (02)
Defense of the Nest (03)

Trolling Prisons (Book 8)
Chosen (Book 9)

Other Books by Ramy Vance

Mortality Bites Series
Keep Evolving Series

BOOKS BY MICHAEL ANDERLE

Sign up for the LMBPN email list to be notified of new releases and special deals!

https://lmbpn.com/email/

For a complete list of books by Michael Anderle, please visit:

www.lmbpn.com/ma-books/

CONNECT WITH THE AUTHORS

Connect with Ramy

Join Ramy's Newsletter

Join Ramy's FB Group: House of the GoneGod Damned!

Michael Anderle Social

Website: http://lmbpn.com

Email List: https://michael.beehiiv.com/

https://www.facebook.com/LMBPNPublishing

https://twitter.com/MichaelAnderle

https://www.instagram.com/lmbpn_publishing/

https://www.bookbub.com/authors/michael-anderle

Made in the USA
Columbia, SC
20 May 2023

17035676R00190